MARCHWOOD

MARCHWOOD

An Essex / Limehouse Tale
(1850s–1945)

ROSALIND CONWAY

Copyright © 2025 Rosalind Conway

"*Stern Realities*" – WM Cat N o FMS – 24-09+ © Cover Image used by permission of Whitby Literary and Philosophical Society

The moral right of the author has been asserted.

Apart from any fair dealing for the purposes of research or private study, or criticism or review, as permitted under the Copyright, Designs and Patents Act 1988, this publication may only be reproduced, stored or transmitted, in any form or by any means, with the prior permission in writing of the publishers, or in the case of reprographic reproduction in accordance with the terms of licences issued by the Copyright Licensing Agency. Enquiries concerning reproduction outside those terms should be sent to the publishers.

This is a work of fiction. Names, characters, businesses, places, events and incidents are either the products of the author's imagination or used in a fictitious manner. Any resemblance to actual persons, living or dead, or actual events is purely coincidental.

Troubador Publishing Ltd
Unit E2 Airfield Business Park,
Harrison Road, Market Harborough,
Leicestershire LE16 7UL
Tel: 0116 279 2299
Email: books@troubador.co.uk
Web: www.troubador.co.uk

ISBN 978-1-83628-339-3

British Library Cataloguing in Publication Data.
A catalogue record for this book is available from the British Library.

The manufacturer's authorised representative in the EU for product safety is Authorised Rep Compliance Ltd, 71 Lower Baggot Street, Dublin D02 P593 Ireland (www.arccompliance.com).

Printed and bound in Great Britain by 4edge Limited
Typeset in 11pt Minion Pro by Troubador Publishing Ltd, Leicester, UK

A story dedicated to children born into poverty, neglect, abuse and hardship and is a tribute to their resilience.

Marchwood

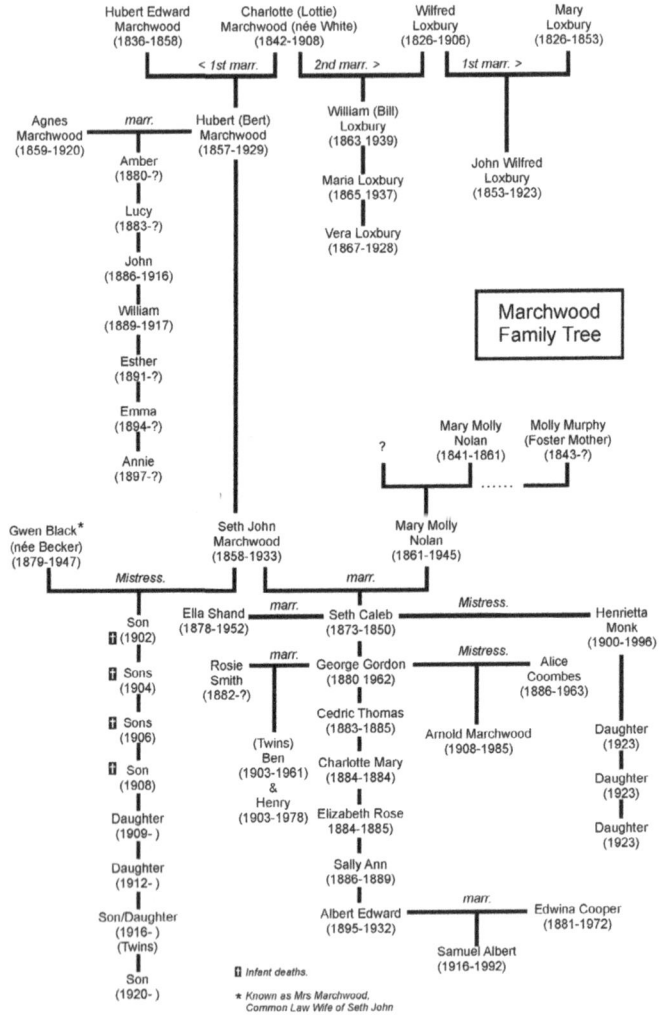

Prologue

London 1861

The young woman lies upon a rancid, bug-infested mound of tattered cloth, strewn in an untidy heap on warped, damp floorboards. Full of jagged splinters that have bloodied many a soft-footed child, spattered with greasy stains from multiple spillages, the floor blemishes are a stark reminder of the many souls who sheltered here. From a single-paned, grimy window in the centre of one wall there comes a faint light. The air is pervaded by the smell of soot from an uncleaned chimney and tallow from a flickering candle on the mantlepiece. The grate, empty of coal or wood, has not had a fire burning in it for six months, for fuel is an unobtainable luxury for paupers who must prioritise food over warmth.

Unable to afford a full week's rent for this miserable place, the young woman leased it for twenty-four hours, hoping that will be enough time for her to birth her child. Despite the draught of air from the ill-fitting window, the pungent stench of body odour in the room is not reduced. Perspiration runs down her flushed face, the droplets pooling at the base of her neck and the threadbare scraps of fabric she lays on are drenched from her waters breaking earlier.

An old hag, wearing a shabby, frayed, blue gown stained yellow-under the arms, and a blood-spattered, cotton apron, bends over the girl with palpable concern. Grunting loudly, head thrown back, the young woman struggles to eject the baby from her belly. Between each brutal spasm, she lies unnaturally still, afraid to breathe, waiting for the next wave of pain to tear her pelvic bones apart and rip the soft flesh of her vaginal canal. Agonised, she pulls out clumps of her long, black, curly hair, leaving trickles of blood to collect around her hairline. Exhausted, she yearns for death to release her from the hell of another contraction. Using a fetid rag, the hag wipes blood-tinted mucus from the face of her patient. Crooning softly, she tries to still the girl's uncontrollable trembling and teeth chattering but it is hopeless. With a last guttural scream the girl cries out, "Jaysus! Playze help me! Help me! Save me babby, Ma Murphy, bu' let me die, fer I am done for."

Frantically, Ma Murphy responds, "Mary Girl! Don't go givin' up. Yer babby wans t' come feet-first. I can feel tiny toes wid me finger. Try one last push t' get d' head 'tru."

Noticing subtle changes in the pallor and breathing of her young charge, the hag knows she is losing the battle to save this young mother, but she also knows it is possible to save the baby. With Mary's last exhale of breath, the tiny infant girl slips out from between her dying mother's pale thin thighs.

Prologue

Whisperings:
I see the moment of my birth. I cannot be sure of the exact date of this squalid and bloody event, but the earth year is eighteen-hundred and sixty-one. As my first gasp of air inflates my lungs, memory is erased, emptied of all that has been before, and all that is to come.

Ma Murphy scurries through putrid cobbled streets and alleyways, dodging the children searching for edible scraps in the gutters. Breathless, she reaches the steps of a slum building near Ratcliffe Square. Holding tight to the swaddled babe with one arm, she grips the iron railing with the other and descends to a dark cellar. Feeling her way along a dank, flag stoned passageway, she turns sharp left, stooping through a low, open doorway, the door long ago used for firewood. Entering a gloomy basement interior, lit by a shaft of muted daylight coming through a broken sash window which is partially covered with crude planks of wood, she hesitates. A candle stub flickers in an iron sconce to the left of the chimney breast in contrast to the ominous darkness of the fireplace, a funnel for bitterly cold draughts.

Slouched on the floor, against the wall under the window, is an ashen-faced, dejected girl not yet eighteen years of age. Her eyes are closed, her breathing slow, and her filthy dress and petticoats dishevelled. Beside her, on the bloodstained, soiled mattress on which she rests, is a naked, new-born boy. His skin is porcelain white and cold to touch in contrast to the blaze of thick red hair that covers his minute scalp.

Ma Murphy leans down and gently taps one shoulder of the slouching woman.

"Molly, Molly! Have yee not moved sins' last ni' when I left yee?"

Muttering, the woman stirs. "Ma Murphy! Yee came back!" In desperation, she begs, "I need yee t' take d' dead babby away, fer it grieves me t' see 'im lying dere, an' me full of milk too. Take his wee cold body away."

She begins to wail, and the hag clumsily wipes her tears with a rag.

"Whist now, Molly! No need t' sob an' weep fer haven't I found yee another babby, a wee orphan girl who needs feedin'. She needs t' suckle soon fer her Ma died hours ago. Listen to me, Molly, d' discomfort in yer swollen bubbies will ease once the child starts to take yer milk. Wid a wee girl t' dress up pretty, yee can get more money ou' cadging."

Reaching up, Molly, draws the infant onto her bare breast and guides the tiny, pursed, rooting mouth onto her leaking nipple. Instinctively, the infant fastens onto the moistened duct and siphons up the rich milk, triggering a wave of contentment in Molly, who smiles broadly on hearing the soft mewling of the baby.

Moving her onto her other breast, Molly asks, "What was 'er Ma's name? I want t' pray fer 'er, Ma Murphy."

"'Twas Mary Nolan, an Irish lassie like yerself, Molly, workin' d' streets, an' brothels. I tried bu' I could not save her, Gawd rest her soul."

Making a quick sign of the cross, she bows her head reverently.

Prologue

A week later, Molly sees the priest about baptising the child.

"Farder, I tink it ri' dat d' wee one has d' name Mary, after her dead mammy. Her second name can be mine, don't yee tink? *Mary* Molly *Nolan* has a grand ring to it now?"

The following day, the orphan infant is christened in the ancient, stone-carved font in St Michael's Catholic Church. Blessed with a plentiful supply of mother's milk, Molly nurtures the new-born, who thrives.

Later, during her toddler years, Mary's life is riven with fear and trauma. Alone at night she hides in nooks and crannies, tense and watchful. When men, invited in by Molly, are violent towards her mama, she experiences terror like no other. Then, she dares not show her face until the rough slapping sounds stop, the door opens, and she hears the man's heavy footsteps fade into the distance. Each night as Molly saunters through dark dockside alleyways looking for business, the child, from her hiding places, listens to the ominous cacophony of sounds reverberating through the inky blackness of the night; women screaming, men bellowing angrily, dogs barking, children crying, and tortured howls of starving, abused horses, mules, and dogs. If brave, she takes a quick peek out the window to watch shadowy figures furtively move crates from warehouses onto waiting wagons.

By the age of seven, her developing character traits reflect the harsh reality of street life. Despite an elfin face topped with wild black curls, and a thin body, she is strong and robust. Her persona is rough, dominant, and unruly. From literate street women she learns to print her name and proudly scratches it onto Whitechapel walls and cobblestones. Molly, and a few trusted pauper women and children, are her family. Amongst them, her days roll by in a collective, monotonous struggle to find food and shelter until one day, everything changes.

Whisperings:
Powerless I watch, but cannot warn, as the child's first lesson in loss races towards her.

1

Mary

Barely past her childhood it required but a glance to discover that she was one of those children, born and bred in neglect and vice, who have never known what childhood is...

Sketches by Boz – Charles Dickens

1870—1875

It is a grey, dreary autumn afternoon when Molly goes insane. The Spitalfields marketeers are clearing up for the day and Mary, underneath a greengrocer's cart, is gathering up fallen pieces of fruit and vegetables and dropping them quickly into her apron pocket. *Ma Molly will be pleased wiv wha' I got 'ere,* she thinks. A sudden commotion interrupts her endeavours. Shrill, raucous laughter, punctuated with screams of fury, pierce the air. Curious, she crawls out from beneath the cart and is shocked to see Molly tossing her voluminous skirt and petticoats over her head while gleefully cavorting about the square. Arms aloft, she hollers bawdy pub-songs, delivering the crude lyrics with gusto. Stunned, the child marvels at Molly's wild elation. Laughing, she runs towards her, paying no heed to the bruised apples and brown onions falling from her pocket.

"Why are y' so 'appy, Molly? What's 'appened? Why are y' so 'appy?"

Reaching out for the small girl racing towards her, Molly hoists her high into the air. Whirled around, Mary's black curls tumble about her small laughing face. As she hangs onto Molly's neck, she sees her mama's eyes gleam with a fierce intensity, and notices with surprise how her rouged cheeks and lips seem redder than usual. Dark, heavy, wooden rosary beads hang around Molly's neck, the small silver crucifix periodically resting between her plump bosoms. Transfixed by the figure of Jesus on His cross, flip-flopping between her Mama Molly's milk-white breasts, the child wonders if He is happy being part of this ecstatic dance.

Abruptly, Molly's mood darkens, and her eyes turn zealous in their focus. She lowers Mary to the ground, and despite the child's frantic effort to cling onto her leg, she sprints away towards the centre of the square, singing loudly. Chasing after her, Mary notices balls of spittle gathering in the corners of her red-painted lips. She calls out, "Will y' stop now, Molly? Stop yer singin', an' yellin', fer yee are scarin' me 'aff t' deff."

Blind to Mary's presence, Molly's agitation and distractibility increase. Exuberantly, she does handstands and cartwheels before fleeing through the archway towards Commercial Street. Mary stands still, shocked, unable to comprehend what she has just seen. She barely hears the muffled murmurings of people around her until a stern woman, holding onto the spherical head of a green cabbage, with a deep intake of breath, loudly exclaims, "Gawd 'elp 'er, fer she is touched wiv d' madness. 'Tis d' loony bin fer 'er now I 'spects. She must 'ave suffered bad t' make 'er lose her wits like that."

Later, that evening, sitting on the doorstep of the sleazy boarding house, where, for the past month, she and Molly have lodged, she hears versions of what happened to Molly.

"I seen 'er chase after d' Catlick priest, shoutin', an' swearin'. Gawd's trufe, she was 'ittin' 'im wiv a broom as he ran into St Michael's."

Daisy Perkins smothers her laughter.

"An' I 'erd she scooped 'oly wawter from d' font into an auld broken cup an' ran up and down d' aisle, splashin' it on people sayin' der prayers."

Those listening, including Mary, join in the merriment and a sombre silence descends as a serious-looking Kathleen O'Toole delivers a sobering account of what became of Molly.

"As Gawd is me witness, I seen it all. Molly was stopped from flingin' 'erseff under a train an' 'ad t' be 'eld down by four burly railway porters. Kickin' an' screamin', she was dragged into a black wagon wiv barred windows and taken to d' asylum."

For weeks after her disappearance, Mary waits, and hopes, for Mama Molly's return. Eventually she accepts that she is gone and instead applies the survival skills that Molly taught her. She avoids low lodging houses,

3

where filthy, vermin-infested mattresses are shared by gin-soaked harlots and drunken men. Instead, alongside other abandoned children, she sleeps behind chimney stacks, inside empty warehouse crates, under parked carts, beneath river piers and in warm stables. As the boys and girls drift into slumber beneath sheets of soiled rags and paper, they hold each other's grime-stained hands and gather close for warmth and safety. In the morning, they rise to carry with them, throughout the day, the noxious stench of dried urine on their soiled, tattered garments.

Masking worries with anger, aggression and an aura of confidence, Mary confronts daily challenges. To get out of threatening situations she spits, bites, kicks, pulls hair, scratches and throws stones. Men, whom she gauges feeble, give her pennies, in return for a few kisses and a grubby-handed fumble beneath her bodice and skirts. Such encounters as these she rigidly controls so she can quickly escape if necessary.

A curious child, she has a hankering to learn. At the age of ten, accompanied by three other street urchins, she visits the Ragged School in Whitechapel. They climb the twelve stone steps up to the huge, black front door of the three-storey, dilapidated corner-house backing onto the riverbank. Mary lifts the heavy brass knocker and bangs it three times. Within minutes, a tall, kindly looking gentleman, wearing a snug green waistcoat, a crisp white shirt, a starched, stiff collar and a red, silk bow tie, opens the door. In a deep, rumbling voice he asks, "Are you little ones interested in coming to my school? I shall go and fetch some pupils to talk to you."

"Gor Blimey!" declares Mary to her companions. "Aint it nice t' be spoke to, so 'spectable like, an' from a real gent too."

Emerging from the shadow of the hallway comes a tall, freckled boy and a ginger-haired girl who happily answer the children's questions. On being made aware that the school provides pupils with clothes, boots and food, and chocolate titbits on holy days, Mary and her companions conclude that learning prayers is a price worth paying for such luxuries. On attending the school, Mary enjoys the many benefits but is sceptical about the true benevolence of Jesus. She ponders, *'Ee didna stop me paur muver from dyin' an' 'Ee let Molly go mad. They do say 'Ee can do anyfink bu' 'Ee did nuffin fer 'em. An' any'ows, 'Is rules are impossible fer me to keep 'cause stealin' is 'ow I survive.* She never stops missing Molly and clings to the memory of a promise made by her foster mama.

"One day, child, we will go together to Ireland, an' paddle in d' cold, salty brine and use cuttle fish shells t' write our names, big and bold, in d' damp sand."

At thirteen, Mary's monthly bleeds begin. Prepared for this event, she has accumulated piles of soft, absorbent cloths to use as pads, which she stores under floorboards in derelict buildings. To keep herself clean, she steals small slabs of carbolic soap from market stalls. Her most treasured possession is a carved-bone nit-comb, thieved from the bag of an inebriated woman. Remembering the horror of being infested as a child, each morning she tips her head forward, scraping the teeth of the comb from her hairline to the end of her long strands, squashing fallen louse between her thumbnail and forefinger, relishing the cracking noise.

In the summer of eighteen seventy-four, Mary encounters a dark-haired, brown-eyed, freckle-faced street entertainer performing card tricks to a modest, good-natured crowd at the east side of The Tower. Lingering, she experiences an inexplicable frisson of excitement and becomes rooted to the spot, unable to take her eyes off him. *'Ee ain't a Cockney boy, fer 'is accent is different. I fink 'ee mi' be Irish, bu' 'ee don' sound like d' Irish I knows 'oo live near Ratcliffe 'ighway.*

"Hello dere! How are youse doin? Let me introduce meself. Me name, 'tis Brian Duffy, an' I am here t' amaze youse all."

His ebony curls, so like her own, peep out from beneath his round cap and Mary has an urge to feel their soft texture beneath her fingers. Her stomach flips over when he catches her eye and winks flirtatiously. A hot flush of pleasure floods her body, culminating in a rosy blush to her cheeks. *Bloody 'ell! Am I goin' red as a beetroot?*

Finding him irresistible, she pushes her way to the front of the crowd, admiring his skill, as he quickly moves cards over the green baize square of the trestle-table. Mesmerised, the world fades as her eyes lock with his. When his act ends, she feels compelled to collect the loose coins that fell short of the upturned cap on the ground before him and drop them into it. Brian Duffy is beguiled and intrigued. He notes the shy glances she throws his way and calls to her.

"Best yee tell me yer name, gurl, 'cause yee know mine."

Cocking her head to one side, hands on her hips, she replies cheekily, "Mary Molly Nolan is me full name, bu' y' can jus' call me Mary."

Grinning, Brian says, "Ahh! Is not that just me favourite name in d' whole wide world. Well! If youse have nuttin' important to do, will yee come for a walk down by d' river *Mary Molly Nolan*?"

Mary nods and her piquant face lights up.

"It mi' sound strange, bu' I feel like I know yee, Mary gurl, though I never seen youse before dis day. 'Ow can dat be, I wonder? Is it because we look alike, wid our black curls an' freckles?"

Lifting the canvas bag containing his props, he hoops one handle over each shoulder and eases it over his back. Then, carrying the folded trestle-table, he walks beside her down to the riverbank where they sit together beneath a wooden jetty. There they chat, enthralled with each other. She learns that Brian too is an orphan. He came down from Liverpool one year before and now lives with a kindly man, George Smith, in Dalston. With unusual ease and openness, both share painful childhood memories; she of the trauma of seeing Molly go insane and he of his bleak time in a Catholic orphanage run by monks.

Looking into the far distance, he speaks haltingly of the cruelty meted out to abandoned, vulnerable boys.

"Evil spooks, dressed in long-brown, cowled tunics, dey crept tru corridors, hidin' bamboo canes under their tabards. For no reason, boys were dragged from der beds, der bare legs and backsides lashed 'til der skin was flayed an' running wid blood. One or two of the younger, delicate boys were usually frog-marched, by the scruff of the neck, out of the dormitory; taken away fer special treatment."

"What special treatment?" asks Mary.

Pausing for a few moments, Brian avoids looking at her before he answers.

"D' wee boys were taken to a monk's cell where, after being whipped, dey'd be forced to do rude tings wid d' brudders. I try hard not to tink of those times, Mary."

He falls silent for a few minutes and Mary, sensing his unease, nuzzles her face into the curve of his neck and whispers, "Y' can tell me, Brian."

"Even now, Mary, dere is many a night when I hear d' tortured, stifled sobs of dose childer on der return to d' dormitory, an' in me head I see dere wee petrified, ashen faces as dey call for der mudders to come and save them."

Shaking himself out of the horror of his memory, Brian looks into Mary's eyes and feels a surge of hope and excitement.

"Meet me tomorra' at me pitch, will yee, Mary?"

That night, preparing for sleep on her rooftop hideaway, Mary can think of nothing but Brian. *'Ees so 'ansome, so funny, so clever. I likes 'im better than I 'ave ever liked anyone afore. Does 'ee fink I am pretty? I 'ope so. Will he be there tomorra? 'Ee 'ad better be, or I will die.* Her last image before succumbing to slumber is of a freckled face, mischievous smile and dark-brown eyes.

Brian walks north, up Kingsland Road towards

Dalston, to the home he shares with George, and the older man's horse Tess, much loved by them both. Fed and groomed at the start and end of each day, she enjoys many an affectionate pat and soft word from them. In return for lodgings, Brian helps George, who suffers with arthritis, load up his cart each morning. The cottage is tiny so Brian either sleeps on a bedroll in front of the warm embers of the fire or outside in the covered cart. Evening time, they sit together at the scrubbed wooden table recounting stories from their day while eating freshly cooked meat or fish.

Approaching the cottage, Brian is preoccupied, unable to think of anything but Mary. He fully expects George to be dismayed on hearing of his feelings for a girl he has just met. He too is astonished to have fallen in love so quickly. Later, as he and George sit in front of the fire drinking ale from battered, pewter mugs, he tells his friend about her.

"'Tis a strange ting, George, bu' I feel like I knows her all me life. Despite her growin' up on d' streets around d' 'ighway, dere is a sweetness in her."

To further impress, he continues, "She goes to d' Christian school for pauper children an' has learned her prayers an' hymns."

George, pulling on his clay pipe, observes the barely contained excitement on his young friend's face.

"I got no objection to y' 'avin' a sweetheart, Brian, me boy. I trust y' t' choose a bonny gurl t' warm yer bed, an' make you 'appy. You are a good lad, wiv common sense. Since me mufver passed, I do miss a woman's company

Brian boy. Indeed, I do. Let 'er come 'ere an' live wiv us an' in time y' can be wedded."

Getting up from the table, Brian, stretching his arm out, touches the older man's hand.

"Tanks, George. Y' have a kind heart an' dat's a fact."

The next day, within minutes of finishing his act, Brian packs up his props, grabs Mary's hand and side by side, in excited silence, they walk to the embankment to sit on a wooden bench facing the Thames. The noisy road traffic competes with the chugging river barges, ferries and wherry boats moving up and down the river. The young lovers giggle at the antics of two scavenging pigeons scuttling around their feet fighting over an apple core discarded by Brian. Slipping his arm around Mary's slight shoulders, looking earnest, Brian asks. "Darlin' Mary! I know 'tis quick t' say I love yee, bu' I do. I spoke wid George an' he said I should ask y' to come an' live wid us and tell you I will marry you as soon as possible."

Momentarily speechless, mouth agape, Mary is stunned. Then she begins to gabble, "Am I dreamin'? Does y' really love me and wan' t' marry me, Brian? I can't believe it. I promise I will be good from now on. I won't fieve or lie. I promise. I promise. I love y', Brian."

Whisperings:
And so, the intensity of first love vanquishes doubt, as it should. It is a gift, albeit a transient one.

Mary runs towards Ratcliffe Highway, to a yard behind a derelict shop, where her few belongings are stashed in a battered wooden trunk, hidden beneath a pile of broken wood. Raising the heavy lid, she lifts out a hairbrush, missing half its bristles, a long hatpin with a chipped pearl bead on its end, and a heavy, linen laundry sack. Untying the ribbon drawstring of this bag, she removes a threadbare, once-white, cotton chemise; a grubby, flesh-coloured bodice stolen from a second-hand clothes cart; a plain, cream camisole; a boy's worn, woollen jacket; she found draped over iron railings near the river; a faded-blue frilled petticoat; and a spare pair of brown, leather boots, two sizes too big. *I 'opes Brian don' mind me not 'avin' no propa ni' clothes. I will jus' 'ave t' wear me bodice an' chemise, or me birfday suit.*

Heat surges through her body at the thought.

She fills the bag with what she can feasibly carry and, slinging it over her shoulder, she leaves the yard and heads to a familiar warehouse roof near Shadwell High Street where she beds down for the night. Next morning, having had little sleep due to her excitement, she trudges her way along the Embankment towards the open patch of land near The Tower where she finds Brian plying his trade. Too intoxicated by Mary's presence, Brian is unable to focus on his performance, so he packs up early and together they start the long walk to Kingsland Road. Mary's throat is dry and her stomach churns with apprehension. Sensing her disquiet, Brian stops, drops his baggage, takes her small hands in his and smiles into her eyes.

"Don't worry yer pretty head, Mary darlin', fer George will love yee, as I do."

Reassured, her desire to be with Brian, to please him, to be loved by him, lessens her misgivings and she walks more confidently towards her new life; a home and a family. Near Dalston Market they bump into two, round-shouldered elderly men, sweeping up rubbish left by costermongers. Brian doffs his cap.

"Evening, Thomas! Evening, Will! I hope yee both had a good day? Dis is me betrothed, Mary Molly Nolan. We are t' be wed."

"Well, ain't that wonderful news. I am glad to see you wid a wee colleen, and her wid d' name of Mary, a fine name, none finer," says Thomas.

"We was wondering why auld George was smilin' like a Cheshire cat when we seen 'im earlier. Now I knows why. Indeed, I do!" adds Will.

On first meeting George, Mary is wary, and it is some weeks before she overcomes her mistrust. Being asked to tend to the beautiful copper-brown horse, Tess, fills her with delight. Alone in the cramped stable, she relaxes, and a close affinity soon evolves between Mary and the mare. While grooming her she basks in the warm smells of straw, hay, and horse sweat and is comforted by the sound of Tess breathing and munching from her nose bag. Her genuine love of Tess endears her to George who takes the young girl to his heart, teaching her to cook, work Tess's reins and drive the cart.

The young lovers share the amenities of George's cottage during the day and at night they bed down on soft rugs, under thick woollen blankets inside the tarpaulin-covered cart. Mary, despite childhood exposure to vice, retained her virginity until Brian. Now her nights are filled with passionate, joyful lovemaking, when she and Brian experience sensual pleasures, and the delight of falling asleep in each other's arms and waking up together each morning. Despite their frequent intimacy, Mary does not fall pregnant, though this does not concern either of them as they want to be married before starting a family.

Months pass. Days are taken up in the rhythmic routines of shared chores; grooming, feeding, and harnessing Tess, loading and securing goods onto the wagon, hanging wet laundry over a rope line strung across the yard or on a wooden ceiling airer in the kitchen, cleaning the grate, setting the fire and sweeping the floors. Mary, so long wayward in her habits, likes routines and structures to her day. Her favourite task is doing the weekly grocery shop, for then she is free to wander in familiar marketplaces; Spitalfields, Billingsgate and Smithfield.

Whenever George and Brian travel south, towards Whitechapel, she hitches a ride, getting dropped-off opposite The Britannia Pub. Sometimes she walks the long route from Dalston, mingling with bustling crowds; women pushing rusting prams full of groceries, men in round caps walking briskly towards the docks, children darting between laden carts and picking up fallen fruit and road traffic lumbering along, leaving trails of horse manure to be picked up by scavengers. Once at the market, she participates in good-natured, costermonger banter and female gossip and is pleasantly assaulted on all sides by sellers calling out their wares, barking dogs, children shrieking, babies crying, sweet-smelling flowers, pungent fish, and heaving men and women pushing to get at bargains. She passes an idyllic year before a tragedy changes her life once more.

On a chilly Tuesday morning, she is dropped off at The Britannia as usual. Jumping down from the wagon, she waves Brian and George a cheery goodbye, calling out over the noise of the traffic, "Ta-ra! See y' bofe later, in this very spot, abou' four o clock."

Brian blows her a kiss as George guides the cart back out into the long, lumbering mass of slow-moving vehicles heading towards Westminster Bridge. From there George hopes to get to Battersea in good time to make his deliveries. Circumnavigating their way through the tumult of horse-drawn carts, over-crowded omnibuses, and hand-cart pushers weaving and dodging their way across the road requires the maximum concentration from them both. That morning, the Embankment is exceptionally congested as horses strain and pull their unwieldy, overloaded wagons; heavy brewers' drays, slow-moving donkey-carts, buses and black cabs. Arriving at the junction of Westminster Bridge, George turns left, relieved to be finally crossing over the river.

"Brian, I 'ope we can make up d' time once we are soufe of d' river."

More convinced than his old friend that they would get to their destination on time, Brian reassures him.

"Don't fret yerself, George! I can help yee offload once we get dere."

The words have hardly left his lips when something

alarming catches his eye. He shouts, "George! George! Watch ou'!"

There is disbelief at the sight that confronts them, and time slows down. A high-wheeled, unstable trap swerves, and judders at speed into the middle of the traffic on their side of the road as the driver frantically tries to bring his frightened horse back under control. Everything is silent. Brian and George are deaf to the catastrophic sounds made as the trap overturns and slews about between screaming horses, wagon wheels and debris falling from surrounding vehicles. Amid these chaotic scenes, they are suspended in eerie silence.

A loaded coal cart, unable to avoid an impact with a vehicle full of logs, swerves into the side of George's wagon. He lets go of Tess's reins and is catapulted to the ground where he is immediately joined by Brian, who hits the road surface head first. In his mind's eye, Brian sees Mary's sweet face, framed by her riotous black curls, and her sky-blue eyes before blackness envelops him. Unconscious, their bodies are pummelled by the hooves of petrified, loose animals; goats, pigs, carthorses and donkeys. Wheels from smashed wagons spin uncontrollably while logs, coal, beer barrels and food produce tumble down. For a brief second, before a last fatal blow to his head, George opens his eyes and calls out joyfully to his dead mother.

When Brian's slender, youthful body is later lifted from the road, an elderly woman remarks on the peaceful expression on his unmarked face and is glad of it. George's body lies close by, pulped and bloodied by the flailing hooves of many frantic creatures. Tess lies beside him; her huge head lays peacefully on his chest near his silent heart. The bridge is closed to traffic for two hours to allow hospital vehicles to take away the injured and the dead. Men jump from vehicles and run to help, while guards on duty outside Westminster Parliament tear, with their bare hands, at the tangled mess of harnesses and broken wagons. Mortally wounded animals are shot. From pavements nearby, women weep and protect their children from seeing the unfolding horror; covering their eyes with their hands or turning their faces into the folds of their long skirts and coats.

Mary stands where she was dropped off earlier, a bulging sack of food by her feet. With just a thin, black shawl covering her shoulders, she shivers, not from the cool evening breeze, but from a sudden feeling of foreboding. Craning her neck, she watches traffic approaching from Whitechapel, waiting for the moment she will catch a first glimpse of Tess's distinctive russet mane. Impatient, she wonders, *Ain't like 'em t' keep me waitin'. Somefink musta 'appened, 'cause George is never late.*

Faintly, she thinks she hears someone calling her name.

"Mary! Mary Nolan, where are yee? Wave your arm in the air, Mary, so I can see y' among d' crowd."

Raising her arms, she stands on tippy-toe and sees Billy, a neighbour of theirs, pulling his pony and trap to a halt at the nearby kerb. Her smile of greeting fades when she sees his pale, drawn face. With tears in his eyes, he looks down sorrowfully at her and instantaneously every bone in Mary's body turns to jelly and her stomach drops down into her boots. Gripped by dread, she shouts at him, "Billy, tell me wha' is goin' on? 'Ave y' seen George an' Brian? I ain't 'aff gettin' worried 'bout them."

Climbing down from his trap, Billy removes his frayed, tweed, peaked cap, holds it nervously, and steps up close to Mary, hesitating to tell her the terrible news and the gruesome nature of the death of George, Brian, and Tess. Putting his big hand gently upon her shoulder, he tells her what he must, though it breaks his heart to do so.

"Mary, y' 'ave t' be a brave gurl, fer d' news is bad. D' news is bad indeed. Yer young man, Brian, an' ole George, got killed on d' bridge by d' 'ouses of Parliament. An 'igh trap did overturn, an' slam into vehicles an' 'orses, an' Tess. They be all dead, little Mary! They be all dead, an' that is d' sad, an' 'orrible, trufe."

On hearing his words, Mary is plunged into a pit of darkness. The world becomes muted and for the first time in her life, she faints. On coming around, she hears unearthly, high-pitched screams reverberating in the atmosphere around her. On and on they go, tortured, piercing cries of unbearable agony that eventually dwindle into low, guttural sobs. Then she knows it is she who screams.

Mary sits, icy cold, in Billy's small trap. In shock, she utters not one word on the ride back to the cottage. Her spirit falls into a pit of despair. Gone from her life is all that made it meaningful. Without Brian, George, and Tess, she has nothing. Once home, and alone, she feels her young heart break, and through the night, in front of the dying embers of the fire, she weeps until there are no more tears to be shed. As dawn breaks, her abject misery turns to bitterness and fury. The power of these emotions gives her a surge of strength and determination. *Best t' be on me own again, t' forget d' life I had wiv Brian an' George. It was good while it lasted bu' in giffin' away me 'art, I lost command over me life.*

Later that morning, she trudges away from the cottage clutching a heavy hessian bag containing her personal belongings. With every step, she repeats set phrases in her head, *Don' look back, girl. Forget Brian. Forget Tess. Forget George. Don' look back, girl.* During the following weeks she resurrects her thieving skills, sauntering through markets snatching silk scarves, purses, hatpins and fob-watches loosely dangling from pockets. Sitting on corners, looking suitably sad, she cadges money from passers-by. No longer reluctant to sell her body for sex, at night she dons gaudy, colourful clothes, rouges her lips and cheeks and goes touting for business. She experiences a resurgence of her independence and truculent personality and is emboldened by it.

Before long, her earnings from prostitution allow her to rent a shared room with Lily, a London girl, the same age as her, who supplements the pittance she earns as a feather curler by working part-time in the sex trade. It is a mutually beneficial relationship for them both and Lily is the first person that Mary grows to trust. Since returning to the Hamlets, she is detached and cold towards others, rarely laughing, and prone to furious outbursts and physical violence when thwarted. Her upper arms carry the scars of secret mutilations made with a sharp knife; a habit inspired by the relief she feels when the pain hits.

On New Year's Eve, eighteen-hundred and seventy-five, Mary and Lily, both nearing the age of fifteen, hear interesting gossip about a Doctor William Raymond. Rumour has it that he owns a splendid manor house in a rural hamlet in Essex and plans on offering poor London girls free lodgings and education. Information leaflets, posted outside ale houses, brothels and churches, invite interested girls to visit the Methodist Church Hall near Whitechapel. On the spur of the moment, Mary and Lily decide to visit the Hall.

Dressed modestly, wishing to make the right impression, they are greeted warmly by a plump, rosy-cheeked woman in the doorway of the Church Hall. She introduces herself as Mrs Susanna Mond, the wife of the church pastor. Turning towards a tall, thin-faced woman, smiling at the girls from inside the doorway, she makes an introduction.

"This is Mrs Hilda Shaw, who is to be the housemother at the Essex Lodge."

Both women show a keen interest in the girls and advise them to return the following week. Seven long days and nights the girls wait in anticipation. Lily can hardly contain her excitement.

"I 'ope we get 'cepted, Mary, fer I never bin in d' countryside. I fink farmyard smells will be a damn sight better than d' stink from rubbish dumps aroun' 'ere."

With relief, Lily and Mary receive the news that they are to be part of the first cohort of girls to leave the

Hamlets and take up residence in *Poplar Lodge*, near the village of Crandon, in Essex.

Whisperings:
Endings and beginnings, beginnings and endings are one and the same. All of us waiting souls know this.

2

Seth

Vices are sometimes only virtues carried to excess.
 Oliver Twist – Charles Dickens

1876

Seth Marchwood, five months short of his eighteenth birthday, confidently sits on the driving seat of a heavy wooden cart loosely holding the reins of a harnessed, sable-black, shire horse. His senses are steeped in the warm, sweet smells of horse sweat and leather bridleware. His mare, Rosie, valuable for her immense strength and stamina, is considered handsome with her roman nose and soft, creamy feathering on her lower legs. She pulls heavy farm machinery for long hours without the need to rest. Seth ponders, as he casts proud glances at the animal's huge flanks, *Ain't it grand t' own such a fine piece of 'orse flesh?* He gloats in the knowledge that his despised stepfather, Wilfred Loxbury, is jealous of him owning such a prize animal at such a young age.

Fifteen hands high, Rosie dwarfs most local horses.

Effortlessly, Seth controls her while they move at a leisurely pace along the country lane. His round cap sits jauntily on the back of his head as he nods to labourers working in the fields. Acknowledging him with a wave or the doffing of their caps, he is aware of the respect and envy he garners as they watch him pass by.

Seth pulls Rosie's reins impatiently to stop her slackening her pace as she plods through deep ruts etched out by heavy cartwheels. Responding, the horse moves to the right of the track, avoiding dangling foliage from a huge copper beech tree. Ducking his head, Seth evades the tangled leafy canopy and his face, thrown into shade by fluttering leaves, is dark as a gypsy's.

Emerging into light, he pulls his cap low over his brow as his eyes adjust to the intense light of the setting sun. Straight, fine, sandy-coloured hair straggles down beneath the back rim of his worn cap where his thick neck springs up from his collar. On his right cheek is a two-inch-long scar, the result of a deep laceration, long ago inflicted by the flailing hoof of an angry horse. His mouth is wide, his upper lip thin and raised on one side, giving him a permanent sneer. His plump, lower lip suggests a hedonistic nature. Large hazel eyes, greener in colour than brown, are a prominent feature in his broad, high-cheek boned face. Muscled arms bulge beneath the sleeves of his jacket and his big, square hands are ingrained with dirt from his physical labours. Tall and stocky, his physique channels a raw strength.

Today, Seth wears his usual working attire; a striped, cotton, collarless shirt with the top button undone, a worn, tan leather jerkin, a dark-green tweed jacket, patched and threadbare, and brown trousers made of thick, tightly woven, woollen cloth. Tied below each knee and around the ankles is string, kept there to keep vermin from running up his legs when working in fields. Sturdy, black, weatherproof button boots encase his feet.

Seventeen years of age and already he is a magnet for local females of all ages, irresistibly drawn to his rough masculinity and earthiness. On warm summer evenings, he strips naked and plunges into the waters of the River Lee. There he wallows in the sensations of cool, rippling wavelets running over his bare skin. Swimming, unfettered by clothes, arouses his physical desires, so afterwards it is his habit to seek out local girls willing to abandon themselves to his lusty overtures.

His reputation as a skilled drover encourages farmers to employ him to drive their animal herds to markets and buy and sell on their behalf. Working at Pickstone Farm as a seasonable agricultural labourer, he can travel, once a month, to London's cattle markets. There he accrues experience buying, selling, and transporting livestock. Referred to by other dealers as *'The Essex Drover'*, he is known for his professional assessment of big horses such as Suffolk Punches, Lincolns, and Drays. Ambitious to become an independent horse dealer, he exercises considerable ingenuity to hide the fact that he can barely read and write, though thanks to his mother, he can sign his name.

From an early age, Seth displayed a passionate interest in working horses and the ploughs and vehicles they pull. Hour after hour, he sat astride field gates watching farm labourers dress the huge animals in their complex bridles and brasses. He also observed labourers skilfully manipulate the reins to successfully steer horse-teams through fields of thick clay. Infatuated by the size and power of horses and in awe of the animals' drivers, he soon learned to copy their behaviour, and by the age of twelve, he was able to gain obedience from a horse and use his whip and voice to good effect.

Despite his huge admiration for the strength and stamina of cart horses and Shires, he is not sentimental about them. In his opinion, they exist to be mastered and utilised by men and if that sometimes involves beating them, there need be no shame attached to it. Owning Rosie has not changed his view, though he would, in truth, be upset if he were to lose her. This sultry evening, as they travel together down Leather Lane, communication flows telepathically between them. The lane, a narrow, rutted, earthen track, is bounded on one side by a thick, tangled, bramble hedge and on the other by a ditch. The gully, usually full of water in winter, is dry, baked hard after a long hot spell. Adjusting his cap, Seth rubs a hand over his clean-shaven chin, musing about the recent weather. *'Tis a good job we 'ad a wet spring, wet 'nuff t' soak d' land. Reckon there be ample waw'er under d' soil, so crops will get as much as they need this year.*

Approaching a slight rise in the lane, he sees a group of workers harvesting a field ahead. A pair of piebald horses stand by as men pitch hay into a cart, piling it high. Once filled, it will be driven to Pickstone Farm, unloaded, and stored in a barn for winter feed and bedding. Further up the field, a youth wielding a pitchfork is building haystacks. It is Bill Loxbury, Seth's twelve-year-old half-brother, a brawny, stocky lad who worships Seth. He spends his days trying to emulate Seth's horsemanship, his self-confidence and poaching abilities.

Working alongside Bill is John Loxbury, Seth's stepbrother, five years older than him, and someone he trusts. John, a kind-natured young man, formed a deep, sympathetic bond with his younger stepbrothers, Seth and Bert, when his father Wilfred Loxbury married their widowed mother, Lottie Marchwood in eighteen-sixty. John was deeply affected by Wilfred's cruel treatment of his stepsons.

Seth calls out, "Evenin', Bill! Evenin', John!"

Downing their tools, they touch the peak of their caps and wave at Seth before resuming their fieldwork.

Neither Seth nor his older brother Bert remember their dead father, Hubert Edward Marchwood, who died two months before Seth was born. Despite being the younger of the two, Seth is the dominant sibling and fiercely protective of Bert. Beaten around the head by Wilfred when he was a boy, Bert is deaf in one ear. Consequently, the brotherly bond between Seth and Bert is strong, forged in the shared miseries of their childhood.

Their mother, Lottie Marchwood, widowed in eighteen-fifty-nine, remarried shortly after Hubert's death. In danger of ending up in the workhouse and losing her children, she willingly married Wilfred Loxbury, a widowed farm labourer sixteen years older than her. He offered marriage and financial security and in return she would bear him more children and do all necessary domestic chores. Three children were born to the couple: Bill, Vera and Maria.

Lottie does not love Wilfred in the way she loved her first husband. Neither does she feel much tenderness towards him, for he is a rough, ignorant, spiteful man. A puny diminutive figure, Wilfred has a ruddy complexion and small, deep-set, black eyes, sunk beneath bushy, jutting eyebrows. Humourless, his facial expression reflects a sour character and meanness of spirit. His attitude towards Lottie and the family is impatient, morose, moody, volatile, and demanding.

As Seth and Bert grew bigger, Wilfred's dominance over them lessened. To compensate for the creeping erosion of his power over the boys, his volleys of verbal abuse became more intense.

"'Member your place in d' family, boys. As my stepsons, you are on d' lowest rung of d' ladda. Y' are not my flesh an' blood, an' glad I am of it. Be fankful that I giff y' a roof over yer 'eds, an' food t' eat. Jus' so y' know, y' bofe mean nuvfink t' me. All y' are t' me is a bloody nuisance."

For years, the Marchwood brothers ate separately from the family, taking their meals in the scullery. Exclusion from the table did not displease them, for it allowed them to avoid Wilfred's glowering face. Fed leftovers, Bert and Seth existed in a constant cloud of resentment, anger, apprehension, dread, and loathing. Hyper-alert to their stepfather's moods, they knew that one wrong word from them would result in a brutal whipping with the leather strap, to this day still hanging on the iron hook behind the scullery door. In time, they found ways to thwart him by hiding their fear behind blank, emotionless faces and by never giving him the satisfaction of seeing them cry. Their lack of response baffled and enraged Wilfred.

When Seth turned fourteen, the family power dynamic changed in his favour. A vicious fight between him and Wilfred spilled out into the lane in front of their cottage. Seth's youthful agility, strength, and years of pent-up rage meant that he left his stepfather beaten and bloodied on the ground. From that moment onwards, Seth became the undisputed dominant male in the Loxbury household.

Now, as he and Rosie draw near to home, he thinks about his brother Bert, and is happy that he is married to Agnes and father of a baby son. *A strong good-natured woman is Agnes, an' she will look after Bert.* In character he knows that they are different; Bert is less ambitious, less inclined to take risks and more sensitive towards others but fiercely loyal to his younger brother who he much admires.

Regular trips to East London allow Seth to enjoy the company of prostitutes in brothels. Carnal experience, acquired in Limehouse whorehouses, inflates his burgeoning ego. Following bouts of energetic coupling in vice dens, he struts about horse markets with an air of smug self-satisfaction, his physical allure palpable. Hampered as he is with overwhelming sexual impulses, he compulsively seeks out sexual trysts wherever he can. He seduces rosy-cheeked, eager daughters of farmers and servant girls working in manor houses. In well-hidden places, beneath hedges, in barns, in carts, atop haystacks and in fields of long grass, he gives, and receives, lustful pleasure and gratification.

Suddenly Rosie whinnies, tossing her mane, as she tries to dislodge flies, dipping into her eyes for moisture. Early signs of dusk turn the horizon soft pink as they near Church Farm Cottages, and home. Pulling Rosie up, he leaps down from the cart seat to open a rusting field farm gate. Together, they amble across a small field to a stone-built outhouse, tiled with a slate roof and having a single, latched, stable door. Once Rosie is unhitched, Seth hangs up the bridle paraphernalia and wipes her down to remove salty, wet traces of sweat from her glossy coat. Finishing his tasks, he strides towards the end cottage of Church Farm Terrace.

Much to his gratification he knows that tonight he, the main family breadwinner, will be served first at the table, and be given the best pieces of meat or fish from the pot. Wilfred will be forced to wait. He is somewhat preoccupied with an unexpected development that occurred that morning and he expects the news to trigger conjecture and gossip within his family and the wider village community. Still, he cannot but feel pleased and excited by the fact that the handsome widow, Bella McKenzie, offered him work at her farm earlier that day. He speculates on her motives. *Why 'as d' attractive widda come an' offered me work, when she could 'ave older, more experienced men from d' village? Is it me young body she is lustin' after or me skills wiv 'orses?* He chuckles lasciviously.

Reaching the cottage door, he removes his boots

and, stooping his head, goes through the doorway onto a bare, grey flagstone floor. To the right of the door is a single-paned window, set deep in the wall. In the centre of the floor stands a rectangular pine table, flanked by two rough-hewn benches, scuffed, and scratched from many years of use. Two wooden high-backed chairs, similarly old, stand either side of the small black range in the fireplace. The once white walls either side of the hearth are smoke-stained and flaking in parts.

Lottie Marchwood is excessively house-proud. She lives and breathes the motto 'Cleanliness is next to Godliness.' Under her stringent supervision, her daughters, Maria and Vera, carry out daily domestic chores. As dawn breaks, they are hard at work. One cleans out the fire-grate, damping down the embers and shovelling cinders and ash into a galvanised bucket. The other sister carries the full bucket out to the back yard where she griddles the contents, separating the reusable cinders and placing them in the coal scuttle with fresh lumps of coal. Once done, they busy themselves blackening the stove before lighting a new fire in the range and placing the kettle of water on the hob to boil.

While keeping a sharp eye on her daughters, Lottie makes bread and prepares vegetables to add to the stock pot. Towards the end of each day, she adds meat or fish, whichever is available. Sunday is a day for roast lamb, a ritual that never changes. When times are hard, Lottie ensures that there is a plentiful supply of fresh bread and dripping.

Seth's eyes alight on his mother stirring the contents

of the stock pot with a long-handled, wooden spoon. At thirty-six, Lottie is a tall, slender, upright woman with a large imposing bosom. Her stiff, formidable appearance compliments her strident, disapproving manner. Deep-set, hard, black eyes glare unblinkingly, and her thin-lipped mouth is always pursed in disapproval and God-fearing self-righteousness. She looks towards Seth.

"Did y' find anyfink in them snares y' laid yestaday? A rabbit or hare praps?"

Seth is struck with resentment at her query.

"I ain't 'ad time t' check 'em yet. Bin too busy, up atta Pickstone Farm, wiv d' 'orses. I will check tomorra."

Sitting at the table are Seth's two half-sisters. Both avoid looking at their father, who sits near the hearth, sharpening his scythe with a whetstone. However, they are acutely aware of their half-brother, furtively raising their eyes to look slyly at him, before exchanging glances with each other. The choking silence in the kitchen is heavy with forbidden thoughts of sexual desire, fear, and hatred. Seth's face is impassive and devoid of expression. Ignoring Wilfred, who watches him malevolently, he crosses the floor and lifts the latch of the scullery door. Entering, he goes to the stone sink to wash his hands with carbolic soap. Using a small, hard brush, he attacks the ingrained dirt on his fingers and under his nails.

Going outside, he uses the earth-closet, a timber-built structure with a corrugated tin roof. For convenience there are two pits, each covered by a wooden seat box. Relieving himself, Seth muses, in pleasurable anticipation, *I 'spec d' buxom Bella will 'ave a h-indoor closet, wiv a propa' basin t' wash in, an' expensive, sweet smellin' soap too.*

Returning to the scullery, he rinses his hands again and hangs his heavy jacket on a wall hook before he goes back into the kitchen. As soon as he sits down at the table, Lottie scurries to serve him. Not a word does he speak until his last mouthful of turnip and beef hotpot then, leaning back, he speaks intentionally slower than usual.

"I be workin' away tomorra night, 'cause, d' widda, a' Down Bridge Farm, she wans' some work done wiv 'er 'orses. Twill be too late t' come 'ome when me labourin' is finished, so I will be sleepin' over at 'ers."

Not trying to hide the sneer on his lips, Wilfred mockingly remarks, "That be d' red 'eded widda, a fine-lookin' woman. I reckon she be wantin' more than 'er big 'orses mastered an' driven 'ard."

Leering, Wilfred looks at Lottie and winks.

"I 'ear say she be always lookin' out fer young bucks t' warm 'er bed an' am told she 'as gone fru most young men in d' village."

Folding her arms across her ample bosom, Lottie spits out, "An' I 'ear she works 'er poor maid, Molly Walker, long hours but favours d' lads workin' fer 'er. There is talk that they are used to satisfy 'er immoral urges."

Ignoring the attempts to goad him, Seth is coldly disinterested. Aware of his mother's reputation as chief scandal monger in the neighbourhood, he expects the news to spread like wildfire. Ignoring them both, he turns his thoughts once more to the attractive widow and imagines sensual encounters with her. He pictures her naked; her creamy flesh, and freckled face, framed in luxuriant russet hair, and her blue eyes alight with passion. Seeing her close today, he had difficulty pulling his gaze from her plump juicy lips and hourglass figure, unmarked by having borne three children.

The following day, he arrives at Down Bridge Farm in pent-up anticipation. His thoughts are scrambled. *Praps 'er desires will get d' better of 'er this very ni'? I 'ope it do, fer I fink I mi' 'ave a problem controllin' meseff. I seen d' way she did blush red, an' look me up an' down? I seen d' invitation in 'er eyes. I will wait fer 'er t' come to me.*

Cordially greeting him, Bella shows him where to stable Rosie and park his cart. Leading him into the farmhouse and up a narrow staircase to an attic room, she shows him the comfortable double bed where he will sleep. On a marble-topped side table, there is a pitcher of water, a plain white, delft bowl and a blue floral soap-dish. Two handcloths hang on a rung beneath the side-table. Telling Seth to leave his belonging there, she seems suddenly self-conscious. Turning to leave the room, she tells him to come down to the kitchen when he is ready, and cook will serve him supper there.

On his second night at Down Bridge Farm, Seth retires to his room after a long day training Bella's horse for the plough. Tired, and replete, after eating a substantial supper of boiled gammon and vegetables, he lies naked upon the white sheets of the bed and is soon asleep. Three hours later, the grandfather clock in the farmhouse hallway chimes midnight. Seth, startled, wakes up hearing a noise close by. The latch on the bedroom door is being lifted. As the door slowly opens, he sees, by the soft glow of moonlight beaming through the skylight, a nude Bella silhouetted in the doorway, her unbound hair hanging loose down to the small of her back. Seth's pulse beats fast. Laughing softly, he springs from the bed. Without uttering a word, he pulls Bella into the room, places his big hands either side of her waist and effortlessly lifts her up. Her long, slender legs loop around his waist and with no sexual preliminaries, he presses her silky back against the bedroom wall and enters her. There ensues a mutually fierce mating, over quickly but followed by multiple fiery couplings until birdsong heralds the dawn.

During the following months, twice a week, Seth and Bella are insatiable in their sexual desire for each other. Bella is Seth's wanton lover, an older, experienced woman who teaches him new sensual tricks. Both are ravenous and inventive during their lustful encounters. Bella's passion, however, soon turns to obsession; she becomes possessive and intensely jealous. To keep him from straying, she overindulges him when he is at her farm; feeding him his favourite cuts of meat, buying him the best quality ales to drink and flattering him at every opportunity. At first, Seth basks in her lavish attentions but after a short while, he feels stifled and bored by her excessive neediness, and her endeavours to control him. Growing increasingly irritated by her cloying tendencies, he stops going to Down Bridge Farm and resumes his dalliances with young prostitutes in London brothels where he does not have to pretend affection. *Payin' fer me pleasures is cleaner some 'ow, easier. Young girls are more me type. Bella is too old fer me I fink.* His thoughts reflect a newfound pragmatism. Paying for sex is business, and in business he is on safe, unemotional territory.

Drinking in The Grapes in Limehouse on a foggy November night, he meets two cheeky harlots, Flo and Dot. What they impart to him is astonishing and piques his interest. Learning that he is from Crandonside in Essex, Flo exclaims, "Crandonside! Why, that is where d' Christian gentleman, Doctor Charlie Raymond, owns a big estate. I bin told that 'ee plans t' take 'omeless girls from d' 'amlets t' liff there."

Intrigued, Seth asks for more information. "Where in Crandonside? "Has d' place got a name?"

Dot, after some thought, replies, "I fink it is called Poplar Lodge. Ain't that ri', Flo?"

Flo nods.

Seth is pleasurably surprised by the news. As he travels back to Essex the next morning, he mulls it over. *Well, I be blowed! Ain't that jus' d' mos' intrestin' bi' of news I 'eard in a long time. Popla' Lodge is only 'alf a mile away from Church Farm Cottages.* Arriving in Crandonside, he stops off at the village pub eager to spread the word. A feverish excitement breaks out among the local men and boys on learning of the imminent arrival of wayward London girls. Their pent-up excitement is, however, dampened by the disapproval, anger and fear among their wives, mothers and daughters.

December eighteen-seventy-six, forty unruly, orphaned young women arrive at Poplar Lodge. From the start, their behaviour is troublesome and difficult for staff to manage. Unused to rules and boundaries, many sneak out at night-time, climbing over the estate wall to cause havoc in the surrounding hamlets and villages. There, they accost farm boys, offering them sexual favours for a price. To the indignation of village womenfolk, husbands and sons squander hard-earned cash on these irresistible privileges.

Charles Raymond, unable to ignore the deluge of complaints, returns the worst-behaving culprits back to the streets of London. Those less troublesome remain. Among them are Mary and her friend, Lily.

Whisperings:
And so, the die is cast.

3

Poplar Lodge

The shadows of our own desires stand between us and our better angels, and thus their brightness is eclipsed.
   Barnaby Rudge – Charles Dickens

1876–1877

Living at Poplar Lodge, courtesy of the charitable Doctor Charles Raymond, Mary, despite hating restrictions on her independence, generally plays by the rules. Her reluctant compliance is a price worth paying for a comfortable bed, three meals a day, clean drinking water, personal washing facilities and a wonderful new wardrobe of clothes. She curtails her learned street behaviours, hiding them behind a façade of innocence and obedience; acceptable characteristics, guaranteed to earn her praise from staff.

She, and Lily, luxuriate in the amenities at the big house. Used to living in squalor, Mary now has beside her bed a tile-topped washstand upon which stands a pretty, pink, floral, ceramic pitcher and basin. Inside the small cupboard of the washstand is a chamber pot for her

exclusive use, not just a plain white cha_
with a rim decorated with pretty, blue c_
accustomed to relieving herself in shared,
privies behind slum dwellings, she feels ju_
have a pot for her exclusive use.

Willingly, she and Lily accept the mandatory daily chores. Their first task of every day, without exception, is to empty the basins of dirty water used for their ablutions that morning. Each girl pours the grey soapy liquid into an enamel slop-bucket that stands at the end of every dormitory bed, after which they empty their chamber pots into the same utensil. Carefully, a lid is placed on top of the bucket to prevent spillages when it is moved. Basins and chamber pots are then wiped clean with a damp rag. The chamber pot is placed back in the washstand and the clean basin is placed on top.

Once these bedside tasks are completed, the girls stand and wait for the house mother to ring a brass handbell. At the first sound of the clappers, the girls lift their heavy buckets and, in a single file, carry them onto the landing and down the wide, curved staircase to the ground floor. Filing out into the back yard, the effluent is tipped into any one of six earthen latrines which back onto a high, redbrick wall. Rinsing the buckets under the yard pump, the girls once more line up and, at the ring of the bell, return upstairs to their sleeping quarters to make their beds and refill pitchers with clean water.

Mary chats with Lily over a delicious breakfast of creamy porridge and fresh bread served in the refectory on the ground floor.

"Gor blimey, Lil, 'aint it grand? 'Ere we sit eatin' creamy oats, an' drinkin' cups of tea, wiv as much bread an' jam that we can eat, I fink we 'ave died an' gawn t' 'eaven. I never dreamed I would be livin' in such a posh 'ouse, gettin' everyfink fer nufvink."

When they arrived at the Lodge, the girls were kitted out with white cotton undergarments for summer, woollen undergarments for winter, a dark-blue weekday dress, a light-blue Sunday dress, woollen stockings, brown leather button-boots and a warm, grey, hooded coat. Like every Lodge resident, they are allocated a shoe box and a brass wall hook in the cloakroom. There they hang their starched white over-aprons and bonnets before going up to bed. Woolly hats and mufflers are kept on a shelf above the shoe boxes, and every item is name-tagged by the girls during sewing class. No longer clothed in grubby second-hand blouses and ill-fitting skirts or fighting infestations of head lice, Mary and Lily can spend time making themselves look pretty. Giggling and jostling one another, they pose and pout, admiring their reflections in the huge, gilt wall mirror hanging in the entrance lobby of the Lodge.

As their first Christmas in the big house approaches, the weather turns bitterly cold. Puddles freeze solid along the winding track that runs down to the imposing wooden gates. Leafless branches of giant copper beech trees, flanking the driveway, sag under the weight of hoary frost. Mary is restless. She struggles with boredom during a needlecraft lesson. Her efforts to produce a sampler with perfect rows of chain stitches, backstitches, cross-stitches and buttonhole stitches is faltering badly. She detests needlework and her lack of concentration on the task results in pricked fingers, which bleed many bright red dots onto her square of hessian cloth. Stifling an urge to swear aloud, she hatches a plan to relieve the tedium of her days and give into her yearning for a bit of fun. Poking an elbow into Lily's side, she whispers, "Lil! Wha' abou' gettin' ou' of 'ere for a bit, once we 'ave finished supper? It is so cold, they will never 'magine us sneakin' ou' over d' gates on such a bloomin' freezin' night. Wha' y' fink, Lil? We 'ave bin good as gold, bu' we need t' 'ave ourseffs a bi' of fun. We can leg it back afore d' lights go ou'. Wha' you say, Lil?"

Offering no resistance to Mary's tempting suggestion, Lily slyly winks at her. When supper finishes, they sneak off to the cloakroom, grab their coats, bonnets and mufflers and leave quietly through the side door of the building. Gleeful, the pair race like the wind down the winding track, slipping and sliding exuberantly over the icy ground. On reaching the high gates, they use the diagonal crossbars to clamber up and over, dropping down into the lane that leads to the village of Crandonside. Laughing, the girls dart one way, then another, in hope of spying a country lad on his way home from the local pub. Fifteen minutes they spend looking in vain for someone to tease. Eventually, giving up, noses blue with the cold, they run back towards the Lodge entrance.

Mary, behind Lil, hauls herself up to the top, where she sits astride, watching Lily slither down to land inelegantly on the driveway. Then, just as she is about to drop down and join Lily from her lofty position, she unexpectedly hears the clip clop of hooves. Turning her head in the direction of the sound, she sees, by the light of the half-moon and starlight, the silhouette of a broad-shouldered youth. He nonchalantly rides an enormous black horse. Holding her breath, she waits, not moving a muscle, quiet as a mouse. When the youth is close enough for her to see his features, she is pleased to see a handsome face beneath a workman's round cap. Strangely, he appears unsurprised at the sight of Mary perched on top of the gate. Letting go of the reins, he raises his right hand in greeting and gives a nod to her. For a split second, the pair look directly into each other's eyes. The brief visual contact startles them both, for it creates a shock wave that ripples between them. Instantaneously, Mary, recovering from the jolt, raises her eyes once more and looks directly at him. She grins cheekily while slowly looking him up and down before swiftly jumping out of sight to join Lily and race back up the Lodge driveway.

Each evening after this occurrence, avoiding staff scrutiny, Mary sneaks down to the Lodge entrance after supper. There she waits, willing the country boy to reappear. Tucking herself out of sight, she watches passing road traffic; two-seater traps driven fast by hunched men wearing long, heavy coats, lumbering wagons piled high with logs, and donkeys pulling small carts; some carrying live pigs to be slaughtered for the festive season. Muffled-up women and children trudge by, carrying bags of winter vegetables, their warm, exhaled breaths creating vast clouds of mist in the freezing night air. The disappointment Mary feels when the youth does not show up is tempered by her conviction that this good-looking young man is her destiny. She has a powerful belief in fate, a superstition fostered by Molly, who told her tales of fairy spirits leading us along a predestined pathway though life. Lying in her dormitory bed in the darkness, she endeavours to conjure up magic spells that will draw him to her.

On the evening of the fourteenth day after their first chance meeting, her forbearance and efforts bear fruit. With a heart thudding in exhilaration, she sees him slowly driving a horse and cart towards where she hides behind the gatepost. He stares intently towards the very spot where she is crouched though she thinks herself well hidden. Then, when he is a few feet from the gate, she scrambles quickly up and over it, jumping down to land with a soft thud in front of his startled horse.

A low, deep voice soothes the animal.

"Whoa, Rosie! Whoa, girl! Easy now!"

Hands on slim hips, flirtatious and provocative, Mary ignores any danger she might have put herself in. Tilting her head to one side, she teasingly says, "Y' took yer time comin' back, country boy. Why? I know you 'ave been finking of me, 'cause I 'ave been finking of you. Gimme yer 'and. Pull me up an' I can sit beside y'. I would like that, fer I am fadin' away fer want of some excitement."

Reaching out, Mary strokes the horse's nose, asking, "That is a fine 'orse you got. Do she belong t' you? You are lucky if she do. Will y' let me 'old d' reins, 'andsome boy? I want t' show you 'ow good I am at 'andlin' 'orses."

He takes so long a time to answer her that she is spurred into another bout of flirting,

"I could promise y' a kiss if y' lift me up t' sit beside y'."

Intrigued by this petite girl's bold, suggestive manner, the youth finally speaks.

"I like d' sound of that, missy. But best tell me yer name first, afore I take y' up 'ere beside me. An' don' fink t' tell me a fib, Missy, fer fibbin' gits me in a mood. Then I mi' be tempted t' giff y' a good spankin'."

In tandem with her racing heartbeat, Mary babbles, "Mary Nolan is me name. Wha' is yours? Is it Thomas, or Alfred or William praps, or is it 'Enry?"

Once more there is a lengthy pause before he answers in a low, drawling manner.

"Me name? Why 'tis Seff Marchwood, an' glad I am t' meet y', Mary Nolan."

Reaching down, he wraps his arm about her slim waist and effortlessly lifts her up. Tucking her close beside him, he hands her the reins,

"Now do as I say, an' y' will soon 'ave control of this 'ansome beast. Bu' best be warned, I won't be controlled by a littl' slip of a thing wiv a pretty face and frilly petticoats, like ole Rosie mi' be."

Enthusiastically taking up the challenge, Mary skilfully drives a few miles down the lane before deftly pulling to a halt by a field gate.

Impressed and curious, Seth asks, "'Ow did a London girl like you learn t' 'andle an 'orse so well? Were y' brung up in a stable?"

Tucking an errant curl back up beneath her bonnet, Mary pertly replies, "That's me secret t' tell, an' fer y' t' 'fin' ou'. An' afore y' ask me questions, Seff Marchwood, best I tell you wha' you will 'ave guessed. I *am* one of the Doc Raymond's orphan girls from Tower 'amlets. Unlike you, I 'ave 'ad a tough life, livin' 'and t' mouff on d' streets. There ain't nuvfink can shock me, Seff. I done fings I 'ad t' do, an' I ain't sorry for 'em. A small girl I might be, bu' I am tough as ole boots."

Captivated, Seth thinks, *Wha' good luck; a dainty, pretty, cheeky madam 'oo could probably teach me a fing or two between d' sheets.* Mary's provocative, bolshie manner and innuendoes about her worldliness imply to Seth that she will not baulk at his lusty sexual proclivities. *Jus' by lookin' at 'er I can tell she is as fond of frolics as I am. I can 'ave some fun wiv 'er, an no mistake,* he muses.

Within days of this encounter, Seth and Mary slake their rampant desire for each other in a hay barn a half a mile from Poplar Lodge.

Back at the cottage, Seth's mother, brother Bill, and sisters notice his uncharacteristic discomposure and they are all agog. Why is he rushing his supper each evening and spending considerable lengths of time washing himself in the scullery? Sniggering, the siblings whisper their suspicions,

"'Ee 'as got 'imseff anuver widda woman, or maybe a loose married woman t' play wiv. She mus' be somefink special fer 'ee is preoccupied wiv washin' 'imseff these days. 'Oo can it be?"

Each night, as Mary waits in the dark for Seth to arrive, she trembles in fevered anticipation of their impending lovemaking. When she gets her first glimpse of Rosie trotting down the lane, she runs towards them. Leaning down, Seth hoists her and holds her on his lap as he drives the cart away from the Lodge gates. Mary presses her hot cheek to his broad chest and snuggles into him. Eagerly, the young lovers seek out sheltered places where they hurl themselves into wild, insatiable lovemaking. Such sessions end abruptly when Mary suddenly remembers that she must get back to the Lodge and sneak into the dormitory and bed before she is missed.

Enthralled by her handsome country lover, Mary likes everything about him; his looks, his deep, drawling Essex accent and his cool, controlled, inscrutable demeanour. Morning, noon, and night, her thoughts are full of him and he in turn basks in her infatuation, which further boosts his already inflated ego. His sensual aura becomes more potent, drawing increased flirtatious attention from females of all ages. Mary is aware of his allure to other women and girls, but she is not possessive or jealous. Rather she is confident in the knowledge that Seth is as enamoured with her as she is with him and their mutual interest in passionate lovemaking binds them together. Lil witnesses Mary's excitement and joy and is happy for her friend. No-one knows better than her the heartbreak Mary suffered when she lost Brian, George and the horse Tess.

Mary's nocturnal meetings with Seth remain secret. During daylight hours, she lives within the consistent rhythm of Poplar Lodge routines. She is outwardly polite and deferential towards staff at the Lodge, obediently reciting obligatory prayers and applying herself to learning tracts from religious scripture. Though she remains doubtful of the dictates of doctrinal rules, she strives to meet most of Doctor Raymond's Christian expectations. To do otherwise would put her place in Poplar Lodge in jeopardy and she cannot bear the thought of returning to a life of poverty and struggle.

In common with Seth, Mary has an in-depth knowledge of the seedy side of life in Tower Hamlets. They are both familiar with corruption, crime, cruelty and vice, a shared knowledge that gives them an enhanced understanding of how to circumnavigate the criminal underworld that populates the rookeries and brothels of East London. Their common experiences are the foundation blocks for building a viable, lifelong partnership. With characters that are manipulative, callous, determined and ruthless, they are endowed with the traits necessary to grasp opportunities and survive against the odds.

During frequent trips to London docklands, Seth mingles with foreign sailors and gangs of petty thieves. Shortly before meeting Mary, he had been making enquiries about combining horse trading on the Continent with trafficking prostitutes between London and Belgium. Seeing nothing immoral or wrong with this ambition of his, he tells Mary about it and pummels her for information about where he can best locate vulnerable, pauper girls who might be persuaded to ply their trade in Belgium. He openly talks about his trysts in brothels and leisure pursuits in gambling dens, instinctively knowing that, because of her past, she dare not object to his dalliances.

Proud of his strength and muscular dexterity, Seth

is a formidable street fighter with a fearsome reputation for violent aggression when roused. Angered when he is pushed to pay his bills, he threatens inn keepers, shouts, swears and uses bricks, horse whips, wooden poles, leather straps and horseshoes as weapons of attack. Villagers are wary in his company; mindful of his ferocious temper. All have heard the tale of when he attacked the local saddler, Jimmy Brown outside The Red Lion Pub.

Jimmy accused Seth of giving him a fraudulent banknote in payment for a saddle. Highly suspicious, he asked the publican, George Spike, to verify the note's authenticity. George, loath to give his opinion for fear of a vicious reprisal from Seth, mumbled under his breath, giving no clear indication either way. Jimmy, refusing to back down, announced he would take the note in question to the bank the next day to have it checked. Leaving the pub quickly, he tried to shake off an enraged Seth who bellowed out a demand for the return of his banknote. Flinging the saddle on the ground, he roared, "Take back yer bloody saddle, y' miserable sod, fer I no longer want it, an' giff me back me banknote."

Ignored by Jimmy, who was walking away, Seth lunged, knocked him to the ground, and kicked and stomped on Jimmy's hands, legs, and arms with his heavy boots. Suffering multiple injuries– a fractured jaw, a broken nose, cracked ribs, broken fingers and internal bleeding– Jimmy's wounds were catastrophic. For six months, he, his wife and his children relied on meagre charitable funds from the Parish to survive. Long after this shocking event, people spoke in hushed tones about seeing Seth calmly retrieve the disputed banknote from the pocket of a bloodied, bruised Jimmy, before he rides away, unconcerned, from the scene. Mary is quickly aware of Seth's aggressive streak, but she is unfazed by it, for she too has a fiery temper and will resort to physical assault when roused.

Smitten with lust for Mary, Seth abandons his usual casual treatment of girls. To his astonishment, their regular bouts of sexual encounters do not diminish his interest in her; rather, he grows more attached to her. With every week that passes, his passion for her deepens. Whenever he looks at her mop of black curls, her dainty hands and feet, and feminine curves, above and below her tiny waist, he is beset with possessiveness. He is puzzled, having never been in such a dilemma of strong feeling before. *I know she mi' not make a good mufver, an' she don' know much of anyfink abou' lookin' after an 'ouse. Bu' she do know 'ow t' pleasure me.*

Driven by something he does not understand, he makes a momentous decision. *I'll ask 'er t' be my wife, t' marry me afore d' end of summer. Ma won' like it much. She will 'ave plenty t' say, no dou'. I am nineteen at d' end of d' year, that makes me old 'nuff t' make up me own mind, an' get wed t' 'ooever I choose, an' whenever I choose.*

On receiving Seth's proposal of marriage, Mary is overjoyed. She knows that she will be told to leave Poplar Lodge as soon as they know of her secret meetings with Seth and their engagement. Lying entwined together in the back of his cart one night, their clothing dishevelled after energetic passion, Mary chatters excitedly. She needs to meet Seth's family, and she needs to meet them soon.

"We can marry 'spectable like, in St James's Church, Seff. A small weddin', jus' me an' you, an' two witnesses. Does y' fink it is time fer me t' meet yer family? 'Ave y' told 'em yet? Will yer mufver allow me t' come an' liff at 'er cottage afore d' weddin'? Tell yer ma that I am a good girl, an' will make no trouble fer 'er. Once I know 'er answer, I will be brave an' tell staff at d' Lodge."

Seth is open to agree to anything she says.

"You an' me, girl. Giff us a few years, 'ere in Crandonside, then we can move t' East London. Workin' t'gever we will make money, Mary. I 'ave a feelin' in me bones. Fer there is easy money t' be 'ad, an' we know where t' find it."

The following day, Seth breaks the news to his mother. Arriving home, he finds her sitting alone in the kitchen, near to the warm range. Removing his thick woollen coat, he pulls up a chair beside her, stretches out his long legs, and leans back, cool and composed. He tells her of his plans.

"I've 'ad opportunity t' meet one of d' girls from Popla' Lodge. 'Er name is Mary Nolan. We plan t' be wed end of summer when she is sixteen. Up at d' big 'ouse she 'as 'ad lessons in 'ousework. She can 'elp you, Ma, an' me sisters, when she moves in next week. No need to worry abou' where she will sleep, as she can share my bed, 'ere in d' kitchen."

Lottie turns a hot, flushed, glowering face towards Seth.

"Those Lodge girls, they be a bloody nuisance in d'

village, stirring up men an' boys wiv their lewd ways, an' loud manners. I 'ope yee knows wha' yer doin', Seff. I 'ear tell that they are all bad girls there, lassies from d' filthy slums of Lime'ouse, an' Whitechapel. But s'pose yee knows that an' don' care."

Sucking in her lips disapprovingly, she pauses expectantly. When Seth fails to respond, she speaks again.

"Well, if this girl is d' one you 'ave set yer 'eart on, then me, an' d' family, will 'ave t' accept it, I do suppose. At least she is near your own age, not like that bloody widda woman, Bella. Speakin' of d' devil, she 'as bin comin' 'roun' askin' 'bout you, wantin' t' know where you are. I tell you this much, Seff, I am sick of Bella McKenzie traipsin' aroun' 'ere boverin' me."

Standing up suddenly, having heard enough, Seth pushes his face close to his mother's and snarls, "Never you min' Bella McKenzie, I will 'andle 'er. If she comes aroun' again, jus' let me know. Of more importance t' me is that y' warn yer 'oul 'usband t' keep 'is lecherous eyes, an' 'ands, offa Mary when she is stayin' 'ere afore d' weddin'. If 'ee puts a damn finger on 'er, or I catch 'im peeping at 'er when she is ou' back in yard, I swear I will knock 'is bloody 'ead off 'is neck."

Scowling, Lottie is silent. She knows that she and Wilfred have no option but to accept the situation because they are dependent on Seth's monetary contributions.

Two weeks later, Mary is living in the Loxbury family cottage. Her arrival there causes tensions and resentments to flourish. Lottie's opinion, that Mary is nothing but a common, lowly trollop, does not shift. She struggles to accept that her second son has chosen the illegitimate daughter of a prostitute to be his wife. Her mortification is extreme, for she knows that neighbours are wagging their fingers and gossiping, spreading embarrassing truths about her future daughter-in-law.

Afraid to arouse Seth's temper, however, she keeps vindictive thoughts to herself but remains convinced that Mary will never amount to much or be good enough for Seth. Her faint hope that Seth will change his mind about marrying Mary is dashed when, in the last week of August eighteen-seventy-seven, her handsome son marries his young, curly headed bride, Mary Molly Nolan.

To the relief of Wilfred and Lottie, and to the newlyweds, a cottage, four doors down from the Loxbury's, becomes vacant, so with the nuptials over the newlyweds take up residence there.

Whisperings:

A villainous coalition is born; dual, contorted emotions blot and fray like ink on paper. Lacking empathy, reckless, without scruples, they will carve a life unfounded on principle.

4

Change

Change begets change. Nothing propagates so fast.
Martin Chuzzlewit – Charles Dickens

1877–1882

During the first three years of their marriage, the weather in England is unseasonably wet and cold. The summer of eighteen-seventy-seven sees little sunshine. Excessive rain results in water-logged pastures, making planting impossible and putting animals to graze in fields unfeasible. Landowners face financial ruin from the inclement weather, the relentless march of industrialisation, and the mass exodus of rural workers seeking employment in factories in East London.

Throughout Essex, abandoned manor houses fall into disrepair. The landed gentry, unable to generate an income, lay off farm workers, labourers, stonemasons, farriers, foresters, woodcutters, and domestic servants. Prolonged periods of harsh weather, combined with the mechanisation of farming, heralds the rapid demise of English village life. London factories, workshops and dockland warehouses are the new landscape for rural workers. The lives of those who remain behind are bleak, riven by poverty and despair.

For the newlyweds, Seth and Mary, the extensive and profound societal changes present them with opportunity. Seth, alert to the personal gains to be had in the rapidly modernising world, takes calculated risks. Astute, adaptable, flexible and ruthless, he gauges that a growing London populace needs an increased number of working horses to pull cumbersome, loaded vehicles through the narrow, congested streets of the capital. In this domain, he is already an expert and is well respected as a purveyor of horseflesh.

Travelling the markets and manor house auctions, he buys popular horse breeds; muscular, chestnut Suffolks to pull wagons, cabs, and omnibuses; placid Black Shires to pull hearses; and Grey Shires to pull the trade-named, brewery dray vehicles. He bulks up his legitimate animal purchases with stolen horses, buying them cheap from known horse thieves. In collaboration with his half-brother Bill, he trawls country lanes at night, stealing ponies and horses from unsecured stables and fields. The animals, along with sacks of pilfered grain, are moved on quickly and sold without delay, the creatures marked to ensure they are not recognised by their rightful owners when placed among herds of legally owned beasts.

As an experienced drover, Seth has the advantage over potential rivals. Travelling extensively between London, Stowmarket, Chelmsford, Ireland and Belgium, he is at home in bustling market environments, mixing with fellow drovers, farmers, and horse dealers, all united in their fevered search for bargains. He confidently fraternises with wheelwrights, bridle-makers, blacksmiths, car-men, horse manure collectors, butchers, vagabonds, horse thieves and gypsies. He is a familiar sight, trudging through steaming mire stirred up by the restless hooves of reeking, broken-spirited animals. He effortlessly blends in with other men dressed in dirty, muck-splattered clothes, smelling of animal dung and body odour.

This melee of uncouth, unwashed individuals, including Seth, is prone to dishonest, fraudulent trading and loud, bellowing disputes. Barking dogs, the whinnying of terrified horses, the baying of distressed donkeys are the vile cacophony of noise that amplifies the fear and terror of the penned animals, as they are continually poked and prodded with sticks.

When Seth returns home, sometimes after an absence of three or more weeks, the first thing he does when he enters the cottage is to go to the larder at the back of the kitchen. Bending down, he lifts some loose floorboards beneath a deep wooden shelf used to store sacks of root vegetables and crates of apples, picked during the orchard harvest. Pushing aside the potato sacks laying on the floor, he gives himself more room and reaches under the floorboards to grasp the handle of a rectangular, iron strong box, measuring twelve inches by four inches and eight inches deep. The box is his secure repository where he keeps rolls of cash and bank drafts.

Placing the heavy container on the upper larder shelf,

he pulls from his trouser pocket an iron keyring, from which hangs an assortment of keys. Selecting the tiniest one, he pushes it into the minute keyhole on the front of the double-locked box. Turning it once, he hears a click; turning it again, he hears another. He lifts the lid and checks that everything is as it should be before he puts in more rolls of banknotes and bills of sale. Hiding his money in this specific cash box pleases him, as it had belonged to his deceased father, Hubert Marchwood, and was ceremoniously given to him by Lottie when he turned fourteen. A part of him likes to think that his dead father watches over, and protects, the contents of the box, from beyond the grave.

Soon after their wedding, Mary falls pregnant. She is surprised to find herself with child, for she had a suspicion that she might be infertile, having failed to conceive a child with Brian. Knowing how important it is for Seth to prove both his virility as well as his fertility, she is greatly relieved. Her consolation is, nevertheless, tempered by acute anxiety about surviving the labour. After all, she is all too aware of her own mother's death while giving birth to her and has never forgotten Molly recounting the gory details, as passed to her by the old mid wife who oversaw Mary's own birth.

Tending to Mary when she goes into labour is her sister-in-law, Agnes, a trained midwife and a calm, reassuring presence during the delivery of her first child, a son, in the month of June eighteen-seventy-eight. Christened Seth Caleb Marchwood, to be known thereafter as Cal, the infant is strong and robust and favours his father in the shape of his face, and his mother in the colour of his curly hair and blue eyes. Becoming a mother at the age of seventeen, Mary recovers quickly from giving birth and wallows in her status as wife of a handsome husband and mother to a healthy bonny boy. Lottie, despite her animosity towards her daughter-in-law, helps to look after the infant, advising on how best to feed and nurture her grandson.

Less than two years later, Mary has another child, George Gordon Marchwood. Away from home at the time of his wife's delivery, it is some months before Seth sees his second son. When he does, he is much humoured by the fact that the boy looks so like him, a miniature version of himself; a high-cheek boned face, light hazel-brown eyes and straight brown hair. Bragging to fellow drinkers in the pub, he tells them, "Lookin a' me son, George, is like lookin' a' me own 'flection, an' that's a fact. I defy any man 'ere t' see 'im in 'is crib, an' not know 'ee is mine."

Living so close to her mother-in-law, Lottie, soon annoys Mary. She is increasingly resentful of the fact that she is heavily reliant on her mother-in-law's help with the children. Her dishevelled childhood, growing up on the streets of Tower Hamlets, sees her struggling to cope with her maternal responsibilities. She is hampered by the fact that, living on the streets of Tower Hamlets, she lacked motherlike role models after Molly was taken away.

She finds suckling her baby sons a tedious chore, even though she has an abundant supply of breast milk. She does not enjoy it, so she hurries through the nursing of her tiny sons, remaining emotionally detached throughout what could be a pleasurable activity. As a two-year-old, Cal spends long hours in a wooden pen in the kitchen, while George lays, tightly swaddled, in his wicker-basket cradle. Both babies are ignored for long periods of time, and often it is Lottie who responds to their cries, rocking George to sleep, and lifting Cal from his pen, so he can toddle about the back yard under her watchful gaze.

When both children are fully weaned, Mary relaxes into her maternal role and interacts more frequently with them both. Her responses to their loud, unruly behaviours, however, are erratic and inconsistent; either she laughs, amused by their antics, or she reacts angrily and gives them a sharp slap. Askance, Lottie observes Mary's poor mothering skills and worries that her grandsons will grow up to be wild and undisciplined. Her strong, dominant personality drives her to continually issue Mary with stridently delivered advice, in the form of familiar biblical texts and proverbs.

"Mary!"

"Spare d' rod, y' spoil d' child."

"Mary!"

"Children should be seen an' not 'eard."

"Mary!"

"Cleanliness is next t' Godliness."

To escape her mother-in-law's endless nagging and criticism, most mornings, weather permitting, Mary walks into the village of Crandon, pushing her sons in the old family perambulator once used by Seth. While there, she buys miscellaneous items for herself and groceries for Lottie, who is teaching her to cook wholesome meals.

Under her mother-in-law's guidance, she is learning how to eke out portions of mutton, pork, beef, or fish and add them to a stock pot of seasonable vegetables. With the meagre bag of flour Wilfred collects each month, from Great Follow Mill, near Chelmsford, Lottie makes bread every day. An experienced bread-maker, she mixes, kneads, and rolls dough to get exactly the right consistency.

Just as she hates doing needlework, Mary has no talent or liking for making bread. Every day she is forced to stand at the kitchen table, under Lottie's critical eye, and roll and pound dough until her arms ache. The older woman's constant barrage of negative comments erodes her self-confidence, and she is filled with an inner rage and resentment that she dares not express, for fear of angering Seth.

Lottie's negative opinions on Mary's overall character persist. As she watches her paltry efforts at domestic chores, her thoughts are dark. *She be nufvin bu' a sulky, slummocky, idle gurl, wiv a foul tongue on 'er, an' sly ways. D' only fink wurfwhile fer Seff is 'er abilities t' keep 'im 'appy in bed. I expect she is an expert in that quarter, 'er 'avin' worked as a trollop.*

Being a married man is no impediment to Seth visiting prostitutes, especially when Mary is pregnant. Like many other males, he believes that it is essential for men, like himself, to relieve their sexual urges freely, and with great frequency, to maintain their vigour and potency. The happy fact that Mary calmly accepts his lusty dalliances leaves him guilt-free, unhindered by fear of retribution from her. She is neither jealous nor possessive though she does attach conditions to Seth's sexual trysts with whores. She insists he take extra precautions when choosing a particular girl from a brothel.

"When y' visit broffels, make sure d' girls are checked regular fer disease. I don' want y' givin' me syphilis or any uver filthy ailment."

Regarding Mary's fidelity to him, Seth takes a very different view. She is his wife, his property, and he is suspicious of men who are too familiar with her, paranoid that they may try to pursue her for sex. His intense possessiveness is based upon knowing that local men rightly guess that she once worked as a street girl in Whitechapel. On occasions, when he broods on the possibilities of other men flirting with his wife, he warns her of the dire consequences if she ever returns to her old ways.

"Don' ever encourage anuver man, Mary, fer if y' do I will kill 'im wiv me bare 'ands. Then I will giff y' a beating y' won' ferget, even though it is not my way to 'it a woman."

By the age of three, their eldest son, Cal, liberally uses a vocabulary peppered with swear words and blasphemous profanities, foul language learned from his parents and the rough men working in the fields. A bully, Cal torments younger children, especially George, who, eighteen months younger than him, suffers the worst of the abuse. Every day he suffers being kicked, pinched, roughly pushed around and has his hair viciously pulled by Cal until he screams in pain.

Cousins, living close by, the children of Bert and

Agnes, hate Cal. Their open hostility manifests in their refusal to let him join in their games, a rejection that drives him into having a tantrum and seeking revenge. He sabotages their childish games; steals their toys, smashes their carefully constructed go-carts, pulls rude faces at the babies in their prams and uses sticks and stones to inflict physical harm. When accused of misbehaviour, he never accepts responsibility but always pushes blame onto his brother.

"Ain't my fault. George, 'ee made me do it. I never done nuvfink."

Cal's unruly behaviour reflects his inner emotional confusion. Mary and Seth's boundaries are unclear and inconsistently applied. Both boys grow up in a perpetual state of uncertainty about what is right and what is wrong. One thing they are certain of is their mother's reaction whenever they whinge and whine, for then she always reacts the same way. She flies into a furious rage, slapping whichever child is grizzling, and screams profanities, as she banishes them to their bedroom.

Although the boys are fearful of their mother's hot temper, they are even more wary of stirring up their father's wrath. To them, Seth is an ominous, intimidating figure; aloof, disinterested and prone to violence. Usually, any attention he gives them is negative. They avoid being in the same room as him for fear of receiving a hard kick to their backside, followed by their father's loud, mocking guffaws of laughter as they cower and cry.

The extended Marchwood family still rely on Seth's financial support. Within the family, he is the most successful, skilful, and enterprising at earning money. Content to carry this extra financial burden, because it gives him high status among his relatives, he determines to maintain his esteemed position through a relentless pursuit of emerging economic opportunities. As his reputation as a successful trader grows, he avoids participating in the act of thieving horses, preferring others to steal on his behalf. Among his wider family, there is an unwritten rule; one of them will take the blame if the law suspects Seth of a crime, for they all recognise the need to keep Seth out of prison, for all their sakes.

To make the most of arising possibilities, Seth knows that he must move, with his family, to Limehouse. London dockland is the place where fraudulent deals, abundant supplies of counterfeit money and trouble-free procurement of stolen horses and goods are readily available. To this end, in eighteen-eighty-one, he begins to look in earnest for cheap accommodation in the overcrowded slums of East London.

Finding somewhere for himself, Mary, and the boys, to settle poses a challenge because the eastern side of the capital is teeming with the influx of displaced agricultural labourers and poor Irish immigrants. The area is also heavily populated by sailors, stevedores, porters, rope-makers, ships' carpenters and costermongers. Pubs, whorehouses and vice dens are integral to the fabric of this community, for it is in these places that criminals conduct their shady deals. The chaotic conglomeration of dilapidated housing, stable yards, warehouses, second-hand clothes shops, pawn shops and street markets are the ideal environment for villains to stay out of sight. In this place, blatant immorality flourishes on street corners, in cobbled alleyways, beer houses, dog pits, opium dens and brothels.

Preparing for their move away from Essex, Seth builds up his livestock trading reputation. He employs his brother Bill to go to cattle markets in Essex and Suffolk to buy, or preferably steal, quality livestock, while he spends his time establishing working relations with horse dealers in Belgium, France and Ireland. He masks his dishonesty behind a confident swagger and loud bluster. Mary's knowledge of East End coiners and forgers gives him a head start in learning the names and whereabouts of small-time felons from across the spectrum of the East London underworld. For a price, counterfeiters provide him with falsified documents to disguise the identity of stolen horses and common horse thieves soon become his favoured drinking companions.

While Seth paves the way for their imminent move to London, Mary grows increasingly restless. Her initial infatuation with rural life is wearing thin. She finds the monotonous daily routines restrictive, and her spirits flag at the drudgery of each passing day. Irritation with her mother-in-law's critical and malicious tongue is taking a toll on her self-confidence. Neighbouring women and girls treat her with suspicion and cast furtive, sidelong glances at her when they pass her in the lane and rarely greet her in a friendly manner.

Reluctantly, every Sunday, she attends church with Lottie. Sitting in a pew, head bowed, she is acutely aware of many malevolent eyes boring into her back. She observes members of the congregation exchanging sly glances and easily guesses their spiteful thoughts. *There she is d' slut Seff Marchwood married. I feel sorry fer Lottie Loxbury,'avin' 'er as a daughter-in-law. 'Ow she 'as d' nerve t' sit there pretendin' to be a decent woman, beggars belief.*

Lottie's contempt towards her daughter-in-law is thinly veiled and prone to erupt when she is alone at night with Wilfred. That her eldest son married a low, common, London tart, ignorant of housewifery, and schooled in the ways of debauchery, is a continuing, festering pain in her heart. She knows villagers gossip behind her back, exchanging stories about her daughter-in-law's scandalous past, and she is mortified.

Relief floods through Mary when Seth asks her to accompany him on a day trip to London. Leaving their sons in the care of Lottie, Mary is ecstatic. Once there, she and Seth part company and she is free to meander through familiar East London markets. While there, she refreshes her pick-pocketing and pilfering skills. When she meets Seth in the late afternoon, she proudly shows him the trinkets she has thieved; hat pins, watch-chains, purses and many silk handkerchiefs.

"Gor blimey, Seff! Jus' look a' d' treasures I got t'day. Ain't I clever then? Livin' in Crandon, listnin' t' yer mufver preachin', 'as not made me t' lose me habilities, fank Gawd."

Pleased by his wife's sleight of hand, Seth grins, as he relieves her of the booty, wrapping the bundle in a small piece of sacking before tucking it deep inside his saddle bag.

"Keep this up, Mary girl, an' ye'll, one day, be paradin' down Cockle Bay pier wearing silks ad satins. We will soon make a permanent move t' London, I promise. Today I bin offered two rooms in cheap lodgings in Lime'ouse. D' people rentin' it now are goin' to America in a few weeks. D' 'ouse is mostly used by sailors visitin' tarts 'oo 'ave rooms there. Still, d' couple 'oo runs it don' tolerate anyone bein' troublesome, so there is no need t' worry. Best of all, I can stable me 'orses in d' yards opposite."

Excitedly, Mary interjects, "I knows d' docks like d' back of me hand, Seff, an' many of d' gang leaders there now were me childhood friends. It won be long afore y' will be in wiv d' gangs there. I knows it."

Nodding agreeably, with a smug smile on his face, Seth stares into the distance before he speaks again.

"I fink, when I've made enough money, I will go back to Essex, an' buy up land, barns an' farm'ouses. D' time is right, fer property is goin' cheap in d' countryside. Then it will be our turn t' liff like propa gentry an' 'ave respec' from family, an' villagers."

He laughs in gleeful anticipation of his future good fortune.

As she listens to his words, Mary cannot imagine she will ever want to go back to live in the country after their move to Limehouse, but she says nothing of her thoughts. For now, she is overwhelmed with delight at the thought that she is soon returning to Tower Hamlets, where she will be free of Lottie's cold, venomous glances and the spiteful whispers of hostile villagers.

Beaming at Seth, words tumble enthusiastically from her lips.

"I will pack everyfink up when y' say d' word. In trufe, I 'ave missed ole London town. I know that I will be welcome there, fer I was brung up there, a pauper girl. I also knows those criminals workin' from d' rookeries will work wiv you, Seff; yes, they will."

Whisperings:
A life stripped of a moral compass reaches out to tempt,
into its embrace, these two souls, seeking a new life.

5

Zephyr Hill

This was far from being a place of doubtful character, for it had long been known as the residence of none but low and desperate ruffians, who, under various pretences of living by their labour, subsisted chiefly on plunder and crime.

Oliver Twist – Charles Dickens

1883 –1887

Autumn fades into the darkening days of winter as Seth and Mary prepare to leave their cottage in Essex. They are finally leaving for Limehouse where they will live in an end of terrace house on Zephyr Hill, situated near to the docks. The owner, Mrs Kate O'Toole, nicknamed 'Crafty' Kate, is a formidable woman with a harsh, uncompromising manner. She and Seth know each other, as his habit is to drink at her illegal drinking den whenever he is in London, spending pleasurable hours consuming cheap, illicit liquor and using the services of resident prostitutes.

Seth takes Mary to meet Kate, three weeks prior to their actual departure from Crandonside. For his peace of mind, he needs the two women to like each other and to get along. Expecting her third baby, Mary's protruding belly has dropped low, evidence of the late stage of her pregnancy. Despite the discomforts of her condition, she is elated to get away for a day in East London. Escaping the dull chores of her domestic routines, the demands of her young sons, and the constant nagging of her mother-in-law puts her in a skittish mood.

The couple set out in their smartest trap, pulled by Mary's favourite white pony, Silver. For once she is oblivious to the villagers' malign looks as they pass them by along the lane. She brims over with exuberance, gabbling and fidgeting on the seat next to her silent, inscrutable husband.

"Gaw blimey, Seff! I can't wait t' see d' crowds an' 'ear d' noise of trams, an' carts rumblin' over d' cobbles. Twill be music t' me ears to 'ear people shoutin' an' bellowin' wiv laughter as they 'aggle over prices. Knowin' we are movin' t' Lime'ouse 'as lifted me spirits no end, Seff. I never did fink I would be so glad t' be returnin' to London town."

Seth shows no interest in his wife's animated chatter. Despite this, Mary continues undeterred by his lack of response. She is familiar with Seth's customary blank facial expressions, and general lack of interest, when she talks to him. Today, as they trot swiftly towards Whitechapel, she refuses to allow anything to dampen her zest for life. With a fluttering heart, thoughts skittering around in her head, she trembles with impatience to get her first sight of the city. Straining her eyes from beneath the brim of her bonnet, she sees in the distance a familiar thick grey smog hanging over the capital's skyline.

Arriving at Mile End Market, as she predicted, her senses are engulfed in a myriad of sights and sounds. She hears raucous calls of costermongers competing for customers and feasts her eyes on the colourful crowds pushing and shoving through the stalls and handcarts. In the general melee; dogs bark, wagon wheels lurch, horses snort through distended nostrils, and shrill laughter springs from the painted mouths of young women hoping to catch the eye of a passing youth. A combination of noxious smells permeates the air; oil, grease, horse manure and raw sewage overflowing from cess pits. From upstairs' windows, men, women and children call down to people they recognise in the bustling throng. They get a bird's eye view of the bobbing canopy of bonnets, feathered hats, top hats, flat caps, straw boaters, and brief flashes of bright mufflers, shawls, and scarves. Dominating the whole turbulent commotion is a repetitive, lone, piercing, plaintive cry, from a young girl dressed in rags.

'Willya spare us a copper, Mister?"

"Missus! Mister! Give us a penny fer crust of bread."

Muffled up in her long woollen coat with a heavy, plaid shawl around her shoulders, Mary stays warm, except for her cheeks, which are whipped red from the chill morning air. The heavy grey sky is occasionally severed by a sunbeam that shafts its way through the dense cloud. Then, for a few moments, intense light dazzles the eyes of those who catch the glaring ray. Mary repositions her blue bonnet to lessen the blinding impact of the powerful flash, and Seth pulls his peaked cap forward to shield his eyes.

The nearer they get to Tower Hamlets, the more Seth mulls over how he might get some time with Mimi, his favourite 'pet' French prostitute. Conveniently, Mimi lives and works from a rundown coffee house, located in the street adjacent to Zephyr Hill. With Mary so close to giving birth, she is not able to satisfy Seth's ravenous and energetic sexual appetite. Unable to tolerate the temporary sensual deprivations, he experiences bouts of despondency and gloom. His feelings are conflicted. When in the company of his pretty, curly headed, pregnant wife, he is proud to show off to other men the proof of his fertility in the size of her belly. Nevertheless, he resents that the lust he feels for his wife must be dampened down while she is heavy with his child. He turns to his brother, Bert, who, with a wry smile, gives him some advice.

"Y' mus' get release, Seff, else y' will lose yer sanity, or worse, y' mi' lose yer ability t' wield yer weapon."

Laughing at the worried look on his brother's face, he adds, "Such a terrible thing as that would bring shame upon y', bruver. Nor would Mary want that, would she? So, git what y' mus' from floosies an' tarts, else y' could end up in d' mad'ouse."

Familiar with the slums of Tower Hamlets, Mary is unsurprised when she gets her first glimpse of what is to be her new home. Kate's abode, at the end of a short row of terraced houses, straddles the corner of Zephyr Hill and Ship Lane. The brick facades of the houses are blackened by layers of soot and grime. Front doors and window frames are dilapidated or missing, replaced by rough planks of wood crudely nailed together.

"I fink d' 'ouses 'ere mus' be crawlin' wiv vermin, Seff. Our boys will be catchin' fat rats an' makin' money from 'em, like their Uncle Bert sellin' 'em t' gamblin' pits 'round 'ere."

Directly opposite the terrace are yards where horses, ponies and donkeys are stabled, and items are stored. The conglomeration of ramshackle lean-tos and sheds, back onto a high, red-brick dockyard wall. Above this barricade loom giant cranes, ship masts and funnels, and a tall, dockland factory chimney belching out thick black smoke. When evening falls, a solitary dim streetlamp at the end of the cul-de-sac is veiled in dense, slime-green fog. The yards are dark, murky places, heavily padlocked, for in these places are the stolen livestock and booty needing to be hidden from the law. Pubs, coffee houses and opium dens proliferate around the area; venues for shady dealings between dockers, horse thieves and those in the vice trade. Limehouse is a sanctuary for the low criminal class. It is a group within which both Seth and Mary will blend comfortably and be protected by its secretive culture.

Leading the horse and trap into the yard, Seth empties a bag of hay, mixed with oats and chaff, into a wooden trough near a hitching post. A galvanised bucket, containing rainwater, is within reach of the horse and the animal immediately drinks from it. Once the trap is safely untethered and parked, he and Mary pick their way over dank, greasy cobbles towards the open doorway of house number one. Entering the narrow hallway, Seth calls out Kate's name. He waits. Not getting an answer, he calls out again before leading Mary through a door to his left into a kitchen about eight feet square. The space, used to serve food, doubles up as an illicit drinking den. It is furnished with several battered wooden chairs, small round tables and six, three-legged stools. Near one wall stands a narrow rectangular pine table, flanked by two long benches.

A twelve-inch brass crucifix is suspended from a rusty nail hammered into the wall above the scullery doorway. Hanging on a hook, left of the doorframe, is a decorative, delftware holy water font, adorned with a gaudy image of the bloodied head and face of the crucified Christ. The lime plaster around the font is grubby from greasy hands touching the surface, as individuals steady themselves before dipping their fingers into the blessed water and making a hurried sign of the cross while mumbling, "In d' name of d' Farver, d' Son an' d' 'oly Ghos'."

Looking at the font, Mary remembers the women she knew as a child. Women who, despite selling their bodies for sex, blessed themselves daily at church fonts, sat together on street corners saying the rosary, and never missed Mass on Sunday.

Hearing footsteps upstairs, Seth calls out again, "Is that you, Kate? 'Tis me, Seff, an' me wife, Mary, come t' see d' rooms we will rent, once d' O'Neils set sail fer America."

From the top of the wooden staircase, Kate answers, "Well! I weren't sure y' were comin' wiv yer missus t'day, Seff, bu' y' are 'ere now, and y' are bofe welcome. Albert's bin askin' when y' were goin' t' arrive. 'Ee'll be pleased t' see y', Seff. Go look for 'im. 'Ee mi' be nex' door in Ruby's place."

Looking down at Mary, Kate speaks directly to her, "You an' me can stay 'ere, Mary, an' get t' know one anuver. Is that alri' wiv you, lass?"

Mary half smiles and nods and Seth heads for the front door, relieved to be free to seek out Mimi and catch up later with Albert. As Kate descends the stairs, the women get a first close look at each other. Although the older woman's face is without expression, her eyes alight warmly upon Mary. A fifteen-year gap lies between them. Somewhat over awed by Kate's confident demeanour, Mary stands mute, struck by the older woman's beauty. She has a pale, delicately freckled complexion, a long slender neck and a glorious mane of curly red hair. Her cheekbones are sculpted high, and her big, vivid, blue eyes are framed with the longest black lashes that Mary has ever seen.

Seth had forewarned his wife of Kate's notoriously brusque manner but had neglected to mention her startlingly handsome face and figure. As Kate's eyes run up and down the younger woman, Mary regrets not spending more time on her own appearance that morning.

"Be warned, Mary," Seth had said earlier, "Kate 'as a brutal way abou' 'er. She is outspoken an' blunt an' don' like t' be crossed. She is more loud-mouthed, bossy, an' fearsome than you are, Mary."

He had chuckled mockingly.

"I seen big, strappin' men slink away from 'er in fear when she singles 'em out for a lashin' of 'er tongue. No-one, includin' me, Mary, ever dares ask 'er 'ow she came t' own 'er 'ouse, though people 'ave their suspicions."

Curious, Mary nagged, until Seth shared the rumours about Kate.

"'Tis said, that when she was abou' your age, she wed an Irish labourer, Mick O'Toole, a 'uge brute of a fellow. Two years after d' weddin', 'ee got 'imseff transported t' Tasmania. 'Is crime being to lead a gang of Irish villains 'oo robbed a ware'ouse. 'Ee got caught, bu' no-one ever found d' stolen goods. Kate knew where it was 'idden because after a few years, when d' police lost interest, she found cash to buy d' Zephyr 'ill 'ouse."

Having Mary's rapt attention, and feeling in a good mood, Seth proceeded to feed her insatiable inquisitiveness. He related other, more serious matters that are whispered about Kate O'Toole. The one whispered about the most being how she caused the death of one of her lodgers; a sickly, desperate prostitute who fell behind with her rent. Ordered to move out by Kate, the pathetic creature barricaded herself in her room and refused to leave. Infuriated, Kate used an axe to break down the door. She then grabbed the scrawny tenant by her thin, greying hair and dragged her out onto the landing.

The story told was that in the struggle, the poor lodger tumbled backwards down the stairs and hit her head hard on the oak newel post. Her neck broken, her limp body slithered to rest on the tessellated tiled floor of the hallway. When the law arrived, Kate brazenly denied any involvement in the death of the woman, and it was registered as a tragic accident.

Now, as Mary stands facing Kate, and sees her beauty, she cannot imagine this woman to be capable of such violence. Kate returns Mary's focussed perusal and instinctively likes the young pregnant woman standing before her. In her, she sees a younger version of herself; streetwise, resilient, and strong-willed. Relieved, her thoughts are positive. *She don' look like a soft simpering girl, even though she be a small, slip of a fing, I know, jus' by lookin' a' 'er, she's as tough as ole nails. No! She won' be shocked a' wha' goes on in dis 'ouse. She will 'andle d' types of drunken sailors, an' dockers, comin' fru' d' door. If we get on alri', an' I fink we will, she can giff me an 'and in d' den.*

Kate is first to break the silence. In a manner that will soon be familiar to Mary, she speaks loudly and emphatically as she stares into Mary's eyes.

"Seff tells me y' are a good little fief, Mary. That's good. Bu' if y' 'tend t' pick pockets 'ere, lass, make sure y' don' git caught. Me an' my man, Alber', we won' 'ave any trouble 'ere. We need t' keep d' bleedin' law from snoopin, an' pryin' into wha' we do. I 'ope y' understand wha' I am sayin, Mary? I 'ave nuffink against y' gettin' up t' tricks, bu' do not get too cocky, or try t' pull a trick on me or Alber'. If that 'appens, I will chuck you, Seff, an' d' children ou' on yer arses, quick as a flash."

Once the rules of the house are made explicit and they each have each other's measure, the talk becomes more friendly. Kate tells Mary of the friendship between Albert, her German lover, and Seth, a friendship formed long ago in The Blind Beggar Pub in Whitechapel. She boasts to Mary of Albert's reputation as a successful, respected dockland thief, known for his meticulous planning.

Not wanting Kate to think that she is an ignorant, naive country bumkin, Mary is quick to tell Kate that Tower Hamlets is familiar territory to her, having been raised on the streets around Ratcliffe Highway. Nor does she want her to think that the children will be an encumbrance to everyday life in Zephyr Hill.

"I promise not t' cause y' trouble, Kate. I will 'elp in any way that y' wan' me to. D' older boys can mind d' baby when it comes so no need to worry abou' that."

Soon after the birth of their third son, Cedric Thomas Marchwood, Seth and Mary relocate to Zephyr Hill with their three children, where they occupy the biggest room on the first floor of Kate's house. The physical upheaval, so soon after the birth, causes Mary's breast milk to dry up so she must resort to bottle feeding Cedric. The substitute milk, bought from the local Limehouse dairy, is adulterated with chalk and starch to make it appear fresh and pure. Its poor nutritious value is reflected in Cedric's slow growth and sickly disposition. With Cal obliged to attend the local parish school, it is left to four-year-old George to look after the new baby while his mother is kept busy by Kate. George, mindful of his mother's fiery temper, duly bottle-feeds Cedric, changes his messy napkins and pushes him up and down the street in an old, battered black perambulator.

Six-year-old Cal feels no brotherly regard for Cedric and refuses to help George look after him. Hating school, he frequently absconds, running back to Zephyr Hill to join other truants; unkempt, unruly urchins, skulking together in alleyways and yards. To avoid being caught by the *chunk*, the children nominate a lookout to keep watch. When caught, and returned to school, Seth and Mary are expected to admonish him for his absences. Both are, however, ambivalent about the compulsory school law obliging children to attend school until the age of twelve. Seth holds the opinion that children learn all that they need from working alongside their parents.

Once George is old enough, he joins Cal at school. Unlike his older brother, he loves being there. School gives him the chance to escape his mother's incessant demands to 'keep an eye' on Cedric, who has recently been joined by another new sibling; a sister, Charlotte. Born prematurely, the baby girl, underweight, cries incessantly. Mary is utterly disheartened to have yet another mouth to feed and yet she feels some small pleasure at having a little girl to tend to, dressing her in pink woolly bonnets and matching pink ribboned booties. Her meagre efforts to nurture the infant fail and Charlotte dies at three months old.

Struggling with her disappointment, Mary hides it behind a flood of rage at the unfairness of her life. Needing to blame someone she turns her ire upon George, accusing him of not holding the feeding bottle correctly. In turn, Seth blames Mary, accusing her of being an uncaring, lazy mother. On the day of Charlotte's burial in a pauper's grave at the local parish churchyard, to her horror, Mary realises she is again with child when she experiences a familiar wave of nausea and sickness.

In late December eighteen-eighty-four, another daughter, Elizabeth Rose, is born. Physically depleted and weakened from her relentless pregnancies, Mary struggles to bond with little Elizabeth. Pessimistic about the child's survival, she resists forming an attachment to her and consequently the infant is badly neglected. Every day the tiny baby lies, tightly swaddled, in filthy blankets, inside a grubby wicker crib. When George returns from school, and in response to his mother's barked orders, he refills the baby's bottle and tries his best to coax her to suckle while at the same time he endeavours to stop Cedric from grizzling.

Just before his third birthday, Cedric suddenly dies after contracting scarlet fever. Too feeble and malnourished to fight off the illness, he passes away one dark, gloomy day, after many hours shivering uncontrollably under a dirty, clammy, woollen blanket in the bed he shares with his older brothers. Mary is assailed with a kaleidoscope of emotions after his death; guilt, hopelessness and frustration combined with a terrible sense of failure. Within hours of watching his tiny wooden coffin lowered into the pauper's grave, beside baby Charlotte, baby Elizabeth also dies of the fever.

This time, Mary masks her grief beneath an outwardly cold, hard, stoic veneer. Cal is unmoved by the loss of his siblings, but young George reacts badly. He blames himself for their deaths and becomes withdrawn, isolating himself, refusing to speak to his mother for many months afterwards. He impulsively kicks holes in doors and punches walls until his knuckles bleed. Struggling with her own inner heavy depression, Mary cannot understand George's erratic behaviour and has no inclination to comfort him. Seth feels the multiple losses of his children to be a slight to his self-image as an excellent husband and dutiful father. Consequently, he vows to immediately take Mary to Crandonside when she next falls pregnant, for there she will be properly looked after by his mother.

The following year, with Mary once more with child, Seth takes her to live with Lottie for the duration of her confinement. Cal and George remain in Limehouse where they attend school on weekdays and participate in criminal activities, alongside Seth and Albert, when not at school. While burgling warehouses and stealing cargo from barges and factories, the adults utilise Cal and George's slender, diminutive bodies and physical dexterity to squeeze through small apertures. Thieving from vessels moored in the docks, the boys are integral to the success of such furtive activities. At low tide, when night skies are cloudy, and moonlight partially shrouded, the men, accompanied by Cal and George, paddle a substantial wooden raft out to moored loaded crafts. Laying up alongside them, the children clamber up the mooring ropes and quickly climb aboard. Creeping about the decks, looking into holds, they locate the desired cargo; casks of liquor that Seth instructed them to find. With soft hooting sounds, they signal to Albert and Seth when they are ready to slither back down onto the raft.

Once told where to find the booty, the men shimmy up the rope ladder the boys had attached to two deck capstans, and, in total silence, they begin the process of lowering casks onto the raft. When this is done, Seth uses a long pole to steer the heavily laden raft over the pitch-black tarry water towards the wharf. Not a single word is exchanged until the heavy loot is taken up the rickety wooden steps, loaded into a covered wagon and driven back to Zephyr Hill.

Both men threaten the boys with harsh punishment if they ever speak about their secret unlawful nightly jaunts. Cal and George adhere to these instructions through a mixture of fear of Seth and pride at being part of the grown-up esteemed criminal fraternity of Limehouse. In this twilight world of wrongdoing, the children are introduced to a world that will shape and mould their futures.

While her sons work their criminal apprenticeship, Mary, safely ensconced in Crandonside, delivers a strong, sturdy girl in the summer of eighteen-eighty-six. The birth of another daughter unexpectedly engulfs her with warm maternal feelings. The baby has an exceptionally pretty face, a creamy complexion and a tiny head topped by a mop of soft, curly, black hair. This time, with plentiful breast milk, Mary takes pleasure in suckling her new baby, whom she names Sally Anne.

Pleased to have fathered another girl, Seth hopes that the child will survive into her early years. Mary lives with Lottie until Sally Anne is six months old. During that time, both mother and baby thrive. Cosseted, fed on wholesome food, washed in clean water, breathing clean country air, the baby is contented. Mary's confidence grows and her maternal feelings flourish. Despite the daily irritation of Lottie ordering her around, she is appreciative of her mothers-in-law's help. As Christmas eighteen-eighty-six draws near, Seth and the boys arrive at Lottie and Wilfred's cottage for the Yuletide celebrations where, as a family, they attend the local church and afterwards feast on fresh lamb and plentiful winter vegetables. Lottie, who has grown possessive of her small granddaughter, worries about Mary and Seth taking her back to Limehouse. *I 'ate t' see d' wee one goin' up t' d' bleedin' filfy slums. I 'ope Mary 'as learned a few fings an' will keep 'er clean an' well fed.*

On the afternoon of Boxing Day, Mary, warmly wrapped in a travelling rug, nursing Sally Anne in her arms, begins the journey back to Zephyr Hill. Beside her sits her silent, straight-backed husband, while eight-year-old Cal and six-year-old George sit stiff and expressionless in the back of the covered waggon. They feel no emotion at their mother returning to Zephyr Hill, nor do they show any interest or curiosity in their baby sister. Instead, the two boys watch impassively as their mother behaves out of character, mollycoddling and gently murmuring to the suckling baby in her arms.

Whisperings:
Detached from her sons, the mother has become a blank in their lives.

6

Detention and Terror

Consider nothing impossible, then treat possibilities as probabilities.
                          David Copperfield – Charles Dickens

1888 1889

Seth, Mary, and their children soon grow accustomed to their bleak, dockland environment. Indeed, they barely notice the unremitting foul stench of human sewage, discarded food waste, animal sweat, horse dung, and oil and tar hanging in the air. Zephyr Hill is a repellent place; a place that deters strangers, and those of an anxious disposition, from stepping onto its slimy street. Residents loiter about. They stand in doorways, lean on the dockside wall, or hang from upstairs windows shouting at children in the street below. Without exception, unknown persons who enter the street are closely watched by the sullen, mistrustful adult inhabitants and unfriendly boys and girls playing in the gutter.

Overdue for demolition, the row of houses in the cul-de-sac deteriorates further while the Marchwood family live there. Kate's corner property is the only building in the terrace that still has an intact front door and unbroken windows. The doors of neighbouring dwellings hang from rusty hinges attached to splintered lintels. Door frames are riddled with dry rot. Most doors bear the scuff marks, and holes, made by heavy boots worn by drunken men, enraged at being locked out by their wives. A portion of the long roof, topping the terrace of houses, is covered with sheets of tarpaulin to keep out the rain. Subsidence is dangerously warping roof rafters, causing chimney stacks to tilt precariously.

For months at a time, Seth is away, travelling between country market towns, buying and selling livestock. His sleight of hand, and easy banter with traders, is so deceptive that he is rarely suspected of passing forged banknotes. If caught, he lies and denies with loud conviction and invariably walks away with no backlash. Once his daily business is done, he either visits brothels or avails himself of eager, naïve country girls who linger around market squares. Away from home, and Mary, he never worries about the well-being of his wife and children.

During his absences, Mary frequently runs out of the money Seth leaves for her to buy food and clothes for herself and the children. Though mindful to always pay the rent, well in advance, for fear of eviction by Kate if he does not, Seth selfishly neglects to take similar measures to ensure the day-to-day survival of his wife and family while he is away. When strapped for cash, Mary, out of necessity, falls back on thieving. She spends hours walking through busy, crowded markets, pilfering from stalls and picking the pockets of unsuspecting shoppers. She relies on earning tips from customers who come to imbibe alcohol in Kate's drinking den at night. No matter how desperate she gets, she is never, even for a moment, tempted to break into Seth's metal strongbox, even though she knows just where it is hidden. To do so would betray Seth's trust in her and invite a violent response from him.

An adept thief, she gradually accumulates tangled bundles of silver and gold trinkets; watch chains, jewelled bracelets, gold hat pins and silk handkerchiefs – booty she hides behind the back of an enormous, black oak wardrobe in their room. When the need arises, she pawns pieces for ready cash.

After one successful spree around Tower Hill, Mary rides the halfpenny omnibus back to Limehouse. Sitting back, she closes her eyes and drifts into a light sleep, lulled by the swaying of the vehicle as it slowly moves through the heavy traffic. Straggling thoughts come and go; *I done well this mornin'; I ain't lost me quickness of 'and. D' ole gent wiv d' tall 'at, was completely blind to me filching d' leather pouch from 'is pocket.* Suddenly, the bus jerks alarmingly and she is jolted from her reverie. Juddering and rocking erratically, the wheels emit a loud grating sound before, with a barking cry, the driver pulls the frightened horse to an abrupt halt.

Heart racing, Mary jumps to her feet. She pushes her way through panicked passengers, all clamouring to get off the bus. Standing at the side of the road, she sees the cause of the sudden stoppage. A costermonger's handcart lays on its side in front of the bus, its cargo of fruit scattered beneath the vehicle, much to the delight of passing urchins who make off with as much as they can carry. Unhurt, the costermonger rushes to rescue as much of his produce as possible, while the bus driver struggles to calm his jittery horse and reassure passengers it is safe to get back on the vehicle.

For a split-second, an image from her past flashes before Mary's eyes. She sees, in her mind's eye, the dead bodies of Brian and George, spreadeagled on a road beneath smashed wagons and terrified, thrashing animals. Time stands still. Everything goes eerily quiet. A kaleidoscope of memories transports her back to the world she once shared with them both; sitting hand in hand with Brian down by the river, a smiling George standing in the kitchen sucking on his clay pipe, and Tess's warm breath on her face as she strokes her long nose. In her head, she hears Brian's lilting voice, whispering, "Sure, I love yee, Mary, me lovely darlin' blue-eyed girl, I love yee forever."

Bumped by a woman scurrying along carrying two bulging bags of groceries, she snaps out of her trance-like state but is left feeling the lingering sadness. Her body seems heavy and cumbersome, her shoulders droop and her chin sinks into her collarbone. Struggling to recover her equilibrium, she takes a shuddering breath and forces herself to think of Seth. She conjures up a picture of him confidently driving a team of big, powerful horses. Only then can she expel thoughts of her previous life with Brian. *Dwelling on d' past ain't gonna do me no good, no good at all,* she thinks. Shrugging her shoulders, she walks back to Limehouse, cheered as she thinks about the profitable morning she has just had, pinching items from unsuspecting men and women going about their daily business.

After ten years of marriage, Mary is used to Seth's possessive, controlling, humourless nature. To openly defy or tease him quickly ignites his anger. If provoked by other men, he lashes out with his feet and fists and, without conscience, uses horsewhips and wooden cudgels as weapons to overpower his opponents. When furious with Mary, he refrains from hitting her, though often threatens it. Instead, he prefers to back her into a corner, thrust his face close to hers, and intimidate with his most menacing voice and physical dominance.

"Bes' fink 'ard, Mary, afore y' cross me. If y' giff me trouble I will abandon y', 'ere in d' rookeries. I will force y' t' go int' d' work'ouse. Cal, George, an' yer precious daughter will then liff wiv me mufver in Essex."

Refusing to be cowed into showing fear when he bullies her, Mary screams, swears, bites, spits, punches, and kicks. These personal, mutually furious outbursts invariably end up in wild, rough, sexual passion which effectively ventilates, defuses, and redirects their vexation into calmer waters. Dependent on Seth for her survival, Mary knows that it is in her self-interest to be an uncomplaining, compliant wife, factors that enable her to ignore Seth's endless sexual transgressions.

Late summer, eighteen-eighty-eight, stifling, muggy days give way to thickening putrid fog that hangs ominously over East London. As she works late one night in Kate's drinking den, she recklessly succumbs to a bit of opportunistic thieving, while serving a man a plate of bread and cheese, and a tankard of strong ale. Gauging he would not notice, she swiftly, and slyly, removes a five-pound banknote from the pocket of his navy-blue, brass-buttoned jacket, hanging on the back of his chair. The owner, a stocky, broad-shouldered German sailor, detects the subtle, furtive movement behind him and swings around. Seeing Mary covertly tuck an item into the bodice of her low-cut, grubby dress, he is immediately suspicious. Undaunted at being in an atmosphere reeking of latent violence, he stands up and loudly bellows in rage as Mary scurries out through the scullery door,

"Komf back here an' zell me vas you ver doing behind mein back!"

Glaring at Kate, who stands mute and furious by the fireplace, he quickly shrugs into his jacket and strides from the premises. Once outside, he checks his pocket and discovers a banknote missing. He can identify the note, for it has a distinctive thumbprint mark in one corner. Convinced that the petite, thin young woman who had served him had taken it from his jacket, he walks briskly to Commercial Road Police Station where he reports the incident. As a man of rank, a ship's captain, the police show him deference and accompany him back to Kate's place on Zephyr Hill.

Despite, loud vehement protestations of her innocence, Mary is arrested and taken to the police station. There she is searched, and the missing banknote is found tucked inside the torn lining of her bodice. Charged with larceny, she is given a date in early September to appear at the magistrates' court. Unable to get word to Seth, she waits for his return, consumed with fear at what his reaction will be to her arrest. She covers her trepidation with belligerent bravado.

Just before Seth's expected return, a shocking, horrific murder takes place in Whitechapel, an event that terrifies the slum populace. Eight days later, another woman is, similarly, brutally slaughtered, her mutilated corpse found in Hanbury Street. Panic, like a contagion, rages through every alleyway, pub, lodging house, and brothel as men and women scurry about their daily business spreading stories of the horrific nature of the murderer.

"They say 'ee is a huge 'airy monster, 'oo rips open 'is victims, an' d' peelers 'ave bin scared t' deff by wha' they seen."

Pauper men, women and children huddle together expressing their opinions on the matter.

"Word 'as it that 'ee is a toff, gone off 'is 'ed, 'oo jus' enjoys killin' women."

"Some do say that 'ee is a butcher 'cause 'ee knows 'ow t' use a knife t' cut up a body."

Police and newspaper reporters swarm around Whitechapel, forcing criminals living there to take urgent measures to avoid scrutiny.

Returning from Ireland, where he had attended annual horse fairs, it is not long before Seth hears the many hysterical stories circulating about the gruesome Whitechapel killings. The closer he gets to Tower Hamlets, the more 'Wanted Notices' he sees stuck on lamp posts and walls, asking for help to catch the killer. Weaving his way through the maze of narrow alleyways, he observes peelers lurking on every corner. He is uneasy as he mulls over the possibility that he might be acquainted with the killer or may even know the victims. *Gawd only knows! I may know d' murderer, fer I knows some 'oo are vicious 'nuff t' kill. Men 'oo 'ates women. Men I could name. Bes' keep me lips sealed, an' me 'ead down, an' advise Kate an' Albert t' do d' same."*

Arriving at the yard in Zephyr Hill, he unhitches his waggon. While tethering the horse, he hears rapid, heavy footsteps crossing the cobbles. Albert appears, uncharacteristically hot and flustered. He steps inside the gate and speaks in a nervous rush.

"Zeff, 'ave y' 'erd 'bout zee murders of zee women in Vischapel? Kate finks das we know 'em by sight, bu' vee do not vant t' be quezioned by zee politz."

Lifting the halter over his horse's head, Seth nods.

"I seen d' posters wiv pictures of what 'as been done t' 'em. Bes' tell y', Albert, d' police are prowlin' fer miles aroun'. We needs t' lay low fer a bit, an' take 'cautions."

Albert nods but still his brow is crinkled with worry. Seth experiences a sudden sense of foreboding as he detects in his friend excessive tension.

"Anyfink wrong, my frien'? I be finkin' there be sumfink in yer manner?"

Contorting his mouth into a grimace of displeasure, Albert speaks.

"'Ave zee 'erd abou' yer missus, Zeff? Mary was arrested fer stealin' an' is goin' afore d' Beak, middle of next veek.

Me an' Kate izz vorried da d' peelers vill be 'ammering on our door soon."

Outwardly, unresponsive to Albert's words, Seth's countenance gives nothing away of the shock he feels on hearing this news. His stomach flips over. He is thrown off balance. Small tell-tale signs– a pulsing jugular vein in his neck and rapid dilation of his pupils– are the only indication of the intensity of his feelings. Overwhelmed by a powerful urge to strangle Mary, he leaves the yard and strides briskly across the road. Shoving open the front door, he aims a kick at a half-starved mongrel cowering in the hallway. Taking a deep breath he bellows, "MARY!"

Kate calls out from the kitchen, "D' stupid, fievin' missus of yers, Seff, is upstairs."

Seth's mood darkens further as he ascends the staircase. Vicious thoughts rampage through his head. *'Ow kin she 'ave bin so bleedin' stupid t' get nabbed? She be a troublesome bitch, 'an no mistake. D' place is crawlin' wiv peelers lookin' fer d' bloody killer. If she is sent t' d' jug, oo is goin' t' look afte' d' boys, an' Sally Anne? We'll 'ave t' move away if she goes t' prison. 'Er careless, sloppy bi' o' stealin' could bring all 'ell upon our 'eds.*

That Seth berates his wife is clear to everyone in the street. They listen to Mary's shrill screams, the sound of breaking glass, splintering wood and hard objects ricocheting off the walls of the upstairs room at Number One. When the ferocious rumpus subsides, Kate raps on their door to stridently inform them that they are to leave the lodging house as soon as possible, regardless of the outcome of Mary's court case. They are drawing unwanted attention upon her establishment, and furthermore, she has been told that the German sailor, Mary's victim, has influence with court officials and is pushing for a custodial sentence.

Mary's hope is that the magistrate will be lenient because, once again, she is pregnant. According to a neighbour, Ma Walsh, having a growing baby in your belly will get sympathy from the court. On the date of her appearance, Mary dresses demurely and adopts a downcast, repentant demeanour. She strives to manipulate the magistrate by outwardly communicating a calm, quiet, timid persona and by speaking quietly. Her efforts fail. Sentenced to five months' incarceration in Millbank Prison, a penitentiary soon due to close, she joins other local petty criminals for the duration of her sentence.

Impassively, Seth watches as his wife is led away to the cells. His most urgent predicament is to get the children away from Tower Hamlets. Not usually prone to anxiety, or doing things hastily, he is galvanised into action when, within days of Mary's incarceration, two more female corpses are found, both slaughtered on the same night.

He and the children immediately leave for Crandonside. Seth informs the school that they need to move temporarily because of his work. Cal and George are jubilant to escape the all-pervading terror gripping everyone in Limehouse and beyond. They are happy to stay with Lottie and Wilfred, where they are free to run about, play in meadows, chase rabbits, catch fish in streams and hide in hay barns. Not having enough room to accommodate her small granddaughter, Lottie arranges for Sally Anne to stay with Bert and Agnes, where the girl will enjoy the company of her cousins. The three children settle quickly, unperturbed by the sudden disappearance of their mother. They neither enquire nor express the slightest curiosity regarding her whereabouts.

Leaving his children in Essex, Seth quickly returns to East London where he rents a single, dingy, damp room in Bethnal Green. Not despondent for long, he actively looks about for fresh money-making opportunities. Assuming various pseudonyms, he covers his tracks, evading unwanted police attention. He avoids taverns and vice dens and does his essential travelling in the early hours of the morning when fog is as thick as pea-soup. Keeping a cool head, he appears impervious to the crippling fear rampaging through Whitechapel regarding the killer, nicknamed 'Jack the Ripper'. Before long he has an idea.

He will capitalise on the alarm and anxiety among wives and daughters of East End residents by running a twenty-four-hour, safe, affordable cab service for those too afraid to walk the streets. He ponders on what he will need to start his transport business. *Bill can 'elp me. I'll pay 'im as a driver. Wiv two small wagons t' start wiv, we can offer 'safe' travel fru d' alleyways running alongside d' 'ighway.* In his mind's eye he sees the words 'MARCHWOOD CABS' in large bold print on the sides of his vehicles. Reinvigorated, he resolves to ignore the gruesome killings, and Mary's imprisonment, and focus on developing his cab business.

This he manages to do until the grotesquely mutilated corpse of Mary Jane Kelly is found in the hovel she rented in Whitechapel, another victim of Jack the Ripper. Returning to his squalid room, a few days after the grisly deed, he finds a note from Albert pushed under his door. The message reads,

ZEFF. KATE SAYS MARY KELLY LIVED HIER A YEAR AGO. BE VORNED! ZEE POLITZ ARE ASKIN' QUEZZIONS. DONT VISIT UNTIL I TELL YOU TO COME. ALBERT.

Struggling to decipher the note, Seth regrets his limited reading skills. He asks a publican he trusts to read it to him and is spooked by the message. He needs to act quickly if he is to minimise the risk to himself, and his business activities. The police are bound to poke their noses into all the comings and goings in Limehouse, and he cannot afford for them to question him too closely. In the dead of the night, he moves his stock of horses and tackle away from London storage yards, into rented farm buildings near Crandon in Essex.

While Mary serves her sentence, he considers ways to circumnavigate recent laws making running brothels illegal. He makes enquiries, quizzing vice den proprietors as to how they are managing to adapt to the new legislation. The advice he gets is to investigate the recent proliferation of small risqué theatres; Penny Gaffs and coffee houses. There, beneath an innocent façade of musical entertainment, tarts can mingle with dolly mops and semi-respectable women looking for excitement. Like bees to a honeypot, men, from all social classes, frequent these venues, where they are sexually titillated with crude songs and discretely serviced by prostitutes.

It is soon an ardent ambition of Seth's to own his own Coffee House and Penny Gaff. He can use profits from the cab business, and from the sale of Mary's horde of trinkets, towards buying himself suitable slum properties. Quenching his thirst one evening in The Grapes, he is approached by Mick White. Mick, an undersized, puny horse thief, with a dark, heavily lined countenance and shifty, beady brown eyes, sucking in his thin lips, leans into Seth and whispers conspiratorially.

"'Ello, Seff! By any chance are y' lookin' fer a fine pair of ponies fer pullin' traps? I 'appen t' 'ave some t' sell, cheap?"

Taking a few minutes to digest Mick's query, Seth answers, "Mick! I am not much interested in buyin' animals a' d' moment. Instead, I am lookin' ou' fer cheap properties in Lime'ouse. It is urgent I get somefink soon. D' y' know of 'ouses due fer demolishment, fer they could suit me purpose nicely?"

Looking pleased with himself, Mick replies, "As it 'appens, Seff, I 'erd of two 'ouses goin' fer a song in Prosperous Way. I spects y' knows it. Plenti tarts t' be foun' there."

Laughing, a dirty laugh, he continues.

"An Irish fella, John O'Grady, is sellin' 'em, I fink."

Next day, Seth visits Prosperous Way, a place similar in character to Zephyr Hill. Flanking each side of the cobbled street are eight, three-storey, crumbling, red-brick terraced houses. Dank narrow alleyways run behind them, from which residents' access tiny backyards. Located a short walk away are Chinese opium dens and gambling houses. The address is ideally suited to his plans. He stops to read the 'For Sale' signs, crudely written on thin pieces of wood nailed to the front doors of No. 1 and No. 7. Both houses are run-down, seedy premises. Running his hand over his chin, he thinks, *Wiv d' 'elp of me bruver, I can do up bofe 'ouses, one t' be a Coffee 'ouse, and d' uver, a Penny Gaff.'* He pictures the scene; a black, cottage piano upon a small stage in one corner of a showily decorated room, sparsely furnished, with wooden tables and chairs. Excited at the prospect, believing that Mary too will like the idea, he buys both properties in January eighteen-eighty-nine.

During the second week of her prison term, Mary miscarries. The foetus, expelled in a deluge of blood, water, and acute pain, in her prison cell, happens one late afternoon. Her predicament evokes unexpected shows of kindness from the screws. Grateful, she settles down and becomes a model inmate. As she once did in Poplar Lodge, she finds comfort and security in the structure of the days and the small privileges to be found in prison.

Each week she gets a piece of soap to use during her ablutions. For the first time in years, she manages to clean off the deep-seated patina of dirt on the soles of her feet and the back of her neck. Provided with a loose-fitting brown, woollen gown, a dark-blue cotton apron, and two close-fitting, white linen bonnets, she is better dressed than when she is at home. To be able to wash her long, curly black hair once a week is a luxury. Given a measure of lavender oil, she rubs it into her hair before using a fine comb to remove any lice she may have. Her temporary loss of freedom is a price worth paying for the hygiene benefits she gets while serving out her time.

The night before her release, Mary is apprehensive. Seth has not visited her in the five months she has been in Millbank. On the actual morning of her release, she finally hears from him. A blunt, brief few words, written on a plain postcard; *Mary, I will pick you up. Seth. X.* Seeing the 'X' after his name heartens her, for she views it as a sign that he is no longer angry with her.

She is pleased she pampered herself during her last evening in gaol, bathing in a hot tub and washing her hair until it shone. She knows she is looking her prettiest as she walks through the big imposing wooden gates of the gaol and hopes her appearance will attract Seth's admiration and desire.

Whisperings:
Losing liberty teaches patience, self-acceptance, and the value of retribution.

7

Rats

There never were greed and cunning in the world yet, that did not do too much and overreach themselves. It is as certain as death.

David Copperfield – Charles Dickens

1889–1894

Armed with useful named contacts, better informed in the art of criminality, and feeling proud that she has served her sentence without complaint, Mary leaves Millbank Prison on that blustery morning in April eighteen-eighty-nine. At 9.30am precisely, the high, heavy wooden gates open slowly, and a smartly dressed, delicately built woman of twenty-eight walks out onto the Embankment on the northern side of the River Thames. Her cheeks whipped by the chilly breeze, she stands, takes a deep breath, and sighs in relief at regaining her freedom.

Glancing around for Seth, she is disappointed not to see him waiting there for her. She is not concerned though, for since getting his postcard, now tucked inside her deep coat pocket, she believes he has forgiven her. She is no longer afraid he will take their children away and abandon her to her fate. When he did not visit her in prison, despite her many pleading messages, she had feared that he would do just that.

Walking away from the gaol, the collar of her long black coat turned up against the morning chill, she clutches the hessian bag containing her few personal belongings. Crossing the road, she drops the bag to the ground and leans over the river wall. Nervously fiddling with the ribbons of her dark blue bonnet, she watches the murky waters lap against the base of the Embankment, and the waves rippling out from heavily laden river barges. Big Ben chimes, striking the hour, and she turns to look intently back along the Embankment towards Westminster Bridge.

On the last chime of the mighty clock, she sees Seth, broad-shouldered and straight-backed, driving a smart black trap, pulled by his sturdy chestnut mare, Ruby. Any mild apprehension she had begun to feel, dissipates. She raises her right arm and enthusiastically waves at him. Her mouth turns up in a wide, beaming smile and her blue eyes sparkle with excitement, and, for a split second, she cannot catch her breath. Watching him approach her, she is reminded of the first time she saw him, when he rode towards the gates of Poplar Lodge. Her thoughts tumble and fly, *Bloomin' 'eck, I 'ad forgot 'ow 'andsome 'ee is, my Seff. I fink we will bofe be 'avin' fun as soon as we can be private. I will stop 'im from finking of tarts fer a while, fer after bein' locked up, I am burnin' wiv lust.* Graphic imagery of their entwined, naked bodies engulfs her in a surge of heat.

Drawing closer to his wife, Seth is surprised to see how well she looks. Her skin glows with health and her eyes shine with flirtatious mischief. Noticing dark curls brushing her forehead from under the brim of her bonnet, he is taken with how wholesome and young she looks after five months' incarceration. Stirred by her cheeky, coquettish smile, he pulls Ruby's reins, calling softly, "Whoa, Ruby! Whoa, girl! Whoa!"

When the vehicle comes to a halt, Mary hands her heavy bag silently to Seth before clambering up to sit close beside him, her thigh touching his. Hiding his astonishment at her transformation from the worn, slovenly woman he saw leaving court six months ago, to this sweet smelling, girlish figure pressing into his side, he is reminded of their early romantic assignations in Crandonside. Like Mary, he experiences a wave of lust. Resentment for the trouble she has caused him abates and is replaced by a powerful sexual desire. He guesses, from the way she keeps looking at him, that she is as eager for physical passion as he is. Impatient to reap what he gauges to be the benefits of her pent-up need for sexual release, he whips the horse into a fast trot.

Almost thirty years old, he is at the peak of his bodily prowess. As father to two legitimate strong sons, and a daughter, his fertility is proven and his potent masculine identity secure. His red-blooded reputation is a major factor underpinning his self-confidence and inflated ego. Unfailingly, he insists that any illegitimate children of his go by his surname, for he is excessively proud of his virility and ability to sire children. Beyond giving them his surname, however, he offers them little else; no financial support for the mother, nor does he show any interest in their ongoing welfare. It is Mary, his legal wife and mother to his sons, who has his loyalty, albeit, at times, begrudgingly.

Driving along the Embankment, towards Tower Hamlets, Mary absorbs the familiar smells and sights while being intensely aware of her husband's thigh pressed close to hers. Seth, much discomforted by her as she perches temptingly on the wooden seat beside him, decides to talk of other matters, to temporarily divert his lusty thoughts until they are safely back at his lodgings.

"We ain't goin' back t' Kate's place, Mary. An' what's more, we no longer 'ave t' pay rent, fer I 'ave bought two 'ouses in Prosperous Way, near to Zephyr 'ill. It will be a familiar place fer d' children. An' they can go back t' their old school. There ain't much furnishment yet. That will take time. Bu' I got us some beds to sleep in."

Struck dumb with incredulity, Mary stares open-mouthed at these unexpected revelations. He continues, "One 'ome is t' be a Coffee 'Ouse, Mary, an' d' uver property will be a Penny Gaff. 'Tis the way fings are now. Cheap 'ore 'ouses are gone. Old' Jack d' Ripper seen t' that. Wiv peelers everywhere, snoopin an' pryin', fings is changin' fast. Gaffs an' Coffee 'ouses are d' future. In Prosperous Way, Mary, there is money to be made from workin' girls, tradin' 'orse flesh, gamblin', an' movin' stolen goods aroun'. You, me, an' d' boys can all work t'gether to run d' businesses."

Laughing quietly under his breath, he places a big square hand on her thigh, squeezing and rubbing it suggestively.

"We be movin' up in d' world, Mary. We must use our 'eds, trust no-one bu' close family."

Mary, flooded with relief, feels her body sag with the sudden loss of latent anxiety. Seth has clear plans for their future together, as a family, and is giving her a chance to redeem herself. With a burst of delight, she babbles excitedly.

"Gaw blimey, Seff! This is such wonderful news I can 'ardly contain meseff. When do we start? I 'eard from uvers inside that undergroun' gamblin' dens is popular. I were told that Coffee 'ouses an' Gaffs are usually ignored by d' peelers."

Easter Sunday falls three days after Mary's release, and that morning, Mary and Seth travel in their finest horse-drawn trap to Crandonside to pick up their children and take them back to London. Apprehensive about meeting her mother-in-law, whose disapproval will have grown since her time in goal, Mary is determined to hold her tongue no matter what the provocation. Begrudgingly grateful to Lottie and Agnes for looking after the children during her absence, she is nevertheless resentful of the fact that, according to Seth, her sons like living in Crandonside. She is under no illusions that they will be happy to see her, fully expecting them to be surly and uncommunicative when they meet. Regarding Sally Anne, however, she hopes that she, at least, will remember her and be glad to see her. She chatters nervously as they travel briskly along the lane.

"Seff, when did y' las' see Sally Anne? 'Ope she 'members me. 'As 'er Auntie Agnes bin kind t' 'er? I know she is strict an' God fearin', bu' she is a good mufver. 'Ave d' boys behaved? I 'spect they 'ave, fer Lottie don' take no nonsense. I know yer mufver looks down 'er nose at me, Seff, especially since she knows where I 'ave been these last months. I promise though, Seff, I will not show me annoyance, fer I 'ave learned t' control meseff better while in Milbank."

The vehicle suddenly jolts over a deep rut in the lane causing Mary's lower back to twinge with a sharp pain, the consequence of two days and nights of satisfying, boisterous sex. She hopes that by douching with vinegar and water, she has prevented herself conceiving. Free of the responsibility of tending to a tiny baby, she craves time to enjoy her new life in Prosperous Way, as the respected wife of Seth Marchwood, a man of property.

Mid-morning, they arrive in the lane outside Church Farm Cottages. Mary glimpses George standing beside his grandmother in the open doorway. Lurking in the shadows behind them is Cal, his countenance surly and ill-tempered. Her mother-in-law, a scowl fixed to her face, nods a greeting to Seth, while pointedly ignoring Mary.

"I've made y' a cheese an' bread platter an' a pot of tea. Figure y' will want 'freshments afore y' go to Bert's place to pick up Sally Anne. D' boys 'ave bin eatin' us ou' of 'ouse an' 'ome. Still, I am 'appy t' say they bin workin' fer their keep, fetchin' wood, an' earnin' shillings, 'elping men prepare fields fer plantin.'"

On entering the kitchen, Mary is subdued as she sits

on the wooden bench by the table. Her stiff countenance, and overall body language, conveys an immense inner struggle to veil her intense dislike and resentment of Lottie. Seth positions himself in front of the range, and from his bulging jacket pocket, he pulls a roll of soiled banknotes, which he duly hands to his mother.

"That should cover d' cost of keepin' our sons, an' more besides, so not anuver word 'bout wha' they cost y' in food. Let me remind y', Ma, you, an' that mean sod Wilfred, get plenty from me, an' will get plenty more, no doubt."

Disliking being beholden to her son, Lottie mumbles through pursed lips, "Don' fink Wilf an' me ain't grateful, son. We are. Any'ow, 'tis no 'ardship 'avin' 'em stay 'ere. I likes 'avin' 'em, an' takin' 'em t' Church on Sunday. Bofe of 'em know their prayers an' d' Ten Commandments. Ain't that ri', boys?"

The boys acknowledge their grandmother's question with a barely perceptible nod, followed by a sly glance between themselves. Lottie continues, "They bin goin' t' d' village school. George, 'ee be a good scholar, an' 'ee can read from d' Good Book. As fer Cal! 'Ee ain't so good at d' learnin'. 'Ee 'as a wicked, foul temper on 'im. I fink that sometimes 'ee needs whippin' t' bring 'im under control. 'Is Uncle Bert sometimes takes 'im to Eppin' Forest, an' teaches 'im foraging fer wood. Bert says, Cal is good a' working wiv dogs when they is ou' catchin' rats."

As Mary listens to Lottie, she broods, sipping her tea and nibbling half-heartedly at the bread and cheese. Seething inside, she thinks, *Wha' a ole 'ypocrite she is, puttin' on a 'God fearing', 'olier than thou' act. She makes me sick, fer she is 'appy 'nuff t' take money from 'er son, even though she knows 'ee steals, cheats, goes wiv tarts, an' don' 'tend church no more.* Observing her two boys, hovering side by side near the scullery door, she senses their ardent desire to be anywhere else except in this room. Standing taller and sturdier since she last saw them, their childish faces are tanned ruddy from working in the open air. She feels as if they no longer belong to her. They have become strangers. Raising her right hand, she beckons them over and, with palpable reluctance, they move towards her.

Wanting desperately to spark their curiosity, she tells them about their new home in Prosperous Way.

"It ain't far from Zephyr 'ill, so y' can attend yer ole school."

At her words, there is a subtle change in Cal's morose demeanour. His eyes show a flicker of interest. During his time in the countryside, he has missed the excitement of being among the local Limehouse gang of unruly boys, Paddy, Mick, Alfie, and Thomas. Hanging around together, they thieved, smoked, fought, drank alcohol, and lit fires for the fun of it. Out on the rampage, Cal was accustomed to regularly participating in frenzied, impulsive acts of aggression. An able fighter, better than most, he has status among his Limehouse peers.

He is impatient to return to re-establish his dominant role within the local gang. He knows that after his long absence he will need to prove himself once more and rebuild his fierce reputation. Confident in his ability to manipulate other wayward boys, he never doubts that he will succeed in playing a key role in their activities once back in London slum territory. Cunning, sly, deceitful, and secretive, both he and George are moulded to survive the cut-throat environment of the criminal youth fraternity, but they thrive within it.

Departing Lottie's cottage that afternoon, neither of the boys look back as she waves them goodbye. They sit, side by side, on the back seat of the trap, mute and sulky while they travel the short distance to Uncle Bert's red-brick, terraced cottage. Both children respect their Uncle Bert and Aunt Agnes, for they are the only adults, along with Lottie, with whom they feel safe and secure. Their aunt, a slightly built, thin-faced, hardworking woman, cares for her family and spends her evenings making and mending clothes for villagers. Born and raised in Yorkshire, in a humble devout Christian family, she is a steadying hand on her partially deaf husband, and her brood of children.

Waiting for her parents to arrive, Sally Anne is smartly dressed in a long-sleeved, blue cotton dress, protected by a starched white apron edged with embroidered blue corn flowers. On her feet she wears soft, black, hand-stitched boots and warm woollen stockings to protect her legs from the cold. Standing quietly at her aunt's knee earlier that morning, her long, brown hair was gently brushed and plaited. The braids, coiled into loops behind her ears, are secured with shiny, pink, silk ribbon bows. As it is Easter Sunday morning, she holds a tiny, woven straw nest, holding miniature balls of marzipan and chocolate-covered raisins. Once home from church she has her aunt's permission to eat these morsels. Fingering the last two, she pops one into her mouth, sucking its sweetness in delight. The recent winter months, living under the tender care of her aunt, Sally Anne has blossomed physically and emotionally. Within this nurturing environment, she stopped wetting the bed and came out of her shell around adults.

Too young to understand that today she is to leave her aunt's house, she climbs up onto a chair to admire herself in the oval mahogany mirror hanging on the wall by the front door. Shaking her head from side to side, she watches her glossy plaits swing and bounce beneath her shiny pink bows. Scrunching up a pert button nose, she squints, trying to get a clearer image of her face through the de-silvering marks on the mirror. Her pleasant reverie ends when she hears the clatter of hooves in the lane outside the cottage. Climbing down from the chair, she peeps through the window and sees a woman who she knows is her mama, with her da and brothers. Uncle Bert strides out to the latched wooden gate and greets them as they alight from the trap. At that moment, Agnes reaches down and takes hold of Sally Anne's tiny hand, giving her reassurance.

Seth and Bert are similar in appearance, each thick-set, square-jawed with high cheekbones and thin lips. Bert, content to live in Crandonside, makes a living working in the forest, felling trees and chopping logs for firewood. He has a yard in Crandon from which he sells timber. He supplements his meagre income by working as the local ratcatcher. Estate managers call on his services to cull rat mischiefs from barns, farmland, and crumbling manor houses. His expertise in deploying ferrets to flush rats from their nests, and train dogs to catch and kill the vermin, is renowned in his locality. When the use of animals is not appropriate, he laces cheese and animal fats with poison and places the lethal titbits near rat holes. Next day, he collects and disposes of the dead rodents. Known as *The Crandon Ratcatcher,* his ability is admired by many and bragged about by his proud children.

"Our da! 'Ee ain't 'fraid of nuvfink. We see 'im pull big brown rats, big as tomcats, from 'ay stacks. Then 'ee swings 'em 'roun' by d' tail, 'fore frowing 'em to d' dogs."

Bert honed his skill at training dogs as a boy. Taken by Wilfred to organised fights in barns, gambling pits and in pubs, he grew accustomed to seeing live vermin pitted against killer bulldogs. In such frenzied, alcohol-fuelled atmospheres, he watched men betting on the outcome of these gladiatorial spectacles. Seeing out his apprenticeship in this low-class entertainment, he is well placed to turn what he learns to his advantage.

Country rats, bigger than puny London rats, are much prized in the fevered East London pits. In collaboration with Seth, who has many London contacts, he supplies Limehouse landlords with huge rural rats for their sporting arenas. On caging the vermin, he transports the pulsating, squirming, terrified, angry rats to Seth's yard in Prosperous Way, where they are kept fed and watered before being sold to the highest bidder. Lifelong fans of the sport themselves, Seth, Bill, and Bert mingle comfortably with rough, low-class, sweaty, foul-mouthed gamblers, tightly packed into cramped airless rooms. The exhilarated punters ignore the suffering of the animals. It is of no consequence to the raucous, hyped-up rabble who gleefully watch blood-soaked hounds, draped in rat entrails and gore, rip and gorge on the wriggling, petrified rats with their vicious fangs.

Standing impatiently waiting, as Seth and Bert arrange the next wagon full of rats to be delivered to London, Mary, eager to lift Sally Anne into the trap, urgently wants to escape the worried, sad look on her sister-in-law's face. Seth is eventually ready to leave and Mary sighs with relief as Sally Anne, pale, forlorn and subdued, is placed between her brothers on the dark wooden seat of the trap. Until the very last moment, she clung to her aunt's hand whispering a plea.

"I don' wanna go wiv 'em. Auntie, please can I stay 'ere wiv you?"

Agnes, heartsore for her niece's predicament, is helpless to console the child as she is driven quickly away. Mary, peeved at her daughter's obvious affection for Agnes, is irked when the child rebuffs her motherly overtures. Muttering angrily to Seth, she complains, "She 'as bin spoilt these las' five mumfs; mollycoddled wiv 'er fancy clothes an' boots. I feel like a bad mufver, when I sees Sally Anne go all lovey-dove wiv Agnes. Did y' see yer sister-in-law gawp at me, as if I were a piece of muck on 'er boot?"

Seth stares straight ahead, glowering but silent. Mary turns to scold her children.

"Y' can stop yer snivelling an' sulkin' fer yer da and I 'ave good news. We are owners of two 'ouses, bofe to be used fer entertainments. We will make lots of money. Cal! You can 'elp ou' at the Penny Gaff an' earn a few shillings. George! You can 'elp me wiv Sally-Anne, an' watch over 'er while I work."

Defiantly Mary looks ahead, her face set in anger and resentment. The boys pull rude faces and make obscene gestures behind their parents' backs, actions immediately copied by their little sister. Stifling laughter, the children are careful not to be caught, for such insolence would certainly earn a beating from Seth.

Within weeks, the houses in Prosperous Way are doing good business. Three rooms, gaudily decorated boudoirs, are leased out on an hourly basis in the Coffee House. The Penny Gaff offers vulgar musical entertainment and private time with loose women. Customers are a conglomeration of down-at-heel toffs, labourers, drunkards, slum dwellers and tarts. Tickets are sold at the door, and long queues form as individuals wait their turn to enter the packed smoky arena. Inside, a black-lacquered cottage piano stands to the side of a modestly sized stage at the back of the room. In one corner of the raised dais is a low, round side-table, upon which stands a decorative oil-lamp, with a milky white globe and black iron base. Scattered around the room are barley twist, wooden chairs, a few circular tables, and long benches placed against the walls. Female performers strut about the stage, singing bawdy, titillating songs and teasing the audience with smutty innuendos.

The family's living quarters are two upstairs rooms in the Coffee House. Seth and Mary sleep in the larger, dank back bedroom, which contains nothing but a well-used, grubby double bed and piles of heaped clothes on the floor. Up a narrow, rickety flight of wooden steps is a windowless attic room where the three children sleep. The boys share a filthy horsehair mattress laying on the bare floorboards, and Sally Anne sleeps on thin, lumpy, bug-infested bedding in an old wooden cot. The air in the room is stifling hot in summer and freezing in winter. It permanently reeks of the stale acrid smell of urine emanating from the foul beds and the children's filthy clothes. Two other bedrooms in the house are leased out to working prostitutes.

While her brothers are at school, or working at the Penny Gaff, Sally Anne, alone in the attic room, stares up at the roof rafters. Her blue eyes are huge and solemn in her tiny, thin face, as she impassively watches black rats scuttle back and forth along the wooden beams. Spiders' webs glisten in the corners of the sloping roof. They remind her of when Aunt Agnes once pointed out a sparkling spider's web in a hedgerow that was shimmering with morning dew. She told her, "That is d' Palace of d' Queen Spider, Sally Anne. We know that. How? Because it is glisnin' wiv 'undreds of tiny, sparklin' diamonds."

Occasionally Mama comes up to check on her, promising to come back to help her wash and dress before George comes home from school. Rarely is that promise kept. Forlorn, the child waits for her brother to appear with something for her to eat. She loves George as intensely as she hates Cal, because he frightens her, especially when he pulls scary faces and roughly tickles her in places where she does not want to be touched. When left alone with

Cal, she holds tightly onto the rag doll Aunt Agnes made for her, nor daring to breathe, willing him to disappear.

Within weeks of the children's return to Limehouse, Sally Anne's health dramatically deteriorates. She cries incessantly. Feeling helpless, and woefully inadequate, as she monitors her daughter's pale complexion, sunken eyes and burning fever, Mary's frustration spills out in a show of annoyance towards George. She nags him. She blames him for not looking after his sister better, shifting responsibility onto his young shoulders, while pretending to herself that Sally Anne is not really ill, just pining for her Aunt Agnes. In less than a month, she must confront the harsh truth.

Returning from school, George finds Sally Anne's fragile, emaciated body lying cold to the touch and stiff in her cot. Nine-years-old, he intuitively senses that his mother's subsequent cold, dispassionate reaction to her daughter's death, masks helplessness, despair, and grief at losing another child another girl, just three years old. On the morning of the day that his sister's skeletal remains are taken from the house for burial, he unties the two dirty, bedraggled, pink bows from her soft, wispy hair and tucks them into his trouser pocket. Turning away from her corpse, he swallows a rush of hot tears which threaten to spill down his cheeks in an unstoppable flow. To reveal such emotion would invite ridicule from Cal.

The flurry of sexual passion in the weeks following Mary's release from Millbank Prison swiftly declines, and Seth's desire for her dramatically wanes. Any physical coupling is perfunctory in nature and affords neither of them much pleasure. Seth views his wife as too old, and too skinny, for his taste, with her flat chest, thinning lips, and wrinkles around her eyes. These days, his lust is only aroused by flirtatious young women with pinched waists, pert breasts, and lively personalities. He seeks out those who can pander to his needs; liberal women; enthusiastic participants in sexual liaisons. With his burgeoning status, ready cash, and handsome appearance, he has his pick of the prettiest whores, as well as fun-loving factory girls looking for a fun time.

Spring eighteen-ninety-four, Seth, on a rare impulse, makes love to Mary. To their consternation, this fleeting encounter results in pregnancy. In the late autumn of that year, another son, Albert Edward Marchwood, is born. His older brothers show no interest in him, for Cal, at seventeen, and George, at fifteen, are youths, preoccupied in establishing their individual identities and striving to earn their father's approval.

Albert's birth coincides with a rapid improvement in the family's material circumstances. Seth is at his physical peak in his mid-thirties. Reflecting his improving social status, he dresses in well-cut, tailor-made, three-piece-suits, made of quality woollen fabric. His stylish overcoats, expensive leather boots, and hats for every occasion communicate to those who meet him that he is a comfortably off, lower-middle-class gentleman. His most prized possession, and one that will remain so for many years to come, is a gold fob timepiece, attached to a heavy gold chain that hangs from his waistcoat pocket. Purchased from a light-fingered servant, in the employ of an elderly gentleman living in Oxford Street, Seth got a bargain. Apart from the floral etching on its case, the watch, when stolen, had no personal inscription. Within days of the watch falling into his hands, Seth has his name engraved on the inside flip-up cover; *Seth John Marchwood, Esquire.*

Whisperings:
Outward stature grows, hiding his baser self.

8

Sons

A man can well afford to be as bold as brass, my good fellow, when he gets gold in exchange!
Martin Chuzzlewit – Charles Dickens

1894–1900

Once over the shock of having another child, Mary is determined that this time she will follow the advice of the midwife, and Lottie, and focus on good hygiene and good food to prevent Albert becoming ill. More confident in the mothering role, she relaxes when breastfeeding and bonds with little Albert. Her obvious devotion to the new baby irritates Cal and George, who feel jealous of the attention she lavishes on him. The subtle softening in her manner is out of character and they are disconcerted by it. They surreptitiously watch while she nurses Albert and are inwardly contemptuous of the way her voice gentles when speaking to him. They exchange sly, scathing glances as Mary smiles into the baby's eyes and cradles his tiny head, crowned with glossy black curls, in the palm of her hand.

The love she expresses for this baby is a bitter pill for Cal to swallow. For months on end he rants and rages to George about it.

"'Ee will grow up t' be a spoilt brat, gettin everyfink 'ee wans, fings we never 'ad when we was children, George. She is makin' a bloody fool of 'erseff, slobberin' an' droolin' over 'im, fergettin' abou' everyfink, an' everyone else."

The broiling rancour both brothers go through is exacerbated by the fact they are working hard for Seth but only earning a pittance for their efforts. Regularly Seth promises proper renumeration for the work they do, but he never keeps his word, and pay packets invariably fall short of their expectations. When intoxicated, which he is often, Cal rails against his father's unjust treatment of them. Full of alcohol-fuelled false courage, he threatens to call out Seth for his stinginess. Despite his furious blustering however, he never does, for he fears his father's rage, and dare not risk falling out of favour, for Seth holds the family purse strings. By nature, George is more measured, taking a longer view of things. He tries to mollify Cal.

"If we aggravate d' ole bugger, 'ee will cut us off wivou' a penny, an' chuck us ou' of d' business. Y' know wha' a temper 'ee 'as, Cal? 'Old yer tongue when y' are wiv 'im.' Be patient bruver. One day we will figure ou' a way t' get wha' is our due. I 'ave no intention of bein' 'is bloody slave fer d' res' of me life. Bu', 'til then, I will 'old me cards close t' me chest an' get everyfink I can ou' of 'im. Only when I am good an' ready will I make my move."

Subservient when in the company of their father, at

all other times, Cal and George are cocky, controlling, and boastful. Neither one of them is averse to using their father's notoriety to bully and demand favours. Years of mendacious practice by both Seth and Mary is replicated by them both. Their fragile self-esteem and delicately balanced egos are masked by aggressive, belligerent facades that effectively shield them against guilt or shame. When not carrying out tasks for Seth, they roam local streets and alleyways with other unruly youths. They congregate outside pubs and loiter on street corners where they menace passers-by and yell profanities at passing girls and women. At night they lurk in the shadows beyond streetlamps and, for their own amusement, pounce on intoxicated individuals, assaulting them for no reason, just for fun. Shopkeepers, who complain to Mary about their disorderly behaviour, are met with a strong rebuttal by her as she vigorously comes to their defence. She interprets any criticism of her sons as personal criticism of her as a mother.

As soon as Cal and George learned to walk and talk, they were taught to be pugnacious fighters; to stand up for themselves and never show cowardice in the face of physical challenge. When attending school, other children, who dare to threaten them, must be able to withstand their cold, hard glares and menacing facial expressions. Their opponents dare not lower their gaze if they are to avoid a beating by the Marchwood brothers. In every physical fight they get involved in, the words of their father ring in their ears and drives their aggression.

"Y' mus' always get in d' firs' punch, boys, an' to their

face, fer blood will blind 'em good an' propa'. Kick d' legs from under 'em, an' break a few fingers by stampin' 'ard on their 'ands. Never show weakness. Fight like dogs. Never giff up, even when bloodied, fer that is d' way you prove yerselves."

By the age of seventeen, Cal has developed a taste and a dependency on strong drink and his daily consumption is excessive. Drinking a mix of beer and strong spirits makes him behave in a hostile, abusive manner, easily provoked to anger and violent assault. Scars on his head, face, arms, and legs are testament to numerous vicious skirmishes; personal trophies which enhance his menacing self-image. Favouring his mother in looks, with an angular face, piercing blue eyes and wiry build, he stands five feet seven inches tall, shorter than George by one inch. His hair, dark and unruly, compliments a swarthy, gypsy-like, complexion which helps him mingle inconspicuously with travelling, itinerant communities thronging the marketplaces. Obvious to those who know him is his restless impulsivity, need for constant stimulation, and his habit of attracting negative attention. His grandmother, Lottie, is vocal in her criticism.

'Ee be nuffin' bu' a bloody 'ooligan, acting like a peacock, struttin' aroun', showin' off, wantn' people to react to 'is drunken escapades."

Wilfred echoes her grumbles.

"Wha' did y' expect Lottie? D' boy 'as bin dragged up in d' slums by 'is sluttish, criminal mufver. Yee 'ave told yer son, Seff, so let's see wha' 'ee will do abou' it."

Affronted by Lottie telling tales to Seth about Cal's

misdemeanours, Mary's anger simmers until it finally erupts into rage. Waiting until Seth is away on business in Norfolk, she wastes no time in driving to Crandonside with Cal. In the lane outside the Loxburys' cottage, they both raise a violent fracas, screaming abuse and threatening physical harm to the elderly Lottie and Wilfred. Neighbours alert the village police officer who, on arrival at the scene, arrests Mary and Cal for causing affray. The case goes to court and Seth is forced to pay a hefty fine for their release. Neither of the antagonists show remorse for the upset caused to Seth's mother and the incident creates a lasting schism in the wider Marchwood clan. Without fail, from then on, each time Seth visits his mother, she furiously reminds him that he had married beneath him.

"I told y', Seff, that she was nuffin bu' a common slut afore y' married 'er. Bu' y' did not listen t' me. It was me 'oo looked afte' d' boys when she was locked up in gaol. She is an ungrateful slut, Seff, an' I will never forgive 'er fer wha' she done; 'oomiliating me an' Wilf an' all d' neighbours watchin'. Yer farver Hubert, Seff, must be turnin' in his grave."

Seth is furious at Mary and Cal's display of uncouth, loutish behaviour, especially at this time when he is endeavouring to better himself. He broods after every visit to his mother, flooded with regret and embarrassment that he is lumbered with a low-class, rowdy wife just when he is moving up in the world and aspiring to be middle class. He pores over the issue. *They 'ave bofe made me look a fool. People will fink I can't control me own wife an' son.*

They are already lookin' a' me wiv sympathy an' I am losin' d' respect of those 'oo knows me. For months on end, he berates Mary with fierce criticism, continually comparing her abysmal behaviour to that of his mother who, he opines, is a paragon of all virtues.

"Me mufver never did approve of me marryin' you. She knew y' were nuvfink bu' a common strumpet, not good 'nuff t' wed a Marchwood. She said I would be sorry one day, an' that day is now. Bes' keep ou' me way fer I am tempted t' break me own rules an' batter y' black an' blue."

Refusing to be browbeaten by Seth's endless barrage of insults, when pushed to the limit, Mary's wild temper, spawned in the slum gutters of Tower Hamlets, ignites. Vicious in self-defence, she swears, screams, and maliciously threatens to expose Seth's fraudulent deals and links with vice to all and a sundry. Spitefully, gauging how best to hurt him, she tells him how indifferent she is to him sleeping with whores, and the relief she feels at no longer being the target of his sexual desire.

Seth's predatory sexual behaviours are not, nor ever have been, hidden from Cal and George. As children, they frequently witnessed his crude, licentious interactions with young prostitutes, his playthings. He would laughingly encourage them to join him in some of these sexual encounters. His belief was then, and still is, that early exposure to the pleasures of sex is fundamental to the healthy growth of boys and an essential part of training for manhood. During his sons' toddler years, Seth basked in their childish admiration and was amused and flattered when they copied his distinctive walk; arms akimbo, straight-backed, distinctly intimidatory and belligerent. He boasted proudly in the pub that the boys had a nickname for him, 'Brown Bear', because in their eyes they equated him with the powerfully strong bears they had seen chained up near the Tower of London.

At twenty, Cal is entrusted to run the Marchwood cab business when Seth makes him responsible for ensuring vehicles are kept in good condition and the horses properly rested and fed in between journeys. At first, Cal limits his drinking as he relishes his new role within the family business, wanting to impress his father with his level of maturity and management of the tasks. Unable to restrain himself for long, however, he soon reverts to drinking heavily and is intoxicated by the end of every working day. Paying passengers in his cabs feel considerable anxiety and fear at his ill-tempered manner and loud belligerent animosity towards other travellers; cyclists, costermongers pushing handcarts, horse riders, and pedestrians crossing the road. Passengers are frequently appalled at his cruelty towards the horse pulling the cab. Women and children become visibly distressed when his harsh wielding of the whip draws copious blood from the flayed rump of the animal and causes it to become nervous, jittery, and unpredictable, affecting Cal's ability to control the reins.

George, aware that his brother's behaviour is jeopardising the family business, discusses the situation with Mary, questioning his father's judgement in handing the management of the cabs to Cal.

"Why did Da 'and over d' cabs to Cal? 'Ee is a drunkard, Ma. I am the one who knows more abou' drivin,' an' mechanics. I can fix d' cabs when they break down. Even when sober, 'ee is useless at sortin' out d' problems. I tell you now, Ma, I am sick of seein' 'im strut around, actin' like 'ee is better than me. It makes me mad as 'ell an' want to punch 'is smug face in."

Watching her son pace about in fury, Mary has some pity for him.

"Bes' be patient George! Compose yerseff, fer it won' do y' no good. Yer farver may get one of them engine-driven buses soon, where no 'orse is needed. An' as y' know abou' these modern motors mor' than either Cal or yer da, I 'spects yer farver will let y' run that side of d' business."

Standing close to George, Mary is, as she always is, taken aback by his striking resemblance to Seth. At eighteen, George is taller than his father, broad-chested, muscled, and handsome. His voice is deep and loud, and he has a hearty booming laugh, instantly contagious to those around him. Better educated than Cal, he is numerate and literate, having completed his compulsory education with a Standard IV Education Certificate. More sociable than his older brother, he enjoys drinking in pubs, flirting, impressing women with his ability to drive teams of horses as well as the latest, motorised cars.

When it becomes necessary to find an appropriate location to accommodate the family's growing collection of cabs and horses, Seth buys Pip Farm near Crandon, a property comprising forty acres of land, a semi-derelict, three-bedroomed, thatched cottage, three outbuildings and a spacious yard with adequate space for wagons, carts, and traps. There is stabling for six horses, and a dry tack-room for harnesses, bridles, halters, and reins. Cal, and his Uncle Bill are to use the property to rest between driving shifts. Once the transactions are completed, the family split their time between the countryside and the Marchwood Coffee House and Penny Gaffe in Prosperous Way.

Since Albert's birth, Mary's attitude towards living in the countryside has altered once again. Her prior delight at leaving Crandonside and relocating to Tower Hamlets has diminished. Seth's frequent absences, leaving her to manage their two businesses in Limehouse without his support, has brought her to physical and mental exhaustion. Almost forty, she has begun to hanker after a more leisurely, slower-paced life. She yearns to have more time to herself and get young Albert away from the rough, crude existence that is their daily life in Prosperous Way. She wants better for him, her youngest son, and nags Seth incessantly on the subject.

"I am bloody sick an' tired of you goin' away so much, Seff. D' older ones are sleepin' over at Pip Farm, along wiv Bill, while me an' Albert is stuck 'ere. You 'ave d' money Seff, so why not buy anuver cheap farm in Essex? A place where we can live comfortably, an' set up 'ome as a family? I worry meself abou' young Albert gettin' sick an' maybe dyin' like poor wee Charlotte, Sally Anne, Elizabeth, and Cedric."

Returning after a prolonged trip around East Anglia, Seth listens patiently to Mary's complaints. Sitting on a sturdy wooden chair placed to the side of the kitchen range, he leans down to untie his bootlaces. Pulling off the heavy footwear he wriggles his toes inside his thick, woollen socks, before sliding his feet nearer to the heat of the stove. He is in a good mood, sexually satiated after spending two nights with a nubile young whore in Whitechapel.

"Was abou' t' tell y' Mary, I do 'ave 'nuff cash t' buy' anuver place in Essex, bigger than Pip Farm. I 'ear there is an interestin' place fer sale near Bildinford. Do you remember Laurel Estate? Well, it is bein' broke up an' sold off. It comes wiv two fields, barns, stables an' a grand manor 'ouse. As it 'appens, I jus' been told that, Prosperous Way is to be demolished at last, on d' orders of d' government. They will be payin' us compensation too."

Pleased with the news, Mary falls silent before getting up to make a cup of tea for them both. As he listens to her pottering about the kitchen, Seth lets his mind wander. *I can jus' see meseff as owner of Laurel 'all. If me plans work, we can be livin' there early next year. Then I shall be a propa squire, an' people will doff their caps when they see me comin'.* He chuckles. *I will enjoy that, indeed I will. Wiv only one year t' go afore d' new century, I fink I am gettin' close to bein' a rich man.* With a contented sigh he opens his eyes, removes his stiff shirt collar and jacket, and drops them to the floor beside his chair before taking the cup proffered by Mary.

During the early months of eighteen-ninety-nine, the family leave Prosperous Way and move back to Essex and into Laurel Hall, where they are immediately elevated to a new social status. Part of the lower middle class, Mary,

Seth, and their sons adapt to their altered circumstances. Seth struts about his country estate in expensive, tailor-made tweed jackets, colourful waistcoats, and fashionable peaked caps, giving orders to the casual labourers he employs. Mary sets out to be seen as a respectable, refined woman, wife of a landowner, a woman who can afford to ride in a shiny black trap pulled by a dainty piebald pony into the town of Bildinford once a week. Strolling along the main street, she exchanges pleasantries with the butcher, baker, and greengrocer, and bestows friendly smiles on passers-by. Cal and George relish their improved circumstances and bask in the increased admiration of local country girls.

When not at school, five-year-old Albert accompanies his mother on her trips to town. Timid, in comparison to his older brothers, he clings to Mary's side and hides from his fearsome father and brother Cal. Seth is too busy to take an interest in Albert and rarely acknowledges his young son's presence. George is sympathetic to his younger brother, especially when he sees the blatant way Seth denies Albert attention of any kind. More sensitive in nature than Cal, George lets Albert tag along with him when he is working with horses and road vehicles. In return, Albert hero worships George and loves him as intensely as he hates Cal.

When George marries his nineteen-year-old sweetheart, Rosie Smith, Albert is elated, and he soon develops a youthful crush on his pretty sister-in-law. As a wedding gift, Seth procures The Three Dogs Pub for the young couple. George becomes the licence holder of the establishment and makes his home with Rosie in the rooms above the bar. Under pressure from Rosie's aggressive, pugilistic, publican father, Harry Smith, the wedding had been rushed so pregnant Rosie could be respectfully married at the time of the birth. George, resentful at being hurried to make an honest woman of her, is temporarily placated by his father's gift of the pub.

Preparing for the ringing in of the new twentieth century, George and Rosie are exceptionally busy. The celebrations are predicted to last for days with copious drinking taking place. Inevitably there are to be many riotous, drunken gatherings so George doubles his stock of liquor and beer to meet the anticipated demand. New Year's Eve, the last day of the nineteenth century, the bar and lounge of the Three Dogs is overflowing with lively crowds, revellers in various states of intoxication. Seth stands in the bar, enjoying the company of a boisterous mob gathered around the piano singing. His intention is to leave an hour before midnight and head to a familiar Soho cafe where he will see in the new era in the company of fresh young prostitutes.

Puffing out his chest, Seth strikes an imposing figure. Dressed in a modern, tightly woven, dark-grey waistcoat, and matching long jacket and trousers, his hat is a soft-brimmed, black fedora. Adorning the little finger of his left hand is a gold ring, inscribed with his initials, and from his waistcoat pocket hangs his favourite gold fob watch. Pinned to his lapel is a gold pin brooch in the shape of a racehorse. Clean-shaven, declining to follow the fashion of growing a moustache, he stands taller than other men in the bar. Women throw him admiring glances, even those accompanied by husbands and lovers.

One exceptionally exuberant, attractive woman, betrothed to a man Seth knows, Tobias Black, catches his attention. Tobias, a skilled horse thief, is frequently engaged by Seth to steal animals to order. When Tobias catches Seth's eye, he walks over to greet him. The dainty young woman on his arm radiates a playful flirtatiousness. She is black-haired, petite, and extremely pretty. Chattering merrily to those around her, she flashes her huge, long lashed, chocolate-brown eyes.

"Seff! Meet me fiancé, Gwen Carter."

Raising his hat politely, Seth is careful to hide his predatory thoughts.

"Glad to meet you, Gwen Carter. Tobias is a fortunate man indeed t' 'ave foun' 'imseff a sweet little filly like you."

Gwen, blushes, and smiles coquettishly before dropping her eyes. Seth's curiosity is aroused. Gwen is well-mannered and charming, not the sort of woman one would expect to see on the arm of a known horse thief. As they make small talk, he is thinking, *Shall I make a play, ri' now, fer this flighty little missy? I can tell she has passion, jus' by lookin' a' 'er plump, rosy, red lips. Praps I need t' fin' meseff a nice young, respectable girl, like 'er, to be me common-law wife, someone wiv good connections; bruvers, uncles 'oo I can do business wiv.* Though the conversation he has with her that night is brief, Gwen leaves an impression on Seth, and he knows that when an opportunity arises, he will seduce her.

On that memorable night, Mary and Albert are in the

bar of The Prize Hen in Bildinford. Union flags flutter in people's hands as they sing and shout in animated celebration. An imposing grand piano is the focal point for merrymakers loudly singing the National Anthem. A picture of the dour, old Queen Victoria is held aloft. The mood turns raucous as crude song lyrics are belted out. Pint after pint of cheap ale is swilled down throats. At the first chime of midnight, not a man or woman stands sober in the bar. Children, if not asleep under tables, jubilantly participate in the carousing. As these loud, happy celebrations echo through the dark night air, Cal Marchwood lies in a drunken stupor in a ditch, oblivious to the ringing of church bells and the excited, cheery voices echoing through the night.

Seth's resolution for the twentieth century is to enter the lucrative world of property development more fully. To accrue the necessary capital, he starts to plan a few, targeted house burglaries where the risk of being caught is minimal. Collaborating with Bill, Cal and George, he executes a flurry of break-ins in Norfolk and Suffolk. The first takes place in a crumbling, ramshackle, manor house, occupied by an elderly, deaf, military man. Known to Seth, the old gentleman had, some months ago, sold him two saddles. By early spring in the year nineteen-hundred, Seth has successfully exchanged a horde of gold jewellery, precious gems, and valuable antique timepieces, stolen from the old man's house, for cash. The shady transactions take place between him and a trusted, crooked pawnbroker, Joseph Goldman.

Seth wastes no time in sinking the ill-gotten gains

into more rundown properties in Essex. One property, an empty farmhouse with arable land, is registered in Cal's name and the other is split up and leased to smallholding tenant farmers. Cal is delegated to be the 'Marchwood Bailiff', a role which primarily involves collecting rents and evicting those who fall behind with payments. He enthusiastically carries out these duties, enjoying the fear he stirs up in struggling tenant farmers. He embraces his new duties with relief as they coincide with the rapid decline of the family's horse-drawn cab business, brought about by the rise in motorised trams and road vehicles. Cal's continued elevation to power within the family ranks stirs up George's anger and bitterness. He broods, tossing and turning in his bed at night. *I am stuck wiv running this bleedin' pub, this 'ell 'ole. D' ole man 'as given Cal d' bes' fings t' do. He 'as a nice farm'ouse to live in an' spends 'is days swaggering about collectin' money. I would be more than 'appy to 'ave a slice of land t' call me own, a place where I can work on motor cars. One day, I will show Da what I am made of. Then I will be me own boss and free t' tell 'em both to bugger off.*

Whisperings:
Sons moulded in vice and criminality are blighted emotionally. How can they not be?

9

Identity

Some people are nobody's enemies but their own, yer know.

Oliver Twist – Charles Dickens

1901-1914

George's job as licensee of The Three Dogs pub continues to aggravate and frustrate him. The place, a thriving haunt for rowdy sailors, dockers, drunken labourers and factory girls, is relentless in its demands for his time and energy. Tall, broad-shouldered and muscular, he enjoys a natural, physical dominance over male customers. His presence alone is usually enough to keep boisterous drinkers under control. Confident in his superior strength, he exudes a natural arrogance that is especially evident when he is with Cal. When they are together, he inevitably feels physically and intellectually superior to his older sibling, as he remembers, extremely well, the numerous brotherly fights they had as children, when Cal suffered maximum humiliation and defeat at his hands.

ults with quite different personalities, they nd leisure time together. George's charisma, and s to laugh, makes him popular with both men and women, whereas Cal is a loner; morose and unsociable. Both men drink heavily, like their father, but George never loses control of his consumption. Cal's reliance on alcohol is obvious to the family. From early morning until late at night, his breath reeks of strong liquor and his moods swing wildly from angry to overexcited and impulsive. His unpredictability troubles his mother, who continually nags him to cut back on his drinking. Her well-meaning advice is ignored, for to go even one day without alcohol would, he believes, be intolerable.

Seth's attitude towards George darkens when he observes women, of all ages, fawning over his second son; batting their eyelids and pouting their plump red lips flirtatiously whenever he is around them. Forty, and beginning to feel middle-aged, Seth's confidence in snaring the interest of young women, is undermined by George's palpable sex appeal. Whenever he is drinking in The Three Dogs, he watches the prettiest females in the bar simper and giggle as they attempt to catch his son's eye. Perturbed, he realises that he is no longer the dominant, potent, sexually vigorous male in the family. Instead, it is George who now has this enviable reputation among the Marchwood males.

Seth's self-esteem plunges. He has difficulty hiding his jealously. Furtively he watches his son, tracking his every movement in the bar. Like a malevolent hawk, his gaze becomes focussed and intense when George is near attractive girls. Watching George becomes an obsession. Plunged into gloom, Seth is plagued by sick headaches from the relentless tension that he feels. His thoughts fester and go round and round in his head. *Marriage to Rosie ain't stopped 'im from chasin' women. I 'ate d' way 'ee is gettin' all d' girly attention, lappin' it up too, like a cat wiv d' cream. When 'ee wed Rosie, I 'oped 'ee would stop chasin' d' fillies. I suppose 'ee cannot 'elp 'imself, fer like farver, like son, they do say.* To assuage his insecurities, he makes cutting sarcastic comments to George, in a futile attempt to reassert his sexual superiority.

"Georgie boy! Bes' concentrate on keepin' Rosie 'appy, an' fill 'er belly wiv babies. Rosie is an 'andsome lass, wiv a glint in 'er eye, d' same look I seen in d' eyes of tarts. A little 'ellcat inbetween d' bedcovers, I reckon. If y' don' look afte' 'er in bed, an older man mi' be tempted t' giff 'er a good seein' to. Best watch ou', my son."

George gloats, aware of his father's envy. *'Ee 'ates that I am young and 'andsome and 'ave women eatin' out of me 'ands. I 'ave t' laugh, fer tis killin' 'im.* Mindful that he is still financially dependent on Seth, he hides his gleeful, spiteful thoughts as he cannot risk being cut off by his father just yet. Recently, George has taken to frequently contemplating a future independent of Seth. He is growing impatient to make it happen. *When d' time is ri', I will finish wiv d' ole bugger, cut meseff loose from 'is control. That day ain't too far away neiffer. I will be boss in me own 'ome, do wha' I please, an' ask 'im fer nuffin.*

The speed of demographic change continues at pace. Seth seizes on emerging ways to make money in land and property development. Suburban housing and roads for the increasing number of cars are spreading like giant tentacles out from London and far into Essex. He never doubts decisions he makes or fraudulent methods he uses to drive forward his plans. He oozes arrogant self-belief. Negative whispers about his unscrupulous scheming, and double-dealing activities, are ignored by him. He only pays them attention if they threaten to impede him from reaching his goals.

Settling down to life in Laurel Hall, the commodious, crumbling manor house, Seth begins, in earnest, to take on the mantle of a country squire. Mary is less trusting of their newfound status in life. She worries that the family's past misdemeanours, and earlier links to London's vice trade, will eventually become known. If they do, she knows that the respectable image she wants so badly to promote for herself, and the family, will shatter. In the hope that this will never happen, she throws herself, wholeheartedly, into running the house and looking after Albert. Unexpectedly, she finds contentment in doing daily chores; practical routines, reminiscent of her time in Poplar Lodge.

When she draws water from the well in the yard, she remembers descending the grand staircase at the Lodge and filling her water jug from the yard water pump. In her mind's eye she sees herself, curled up, with Lily, on a soft squishy settee in front of a roaring log fire. She lets her mind wander. *Livin' 'ere is like bein' a' d' Lodge all of them years ago. 'Appy days when I fink of 'em now. A time when I 'ad freedom t' primp, an' pamper meseff.* Her favourite time of the day is early morning.

On rising, she breathes in the fresh air, delighting in the dank, moist smells of wet grass, and the sweet odour of horse dung wafting up from the stables. Her previous fervent desire to live in London is gone, as is her prior loathing of the countryside. Today she is mistress of a substantial home and elevated to a position in life that she never dreamed of. Here, time drifts by slowly. Embedded in this tranquil environment, Mary softens in character. Tending to her modest vegetable patch, feeding hens and collecting their eggs, she finds an inner peace.

In summer months, she sits on the wooden seat of the outside privy, door open, and wallows in the sights and sounds of nature all around her, noticing things she had never paid attention to before. Beautiful things, like the array of colourful wildflowers, bees flitting from bloom to bloom, magpies gathering sprigs of dry grass, and white fluffy clouds scudding across the blue sky. Looking up to the sky, she recollects how once she stood on a London rooftop, craning her neck, to catch a glimpse of the blue heavens through the murky smog. *'Ow lucky, I am t' 'ave been given anuver chance to live in a place like this,* she muses.

Her bond with Albert is strong. In her relationship with him, at last she experiences warm, maternal love. By the age of eight, he is a healthy strong boy, most like George in looks, with an emerging temperament like Mary's. He can be truculent, and hot-tempered when provoked, but is exceptionally sensitive and kind towards animals, especially horses and dogs. An apt pupil at the local parish school, he excels at numbers, something that duly impresses Seth, who, at last, gives his youngest son some positive attention.

Albert's position as favoured child dramatically changes when Rosie gives birth to twin boys in nineteen-hundred-and-three. All adult attention, especially Mary's, switches to the new arrivals. Accustomed to being the youngest child, Albert is resentful of his changed status within the family and has difficulty adjusting. Seeing his mother lavish attention on her grandsons fills him with dismay. He feels abandoned, neglected, and his ire drives him to be spiteful towards his tiny nephews whenever he is alone with them. Then he slyly pinches them, pushes them over and pulls scary faces to frighten them.

Rosie turns to Mary for support with the children, and before long confides in her the distress she feels at George's continued pursuit of girls for sex and his strange, indifferent detachment towards his baby sons. Listening to her, Mary is sympathetic, seeing parallels between her early marital struggles with Seth and her daughter-in-law's current plight. Endeavouring to help, she advises Rosie on how she should react to George's behaviour.

"I know y' 'ate George chasin' uver women, Rosie. Bu' if y' nag 'im to stop, y' will jus' be beatin' yer 'ed agin a brick wall. Like farver like son. Seff 'as never changed in that respect, an' George is probably d' same. It is d' way fings are. Turn a blind eye, Rosie dear, fer stirrin' up trouble will make no difference. You are 'is lawful wife, an' d' mufver of 'is sons, so I doubt 'ee will ever leave you."

Tearfully, Rosie responds.

"Tis impossible fer me t' stop imaginin' 'im wiv women,

Mary. Every time 'ee is away from d' pub, I am twisted up inside. It 'urts to see 'im ignore d' babies, 'is own flesh an' blood after all."

Trying to give Rosie reasons for George's infidelity, and his lack of warmth towards the twins, she tells Rosie something of George's childhood.

"I fink it is my fault, Rosie, that George finds it 'ard t' show interest in d' boys. When 'ee was little, I put upon 'im too much, askin' 'im to mind 'is dying bruvers an' sisters. I fink that affect'd 'im bad, Rosie. As they get older, I am sure 'ee will take more of an interest in them."

The status of grandmother boosts Mary's self-esteem. After a lifetime trying to understand herself, now, settled back living in the country, older and wiser, she feels more self-assured. Every morning, she stares at her reflection in the swivel mirror on top of the old pine chest in her bedroom. Contorting her face, she practises smiling, liking the way her lips turn up and how her eyes sparkle underneath her mop of unruly black curls that are now flecked with strands of grey above her ears. Taking a deep breath, shoulders back, she gives herself an uplifting pep talk before going downstairs to the kitchen.

"Mary girl! Y' are still an 'andsome woman, wiv yer curls an' eyes as blue as cornflowers. Anyfink bad y' done in d' past, y' done fer d' best, an' it does not mean that you are a bad person. Y' can 'old yer head up fer when fings were agin you, y' always came fru and survived."

Once this morning ritual is over, she splashes chilly water on her face, gets dressed, and brings her hair under control by pinning it into a loose bun on top of her head.

Savouring the last few minutes of her ablutions, she dabs rouge, from a tiny round pot, onto her cheeks and lips, and fondly remembers the friendly London tart who gave the powder cake to her. Once applied, she takes a last look at herself in the mirror before leaving the bedroom with a spring in her step to make an early morning cup of tea while she waits for Nellie to arrive.

Nellie Brown is a sweet-natured spinster of indeterminate middle-age employed by Seth to help around the house. When he originally told Mary to engage a local girl to help in the house, he assumed she would find a comely, buxom village lass in need of work. He hoped for the convenience of having a rosy-cheeked girl about the place, who would welcome his lusty innuendoes and sexual overtures. Mischievously, Mary thwarts his ambition in this regard. When Seth is away from home, she chooses Nellie, grey-haired, short-sighted, a simple-minded spinster to be her home help. Conveniently, Nellie lives just outside the gates of Laurel Hall, in a two-roomed thatched cottage.

Mary and Albert are quickly won over by Nellie's childlike sense of fun and playfulness. She likes nothing better than to see them both howl with laughter at her silly antics as she goes about her chores. Her infantile tricks, and the way she throws her long white apron over her head when she laughs, injects enjoyment into both their lives and they love her for it. In return, Nellie gives total loyalty to her new mistress and the boy, who she regards as if he were her own son.

One warm, memorable summer's afternoon, while

paddling in the farmyard pond, Nellie, her skirts hitched up, tries to cool herself down. Suddenly, a duck, tying to protect its ducklings, skids and squawks its way across the pond towards her. Startled, she falls fully clothed into the murky, two-foot-deep water. Shrieking and screaming for Albert and Mary to come quickly and help her, she pulls herself up and sloshes her way back to the bank where she collapses in a sodden heap. Convulsed in hysterical laughter, Albert had never before experienced such wild merriment. The wonderful sight of Nellie in that moment is etched into his memory and will be retrieved in the darkest moments of his adult life.

Needing to be part of her local community, when Seth is away, Mary spends her evenings in The Cock and Hen, either walking or driving the single trap there and back. Settling herself in the dark, oak-walled snug, she drinks a few glasses of stout and exchanges pleasantries with neighbours and casual labourers passing through. Their topics of conversations range from recent weather conditions, current crop yields and troublesome landlords. Although one of the landlords most complained about is Seth, these opinions are never expressed in front of Mary as she has the respect of villagers, as well as their sympathy, for it is common knowledge that Seth keeps a young mistress in London.

When Mary is not in their company, Seth's tenants, and the casual labourers he employs, grumble about him being a neglectful landlord who is too mean to maintain their properties or pay workers what he rightly owes them. They also detest and fear Cal Marchwood for his bullying, aggressive tactics when collecting rents, and his sadistic brutality when evicting those who have fallen behind with their payments.

In spring nineteen-hundred-and-four, Seth can no longer avoid bankruptcy. Having sunk so much of his capital into property, he is unable to muster up the cash to settle his many bills. Under pressure from creditors, he finally shares with Mary what he needs to do to get himself out of his current predicament.

"I 'ave t' sell Pip Farm, an' d' cab company. I knows that d' 'orses won't fetch a decent price, nor will d' cabs they pull. No-one wants 'em, fer all d' latest vehicles 'ave engines, or are 'lectric, like trams. 'Member Liam Murphy, Mary? D' forger livin' in Zepher 'ill? 'Ee is goin' to draw up false papers fer me that will show Cal as d' legal owner of property I owns. That way they cannot take 'em away to pay me debts. I need to see Cal an' I need to see 'im urgently so I can put 'im in d' picture."

Mary has profound fears about Cal's reliability in lending Seth constructive help. She has deliberately kept from him the stories circulating about their eldest son's unstable, dangerous behaviour when drunk. Fearful of Seth's fury when he knows the full extent of the matter, she chooses to stay silent on the subject. When the Bankruptcy Court date draws near, Seth visits his elderly mother still living with her aged husband, Wilfred, in Crandonside.

Two years of relentless rain throughout England has turned the lane leading to Lottie's cottage into a quagmire. Seth manoeuvres his pony and trap through squelching ruts and deep oily, black pools of water. He has not seen his mother for three months and he needs to put her mind at rest about his looming court case, before she hears rumours about it. To divert his troubling thoughts away from his money problems, he thinks about his latest love, Gwen Black, who he left earlier that morning. Being with Gwen has reinvigorated Seth. With her, he has regained his sexual prowess and the angst he felt about George's youth and sex appeal has abated.

Tobias Black, Gwen's husband, is serving four-years in gaol for horse theft. Within days of his arrest and imprisonment, Seth had seduced Gwen, satisfying a long-held desire to do so. Since meeting her four years previously, at the ringing in of the new century, Seth had fantasised about her dark eyes, rosy lips, slender waist, and rounded womanly curves. Young and vibrant, at twenty-two, she is less than half his age. Even more appealing to him is her modern, liberal outlook on life, her streak of independence and the fact that she willingly works in a sweat shop to earn just a pittance. Already acquainted with an influential uncle of hers, Joseph Carter, who runs a substantial pub in Bethnal Green, Seth hopes that through his relationship with Gwen, doors will open to him from within the East London business community.

Arriving at his mother's cottage, Lottie greets him at the door and expresses both surprise and pleasure at his visit. No sooner has she poured him a cup of hot tea and handed him a plate of fresh bread and dripping, through pursed lips, she recounts what neighbours are saying about Cal's appalling behaviour.

"I 'ear that Cal is too fond by 'alf of usin' 'is whip,

an' maltreatin' 'is 'orses. People are scared t' deff when travellin' wiv 'im. Accordin' t' Mrs Andrews, from Bumble Cottage, Cal often deliberately swerves at people walking across the road, frightenin' them bad."

Shaking her head, she furrows her wrinkled brow and continues.

"If that ain't bad 'nuff, Seff, Mrs Buggins, 'oo was a passenger on Cal's waggon, says she saw Tom White fall off 'is cycle, 'cause Cal deliberately swerved int' 'im. She then 'eard Cal laugh at Tom, finking it a fine joke t' see 'im struggle to get up. When passengers tore into Cal, fer 'is dangerous drivin', 'ee swore at 'em, an' said 'ee would frow 'em off if they didn't shut up."

Struggling to hide his rising anger at her words, Seth gulps down his tea and deftly changes the subject; telling her of his current debt problems, though pride drives him to make light of it. Lottie is not worried by his news, for she is convinced that her clever son will find a way out of his predicament because he always does. Wilfred arrives back at the cottage after a long day in the woods foraging for kindling, just as Seth takes his leave. With a tense look about his jaw, Seth steps up into his vehicle, shakes the reins, and, without a backward glance, disappears down the muddy lane. His abrupt manner of departure leaves Lottie in no doubt that, despite his outward calm, Seth is seething with fury. Turning to Wilfred, she says, "I wouldn't want t' be in young Cal's shoes when Seff gets 'old of 'im. Afte' wha' I told 'im, 'ee is in fer a good beatin'. I ain't got no sympathy neiffer, fer 'ee is a badun', that Cal."

As the sky grows dusky, Seth arrives at Laurel Hall to find it empty. Pensive, stony-faced, and emotionless, he enters the kitchen through the open back door and stands, silent and still, in the dim light of the glowing embers in the range. He does not move a muscle until twenty minutes later when he hears unsteady, heavy footsteps approaching from the yard. Then the veins in his thick neck begin to pulsate; pent-up anger about to be unleashed. He stares toward the doorway.

Reeking of beer and whisky, Cal lurches over the threshold into the kitchen. Putting a hand on the edge of the pine table to steady himself, he sees a dark ominous figure out of the corner of his eye. He desperately tries to unscramble his muddled, drunken thoughts and find some Dutch courage. So, *d' ole man is 'ome afte' bein' wiv 'is floozy in "Ackney. We all know wha' 'ee is up to, an' I ain't 'fraid t' say it t' 'is face.* Infused with alcoholic bravado he adopts a hostile attitude. He sneers at his father and launches into an attack on Seth's personal affairs.

"So 'ere y' are, d' big man, back 'ome afte' spendin' time an' money you ain't got on yer trollop. Half yer age, d' same age as me from wha' I 'ear. I 'spect she finks she is d' only one, eh Da? Well soon 'nuff she'll know that she ain't."

Too intoxicated to be aware of the imminent danger to himself, he smirks and stumbles his way over the flagstone floor towards the scullery. In that moment, Seth erupts in rage. Lunging at Cal, he grips him by the throat with his left hand and pushes him backwards, slamming him against the kitchen wall. Holding him suspended there for a few minutes, he uses his right hand to slap his son's mocking face until it runs with blood and mucus. Throughout the ferocious beating, he speaks not one word. The only noise in the room is flesh hitting flesh; weighty, walloping thumps, and the laboured breathing of both men. With a last mighty kick to Cal's shins, the savagery stops. The stultifying atmosphere in the kitchen expands into eerie silence, broken by muffled sobs and bitter expletives from Cal, as he slithers slowly down the wall to slump limply on the cold floor.

Viewing his son's rapidly swelling face and blackening eyes, Seth speaks quietly, and menacingly.

"Y' be nuffin bu' a menace, Cal, a man 'oo cannot 'old 'is drink is not wurf a damn. I enjoys 'avin' a few drinks. I likes nuffin better than a good fist fight, bu' some fings I never do. I never try t' scare ole men an' women. I never drive 'orses recklessly. I never deliberately cause accidents t' 'appen. Yer gran-mufver tells me that y' 'ave been 'ollerin' an' shoutin' yer mouff off, terrifyin' payin' customers. I could kill y' fer losin' us trade, drivin' people away from usin' our vehicles, jus' when I needs all d' money I can get t' pay off me debts. You best do somefink quick t' impress me, Cal. Show some gumption. D' cabs are bein' sold so you best be lookin' fer anuver job to do besides yer bailiff duties."

Staring down at his son, a pathetic, beaten figure on the floor, Seth has a flash of inspiration. He recalls a conversation he recently had with a London docker who used to work as a porter on a big liner, sailing between America and Southampton. If Cal were to join the navy, he could become an asset to the family, instead of being a continual embarrassment. Leaning down over Cal, his voice takes on a more conciliatory tone.

"Cal, why not fink abou' goin' t' America t' seek yer fortune? I 'ear there is lots of work t' be 'ad on ships sailin' t' America. If they take you onboard, you can praps smuggle jewels an' gems, fer I 'ear there is a ready market fer such trinkets in New York. Me an' d' boys in Lime'ouse will provide you wiv d' loot, an' arrange contact wiv receivers in America. If you are successful, it will go some way t' makin' up fer all d' trouble y' caused me an' yer granmufver."

His black mood lifts when he notes the flicker of interest in Cal's rapidly swelling eyes. He has no regrets about inflicting such injuries on his own flesh and blood, believing that the harsh, physical punishment is well-deserved.

In November of that year, Cal, muffled up against the frigid wind, joins the crew of the *SS Merion* as a steward. To avoid being turned down by the navy, he travels under false papers, *Stuart Callum Borewood*, born in Edinburgh in eighteen-eight-two. Without these forged documents he would be denied entry to the United States because his criminal record for violent affray would go against his application.

He sets sail from Liverpool to Philadelphia, imbued with a sense of adventure, and committed to making a success of his new role, wanting to make his father proud of him. Once settled on board, he embraces his on-board duties; lifting, moving, stacking, and securing heavy cargo, cleaning officers' quarters, serving drinks, doing deck duties, and collecting passengers' baskets of laundry. He works hard, keeps his head down, and, for him, consumes extraordinarily little alcohol. On his second trip, he has the confidence to carry stolen jewels to sell in America. Hidden in a tight-fitting, pocketed, flesh-coloured cloth belt, under his undergarments, the fine gold chains, pendants, diamond rings and other precious gems are safe and secure during the voyage. Once the ship docks in Philadelphia, he meets Guido Giofanni, his father's trusted American receiver. A fat, balding, middle-aged Italian, Guido has long-established links to Limehouse gangs. Once the handover is done, Cal returns to the ship where he hides rolls of dollar bills under the false bottom of his seaman's bag.

Back home in England, Cal hands the money over to his father, who is responsible for exchanging the American currency for sterling through East London criminal bankers. The money is speedily invested in property and land in Essex and Suffolk, familiar territory to Seth and his sons. Declared bankrupt by the court, Seth is, for the time being, unable to hold property in his name, so farms and estates purchased are legally owned by Cal and George. The relationship between Seth and Cal improves with each successful trip to America. Cal tempers his more destructive behaviours as his confidence grows and he is filled with a newfound sense of power and status.

Whisperings:
An exaggerated sense of self-importance is reflected in a distorted view of actual abilities and achievements, where truth is not recognised.

10

Manors-Mistresses-Matrimony

Everyone may not be good, but there's always something good in everyone. Never judge anyone shortly because every saint has a past, and every sinner has a future.
— Oscar Wilde

1906–1914

By the time Seth's bankruptcy draws to a close, the family coffers are full of money accumulated from lucky trading in stolen gems. Seth's main task at this time is to liaise with East End pawn brokers, willing to exchange the stolen jewels for cash, and property owners, willing to sell land and buildings for hard cash, no questions asked. When Seth's period of bankruptcy finishes, he fully expects some properties, lawfully registered in the names of his sons, to be sold so he can be remunerated, for he considers himself the sole architect of their current financial gains.

Heavily involved with known thieves and fraudsters in

Tower Hamlets, Seth is in constant danger of either being investigated by the police or caught up in vicious rivalries between London's criminal gangs. Forced to conduct his business furtively, he exercises cunning, pulling on a lifetime of experience ducking and diving. Whenever he is challenged or questioned by police, he vehemently lies and denies any involvement in fraudulent activities. While Cal is away, he meets up with George every week, in the snug of The Three Dogs. There they confer with jewel thieves, who supply the booty for Cal to smuggle to America, and together discuss and plan for the continued laundering of the money flowing in. It is soon apparent to Seth that George must give up his publican role so he can get more involved in the property side of the Marchwood business. He speaks persuasively to him.

"Georgie boy! Bent money is pourin' in so fast we urgently need t' 'ide it quick from d' authorities. I fink y' should leave off runnin' d' Dogs, fer y' need to be free to 'elp me an' Cal get our money into bricks an' mortar as soon as possible. As a recent bankrupt, I will be under suspicion so it will be down to you, George, as a respectable licensed victualler, to sign off on property contracts while Cal is away."

George jumps at the chance to get free of running the pub and become more involved in the lucrative property schemes devised by his father and Cal. Profits he makes from the pub do not compensate for the nightly drunken brawls he has to quell with his fists. Though an able fighter, he nevertheless sustains regular physical injuries from grappling with rough customers. Proud of his handsome face, he resents the cuts and bruises that frequently mar his good looks. Managing the pub, while living in the cramped first-floor apartment with Rosie and his growing family, is becoming a strain. He feels trapped in his marriage and is increasingly resentful of his domestic responsibilities.

His father's unexpected invitation comes at a time when George is restless and deeply frustrated. He yearns to be part of the modern, technologically advanced, Edwardian society. He wants to travel, to see the world, to drive fast motor cars and to be free to make his own personal and financial decisions. He calculates that by initially going into property development with his father and brother, he can get what he needs to tide him over, until he sees a way to become self-sufficient and independent. After some thought, he questions Seth.

"Where will me, Rosie an' d' boys live if we give up the pub, Da? Are we goin' t' 'ave an 'ouse to live in?"

'Course, my son! Y' can choose d' bes' place fer yerseff an' yer family, an' make it yer 'ome. Rental from uver farms we own will be our income 'til developers come sniffin' aroun' fer land t' build on. An' they will. Of that I 'ave no doubt. Then we will all 'ave money t' burn."

Both laugh at the prospect of getting rich, inwardly marvelling at their own cleverness and devious manipulation of the law. As far as George is concerned, the real bonus is that he has, at last, got power over his father, a man he has feared for so long. He gloats inwardly that Seth is dependent on his help to tide him through his period of bankruptcy.

George spends hours cogitating on the unexpected and novel situation he finds himself in. *What a Godsend! The old man's bankruptcy is a gift. If I play me cards right; I can use the situation to milk wha' I can from d' old bugger. If I can 'ave enough land, as well as an 'ouse in the country, I can start me own motor vehicle trade. 'Ee won't dare to stop me, fer wivou' me an' Cal covering d' legal stuff 'ee could lose everyfink.*

Within months, the purchase of Knowle Farm, near Brayridge in Essex, allows George to move away from East London, and his gruelling life at *The* Three Dogs, and begin anew in the country. Leaving the smog and the dirt behind, he is rejuvenated. As the official owner of a fine country house, with land, he launches himself into the local community in pursuit of self-improvement and status. Long attracted to modern, feisty, independent women who passionately support the suffragette movement, he desires to be part of the young set of societal game changers. Forward thinking and nakedly ambitious, it is in his best interest to block from his mind all memories of his slum childhood years in Limehouse.

Blizzard conditions descend on England in December nineteen-and-six. Deep snow blankets rural landscapes and many roads are impassable. On Christmas Day, Seth, Mary, Cal, and Albert enjoy a festive meal of roast beef and lamb in the kitchen of Ennis Lodge, a six-bedroomed manor house outside the town of Chivelbank. The men are elated at their recent purchase of the Ennis Estate, along with two smallholdings in Essex and Suffolk. They copiously imbibe Jack Daniels whisky from a bottle, one of a dozen brought from America by Cal. The drunker they get, the more ebullient they feel as they sit in the two-hundred-year-old mansion on a three-hundred-acre estate.

Ennis Estate is a secluded property, surrounded by a high, red-brick wall, entered, and exited through ornate, rusting iron gates. Shielded from prying eyes by huge beech and oak trees, the family have complete privacy to enjoy the festive season together. At twelve, Alfred hovers close to his mother, avoiding the company of Cal, who he wishes was not there with them. *If only I 'ad gone t' spend Christmas wiv Rosie an' George, at Knowle Farm,* he thinks with regret.

Though pleased for Seth, and her older sons, that they successfully acquired such prestigious properties, Mary misses life at Laurel Hall. She is grieved at losing the companionship of Nellie. On the day they left, wagons loaded up high with their belongings, Nellie stood in the lane outside her humble cottage and wept to see them go, wiping her eyes on the hem of her long apron. Mary knew, with certainty, that they would never meet again, and she was struck low with sadness. Young Albert showed no emotion as they passed her, unsure how he should respond to her obvious distress. Still a child, he was sensitive enough to know that this simple woman was someone he would never forget.

During this first winter at Ennis Lodge, Mary struggles to create a warm space outside the flagstoned kitchen, where an enormous range throws out constant heat. Once, there had been fires burning in every room, tended to by house servants. Today, fireplaces throughout the house stand empty, unlit; black gloomy recesses, no longer the bright welcoming heart of every room. Many leaks, caused by missing roof tiles, make the house interior dank and musty. Upstairs rooms are unusable because plaster walls are crumbling under the weight of rainwater coming through the ceiling.

As the weather improves, Seth sets about establishing himself as Lord of the Manor. He hires hedge trimmers, gardeners, and farm labourers on casual contracts. He treats them badly. He is rude, arrogant, and intimidating towards them. He criticises their workmanship and frequently refuses to pay them for their labour. A recently introduced law, giving rights to ordinary workers, is contemptuously ignored by him, until he is reported to the authorities. Being fined and compelled to settle his bills has minimal effect on his continued attempts to swindle his employees.

Approaching fifty, he has come to realise that he is not as agile and strong as he once was, and that he is vulnerable when pitted against younger, fitter men in a brawl. A recent fracas outside an Epping pub culminated in personal humiliation. The dispute, over his non-payment for drinks, led to him being set upon by the landlord and his burly son. During the ensuing physical fight, Seth bellowed obscenities and threatened to do them both serious harm, but he was overcome and knocked to the ground. Winded, struggling to get up, he was kicked hard on his buttocks, before being yanked up by the scruff of his neck and punched hard in the face. Staggering away from the inn, holding his bloodied nose, his mortification was amplified when he heard raucous laughter and cheers from the men and women thronging the doorway of the pub. For weeks, he lays low, licking his wounds, waiting for the bruises to fade. He did not visit Gwen, for his vanity would not allow her to see his swollen, battered face. To see him so disfigured might lead her to believe him a weakling, a victim, and a man past his prime. He sends her messages, via his London contacts, telling her that he is detained on important matters.

For the first time in his life, Seth is genuinely enamoured with a woman. Gwen's light-hearted, jolly, affectionate, trusting personality charms and beguiles him. She is the antithesis of his jaded, cold, suspicious character. When in her company, he strives to be a better man, an upright man, a man of integrity and class. He hides the worst aspects of his disreputable nature beneath a thin veneer of generosity and mannerliness. Wearing expensive, tailor-made, woollen suits, he moderates the tone of his voice, and East London accent, to hide his roots, wanting people to see him as a well-off, middle-class gentleman.

Their relationship is an open secret, and they are frequently seen out together. Ardent fans of music-hall entertainment, they spend happy hours being entertained at the Hackney Empire and riding together through Hyde Park in Seth's pony and trap. They are familiar figures in Hackney pubs, where piano music is played and risqué songs are sung. In the three years after becoming his mistress, Gwen has two sets of twin boys, proudly sired and acknowledged by Seth as Marchwood babies. Weak and sickly at birth, the infants sadly die within weeks, despite the loving attention lavished upon them by Gwen.

When her husband, Tobias, is released from prison, having served his sentence for horse theft, he is warned by Seth to stay away from Gwen. Tobias, with no means to support Gwen and intimidated by Seth's aggressive attitude, complies and does not attempt to see his wife. Tormented by jealously at the thought of a reconciliation between his young mistress and Tobias, Seth demands that she keep herself exclusively for him and in return he will pay rent for the dingy room in Hackney where she lives.

Mary finds the intensity and longevity of Seth's attachment to Gwen unsettling. Needing to better understand his continued attraction to the young Mrs Black, she arranges to meet with Tobias, whom she was acquainted with before his imprisonment. They meet in Chivelbank town square and retire together to a private booth in the bar of the local hotel. Tobias willingly answers Mary's curious questions about his estranged wife and shows empathy and understanding for her current predicament as helpless bystander, unable to halt the relationship between Gwen and her husband.

"Gwen ain't a bad person, Mary! She 'as an 'appy-go-lucky nature, an' never 'as a bad word t' say t' anyone. She likes nuvfink more than bein' in d' 'Ackney Empire, singin' 'er 'art ou,' after an' 'ard day in d' sweatshop. Kind 'arted, she is. Would giff 'er las' penny to beggar children, 'oo flock around 'er like bees t' an 'uney pot. She ain't never 'appier than when children are 'angin' on 'er skirts."

Pausing for a moment, Tobias senses impatience in Mary as she listens to him. He knows he is not saying what she wants to hear. Nevertheless, he continues the personal appraisal of his wife.

"It be difficult fer me t' say a wrong word abou' 'er, Mary, an' that's a fact. Fer didn't I land 'er in a desprit situation when I got meseff in trouble. It 'appened just afte' she 'ad lost d' baby we was spectin', an' 'er soldier bruver was killed in Africa. I fink she can never fergave me fer wha' I done, an' I can never fergive meseff."

Mary, battling loneliness at losing the companionship of Nellie, feels the words of Tobias as a physical blow to her gut. This Gwen is obviously different from the type of girl Seth usually seduces; passing fancies and prostitutes, women who pose no threat to her position as his wife. She is frightened by what Tobias tells her, for it confirms the stories she hears from Cal and George about their father's blatant association with this young woman. She broods. *Wha' if Seff abandons me fer this young missy, wiv 'er fancy modern ways an' 'appy-go-lucky manner? If 'er own 'usband defends' d' way she is carrying on wiv 'im, she mus' be somefink special. Should I be worried this time?*

She gets a crumb of comfort from watching Seth's growing fondness for twelve-year-old Albert. He is more indulgent with his younger son than he ever was with the older boys. Mary consoles herself that Seth's affection for Albert may keep him loyal to her in the future and stop him from setting up house with Gwen. Nevertheless, she ruminates over how she might handle the situation. *'Ee can stay weeks wiv 'is floozy, even set 'er up in 'er own place, bu' if 'ee completely deserts me, or stops giffin' me 'ousekeepin', I will shop 'im into d' police, quick as a flash.*

The sixteenth of April nineteen-hundred-and-eight, Cal, signs off the ship and walks briskly down the gangplank of the *SS Merion* for the last time. His time at sea has transformed him from lowly sailor to a man of property and wealth. Soon he is to marry prim Ella Shand, the ship's nurse. Their courtship, conducted during their time on board together, resulted in Ella agreeing to marry him. At twenty-nine, she is grateful to have procured a proposal, for she assumed, at her age, she was destined to remain a spinster. Barely acquainted with Cal at the time of their engagement, she is unaware of his dark, violent side, a side carefully hidden from her. So, blind to his faults, she anticipates her wedding with mounting excitement. Needing to work out her contract on the ship, she remains on board for some months after Cal returns to civilian life.

Despite his betrothal to a respectable woman, Cal continues to use the services of pubescent whores and has every intention of continuing this habitual behaviour after he is married. He prefers to pay for his carnal pleasures, for, as a simple business transaction, there is no emotional involvement. Surprising his family by suddenly marrying a woman his own age, he hopes to finally allay their suspicions about his sexual preferences for noticeably young girls. Travelling to Ennis Lodge for Easter, he arrives just as Essex is hit by a snow blizzard.

The inclement weather keeps him, Albert and his parents trapped together for days. Spending such an extended period of time in each other's company, family tensions rise. Seth and Cal get embroiled in frequent drunken arguments as each vies to be the one to control their ever-increasing property portfolio. Cal's imminent marriage to Ella is the one piece of news guaranteed to settle all their nerves. Relief is the overriding family emotion when they think of Cal finally settled with a wife. Mary expresses her delight to Cal while secretly thinking, *fank Gawd 'ee is gettin' wed to a woman 'is own age, fer a younger one could not 'andle 'is foul temper. An' a nurse too? Does she know wha' she is lettin' 'erseff in fer?* Seth is hopeful. *Marriage will settle 'im down, cut down 'is drinkin' an' braggin'.* Albert struggles to suppress his whoop of joy at the prospect of Cal moving out of Ennis Lodge and into a grand farmhouse five miles away in Great Widewater, where he will live with his bride.

On the wedding day, in the Registry Office in Chivelbank, Albert watches Cal and Ella take their vows, and cannot help worrying for his new sister-in-law. His impression of Ella is that she is a kind, shy, gentle person. During the brief ceremony, he dwells on the matter. *Does she know wha' Cal is really like? 'As she seen 'is filthy temper? 'As she seen 'im mad drunk? I don' fink she 'as. If she knew wha' a nasty bugger 'ee is, she 'would never 'ave agreed t' marry 'im.*

His fears are well-founded, for six months later, Ella's face and arms bear dark bruises left by physical beatings at the hands of Cal. When she is seen in her husband's company, she appears fearful, cowed and unnaturally submissive. Rosie tries to befriend her but is apprehensive of Cal's reaction if she shows too much concern. Having nothing in common with Mary, Ella becomes increasingly isolated and withdrawn. George shares Albert's concerns but is too wrapped up in his own business developments to give her situation much thought.

He and Rosie still live at Knowle Farm with their sons. The main bulk of their income comes from the lease of four tied cottages on the farm. At last, George is able to pursue his own interests and build a trade servicing motor cars and mechanised farm vehicles. Proud of himself, and his mechanical skills, he no longer allows his father's disparaging remarks to affect him. He remains resolute in his determination to break free from his father, and older brother, and make his own way in life. Impatient, he vents his pent-up frustration by having frequent arguments and disagreements with Rosie.

Six years married and George is bored. He feels little loyalty to Rosie, and shamelessly beds numerous women, making no attempt to hide his casual dalliances. Rosie's spirit shrinks under the weight of George's neglect, and her unhappiness shows in the set of her face and the drooping of her shoulders. She grows used to his petty cruelties, so is suspicious when his behaviour unexpectedly changes for the better. Unexpectedly, he becomes kinder, gentler, more generous, and good humoured. Rosie's instinct tells her that something is amiss, and her intuition is correct. George is head over heels in love with the beautiful wife of the new landlord, Charlie Coomes, who manages The Wheatsheaf Pub in Seldon. The recipient of his ardour is named Alice.

Curious to see the woman all men in Seldon are talking about, George went to the pub, where he stood at the bar, patient and watchful, waiting to catch a glimpse of Alice. Leaning nonchalantly against the dark mahogany counter on that particular morning, he frequently looked into the enormous gilt-edged mirror hanging above the bar. Suddenly, his eye was caught by the reflection of a tall, willowy woman, with almond-shaped green eyes, pale skin, and prominent cheekbones. Her rich auburn hair, pinned into an untidy bun on top of her head, framed her ravishing face, and wispy curls touched the back of her long, swan-like neck. Wearing a full-sleeved, tailored blouse and a softly pleated, clingy black skirt, pinched in at the waist by a wide ribbon, she was the epitome of a modern Edwardian woman. He was instantly smitten.

Extremely glad that he paid attention to his appearance that morning, in his favourite white shirt, with double-rolled collar, a red bow tie, and a black waistcoat and jacket, he knew he looked particularly dapper and handsome. The straw boater, tilted back on his head, lent him a jaunty air and his heavy gold watch chain, and red Ford Model C automobile parked outside, were indicators that he was a man of affluence and status. Turning his gaze from the mirror, George looked towards Alice and experienced a surge of excitement at the flash of a filmy white petticoat, peeping out from beneath the hem of her skirt. At that moment she turned, looking directly at him. Her soft, rouged, reddened lips broke into a flirtatious smile, and her pink-tinted cheeks grew brighter, as their eyes locked. As the minutes passed, and encouraged by the number of times she continued to peek at him from under her eyelashes, George moved towards her. Leaning in close, he whispered softly. "I can only fink that you are Alice, Charlie's wife, for I 'ear tell that she is a bewitchin' woman, an' you match that description."

With a half smile, Alice blushed a deep red as he continued,

"I seen yer 'usband, Alice, an' I can't 'elp wonderin' 'ow such an ordinary man snared a vision of loveliness to be 'is wife. 'Tis a mystery t' me, an' no mistake."

Sensing Alice is as affected as he by strong mutual attraction between them, he tells her his name and whispers an invitation, "Meet me soon, beautiful Alice, an' let me get t' know you. If you could feel my 'eart, you'd know 'tis racin' in me chest as I wait fer yer answer."

With a slight toss of her head, a shy smile, and in a voice just above a whisper, she replies.

"I plan to go into Seldon town, the day after tomorrow. I shall travel by bus. Meet me in the square at noon, outside The Hare and Hounds. We can take a walk, or a short ride in your car, which I would like very much."

The following forty-eight hours dragged for them both. They met, as planned, and, eager to find privacy, they drove out of town to a small secluded wooded area. There, gripped by irresistible passion, oblivious to everything except each other, they made wild, abandoned love to one another. In this mutually explosive expression of sexual desire, they were emotionally forged together and bonded for life.

The certainty of her feelings for George pushes

Alice to leave her husband within a month of them first meeting. Turning her back on her marriage to Charlie, she moves into a recently vacated cottage owned by George finds employment in a local bakery, and commits wholeheartedly to being with her lover. Finding love with Alice, George's restlessness dissipates. Alice's character and intellect are a powerful support and encouragement to him as he prepares to take a separate path from his father and brother. Basking in Alice's admiration and affirmation, he grows in confidence. Both are overjoyed when Alice falls pregnant with his child. In December nineteen-hundred-and-eight, soon after the wedding of Cal and Ella, Alice and George have a son, Arnold Marchwood. The obligation is now on George to find a bigger place where he can live comfortably with Alice and Arnold, a place that will be their proper home.

Within weeks of Arnold's birth, Seth's mother, Lottie, dies. The old lady fell, hitting her head on the edge of the stone step leading out to her back yard. Widowed, the previous year, it was down to her sons to arrange her funeral. The situation posed a dilemma for the family, as tensions, linked to old hostilities, threatened to sully the magnificence of the event that Seth has in mind. As the wealthiest in the family, he was keen to impress his siblings, his children, and his grandsons by funding a lavish service and burial for his mother. Meeting up with his brother to plan the event, Bert advised him, "I best warn you brother! Many in d' family don' wan' to clap eyes on Mary, or yer braggard son, Cal. Sure as eggs is eggs, they will be ignored by me an' Agnes, an' me sons an' daugh'ers. Ever since they attacked Ma, ou'side 'er cottage, d' family 'as not forgiven or forgotten. Bes' warn them both wha' to expect. They will be cold-shouldered, bu' 'opefully you and I will make sure there is no brawling, or bad talk while Ma is laid to rest."

Determined to control Mary and Cal's behaviour, so his mother is afforded due respect during the sombre ceremony, Seth reassures him.

"Yee can count on me, Bert. I will keep 'em in line for d' day. There will be no trouble from 'em. Ella will look out for Cal an' tell me if 'ee is drinkin' too much. For it is always drink that makes 'im do an' say bad fings. Do not worry 'bout Mary. She is a respectable lady now. She won' giff you any trouble. She 'as changed, Bert, an' I fink y' will be surprised when you sees 'er."

On the day of the funeral, Lottie's body lies in an ornate, glass sided, ebony coffin. Carrying it slowly into the Seldon Parish Church are six pallbearers, Seth, Bert, Bill Loxbury, and three of Lottie's grandsons, including George. At the top of the aisle, the coffin is placed in front of the altar. The funeral procession proceeds into the church before the individuals take their pews. Mary, stoic and tight-lipped, is accompanied by Albert and Ella. They sit together in the front row, where they are eventually joined by Seth and Cal.

Mary is determined to studiously ignore malicious glares thrown her way. Dressed fashionably in a long, tailored, black woollen coat, with squirrel fur cuffs and collar, and wearing a wide-brimmed, black velvet hat, festooned with black feathers, and coiled, black silk ribbons, she oozes confidence. She wants the whole congregation to see how she, Seth, and her sons, have risen from low-class beginnings and become gentrified. She hopes her sanctimonious, judgemental in-laws will be envious of her elevated station in life. Sitting, stiff-backed and proud, she is unaware of the unknown attendees who sit at the back of the church. Strangers to each other, these two young women sit, heads bowed, in separate, shaded pews.

Unobserved by the main party of mourners, from beneath their wide-brimmed hats, the pair furtively watch their lovers, Seth and George. Gwen tracks every movement that Seth makes, willing him to glance her way, wanting to get a warm, secret look from him, while Alice never once takes her eyes off George. Both men are aware of the discrete presence of their mistresses, for they are there at their invitation. Neither man cares about hurting their wives; indeed, Seth enjoys flaunting his relationship with a pretty woman half his age. It panders to his vanity. George too relishes the fact that he is envied for having a stunningly beautiful woman as his lover. Sitting behind Mary in the church, Rosie dwells on a recent conversation she had with her mother-in-law about George's affair with Alice. Mary had advised her. "As long as 'ee gives y' money fer d' children, an' keeps a roof over yer 'ed, let 'im 'ave 'is lover. Keep quiet, Rosie, say nuvfink. If y' ever run short of cash, come t' see me, I can 'elp you."

Older, and wiser, Mary has long been resigned to Seth's philandering. Nevertheless, when she learns that Gwen and Seth have a daughter, born in nineteen-hundred-and-nine, and another girl born three years later, she is unnerved. According to information gleaned from Cal, the infants carry the Marchwood surname, and Gwen calls herself 'Mrs Marchwood', When told that Seth has set Gwen up in a big house in Hackney, she is furious, but reluctant to challenge him on the subject, afraid he may desert her and go and live permanently with Gwen and their children. *Best to let sleepin' dogs lie fer d' time bein'*, she thinks.

Turning thirty-three, George finally ruptures his relationship with Seth. He takes the decision to sell Knowle Farm, and all its assets, without consulting with Cal and Seth. The situation is worsened when, refusing to be intimidated by their threats, he takes the matter of his ownership rights to court and wins his case. Knowle Farm, and other properties registered in his name, are declared as legally belonging to him. Despite protests made by Rosie and Mary, he sells Knowle Farm and moves Rosie and their sons into a modest mid-terrace Victorian house on the outskirts of Seldon. The twins, now lads of working age, accept that their mother and father are estranged, so George feels no pangs of guilt when he sets up home with Alice and Arnold. Heartbroken, Rosie placidly accepts the intermittent payments that George gives her and is grateful that he is, at least, providing her with a house to live in.

Meanwhile, George purchases a substantial, prestigious, secluded, moated estate in rural Suffolk, ten miles from Stowmarket, as a home for himself, Arnold, and Alice. As a family unit, they adopt the ways of the middleclass. Seen as comfortably off, they declare themselves married and immerse themselves in the life of the local community. George drives about in an open-top car, taking day trips to Cockle Bay with Alice and their small son. Wealthy neighbours invite him to pheasant-shooting weekends, and he and Alice are seen in all their finery at hunt balls and enjoying days out at Chelmsford Races. Despite having an air of mystery about them, they are invited to the best social events and treated with courtesy and respect.

Nineteen years old, in nineteen-fourteen, Albert marries his sweetheart, Edwina Cooper. He desperately wants his brother George to come to his wedding, a decision that is vehemently resisted by Seth, who deems George to be a traitor. A temporary truce is agreed between them, and on the third of April, the family gather in the ancient stone church in Ickle Bow. To avoid trouble erupting during the service, George sits at the back of the church, far away from the rest of the family, quietly watching Albert marry his pretty Edwina. Seth coldly ignores him, and Rosie sits dejected, religiously avoiding looking his way.

Ella, still childless after two miscarriages, looks pale, stiff, and unhappy sitting beside a glowering Cal. The only guest there who appears comfortable is Mary. She sits, the proud matriarch of the family, beaming pride as she watches her favourite son marry. Sensitive to Albert's feelings, George leaves the church directly after the service; to stay longer would risk unpleasantness occurring between him, his father and Cal.

Seth's wedding gift is a substantial farmhouse in the

heart of Ickle Bow. It comes with farmland, rented out in smallholdings to agricultural workers. Helped by labourers, Albert works his farm, grows crops and keeps a small stable of horses. His income is bolstered by the payment from his father for collecting rents. Things are good for the newly married couple who are undisturbed by the rumours of war with Germany.

Whisperings:
A laughing bride and groom, flanked by mossed tombstones, weave their way out of the churchyard into bright sunshine, blind to the encroaching dark shadow of war.

11

Profits of War

In time of War, the loudest patriots are the greatest profiteers.

– August Bebel

1914–1920

Rumours abound that war with Germany is imminent. Seth is alert to potential profits to be made from the conflict. Thousands of horses and mules will be required by the army, and his experience in the trade places him at the forefront for military contracts. One warm summer evening at the end of July in nineteen-hundred-fourteen, three months after Alberts and Edwina's wedding, Seth and Cal sit on a wooden seat in the yard of a village inn. Both sup pints of ale from battered pewter mugs and throw back whiskey shots in between. They are disinterested in joining in with excitable, patriotic drinkers inside the pub, belting out rousing renditions of *Goodbye Dolly Gray*. Huddling close, elbows on a roughhewn oak trestle table, Seth adjusts his peaked cap, protecting his eyes from the glare of the low evening sun. He speaks slowly and conspiratorially.

"Son, wha' do y' fink of d' rumours that war will be declared this week? Everyone expects it. People is workin' demseffs into a righ' ole frenzy, predicting that if we go in an' 'elp d' French, d' war will be over in weeks."

Seth pauses, trying to gauge Cal's thoughts.

"I 'ear that men good wiv 'orses get paid more than ordinary soldiers, especially if they can drive teams of eight or more, pullin' 'eavy waggons. Bein' older, Cal, y' 'ave years of experience, so I reckon d' army will snap y' up. Is y' finking of enlistin'? I tell y', boy, if I were younger, I'd join up an' be proud t' do so."

Taking a swig of ale, he watches Cal, with a combined quizzical, sly expression. He wonders if his son realises the financial opportunities war brings. Their previous and current successful partnerships in the jewellery and property businesses have given Seth a respect for Cal, though he is not blind to his weak character traits. Between the men there is scant affection; old grudges linger just below the surface. Common to both is a desire to manipulate the other and bend them to their will. Seth subtly manoeuvres the conversation to what he wants to discuss, while Cal maliciously keeps his father guessing. Both stroke each other's ego, in a display of mutual self-interest.

Cal, ebullient with alcohol, fidgets. Twitching his shoulders, he gesticulates expansively with his hands, fiddles with his collar and moves his legs restlessly. His scowling angular face, poor eye contact and physical agitation communicate a hyper-vigilance, someone ready to fight at the slightest provocation. Sensing his father wants something from him, Cal decides to keep a clear head and drinks more slowly. Leaning across the table, he says to Seth, "I've been 'earing d' same talk, Da. I cannot deny I 'ave an 'ankerin; t' join up, but I 'ave a problem. Ella cannot be trusted t' manage d' rent collections. She is too soft 'arted, an' too stupid t' look after d' farming side of d' businesses. Six years married, she do nuffink except snivel an' complain, an' she takes no interest in anyfink since she lost d' babies. She finks she is past d' age of getting pregnant an' I agree. Truth is, Da, I 'ave no desire t' touch her no more. I takes after you, old man, for I likes 'em young an' fresh."

He laughs suggestively and continues, Any'ow, I 'ear farmers are t' stay 'ere in Blighty, an' plough, an' plant an' 'arvest d' crops, fer d' army needs feedin'. I 'ear from Rosie, 'oo seen George recently, that 'ee is plannin' on joinin' d' Veterinary Corps. Just like George to want t' be in d' best paid army squad? 'Ee wont 'ave no worries fer I 'ear Alice is one of those clever, modern women 'oo will manage 'is business while 'ee is away."

Immediately alert, Seth responds.

"That be a good thing in d' long run, Cal, for most men will be off fightin' d' bloody war, an' women will 'ave t' take over men's work. It mi' be in our interests to bury d' 'achet wiv George. Your ma will be 'appy if we get back on good terms. It will be 'ard to let go of me anger t'wards 'im, but if I don', we cannot make use of 'is farm when 'ee goes t' war. I want t' meet wiv 'im, in a friendly manner.

We could meet in The Boar's Head? You arrange it, Cal. I will bring young Albert along. 'Wiv 'im bein' there, it will soften George up. Then I can discuss my ideas wiv 'im."

Pausing, he lifts his mug, gulps down some cold beer, then looks at Cal expectantly.

"Best tell me your grand ideas afore we meet wiv George, Da," says Cal, grinning.

For the next few hours, Seth lists viable opportunities to be grasped from the logistical consequences of war. There is an urgent, ever-increasing demand for horses and mules for the army. With his extensive experience in the trade, he can, on behalf of the army, assess, purchase, and transport vast numbers of livestock. The farmlands currently owned by each of them, in Essex and Suffolk, can be used to grow fodder for thousands of horses. Transport of animals and goods can be arranged by the Marchwood Livestock Company, while clever young Alice, if she is willing, will draw up and monitor contracts with Military Logistics.

"Cal, my boy, if you join d' Royal Field Artillery, your 'orse drivin' skills will be put t' good use. Quick as a flash, they will take you in. Your mufver, me, an' Albert will work yer farm, collect yer rents, while you keep us informed of wha' d' army needs most. Chances are 'twill all be over in six mumfs. Still, it should be long 'nuff fer me, you, an' d' family t' make money an' at d' same time do our duty fer King and Country."

Listening to his father, Cal experiences a flood of nationalistic fervour. Draining the dregs from the whiskey bottle, he acquiesces to Seth's suggestions, before swaggering off towards his loosely tethered mule. Being pivotal to his father's ambitions is gratifying. His mood is high as he arrives home. Entering through the back door of the farmhouse, he finds Ella, tipping coals from the wooden coal shuttle into the range in the kitchen. She does not look up, or greet him, as he picks up the open bottle of rum on the table and swigs from it. Tension in her shoulders eases when she registers his good humour. She listens, with heightened interest, as he relates the discussion he just had with Seth. Wrapped up in his inflated sense of self-importance, he fails to notice the excited gleam in her eyes. Ella's thoughts are cascading in a torrent of hope and exuberance. *The day that bastard goes into the army will be the best day of my life. I will escape his detestable presence and go to America. I will get a job nursing in a hospital there. He will never find me; I will make certain of it. I will be liberated, free of his vicious tongue, and his beatings.*

Within weeks, Seth, Cal, George, and Albert agree on how to pursue, and manage, the considerable wartime opportunities. Cal and George are to enlist, Albert will oversee the production of farm produce, and Seth will organise the purchase and sale of horses and mules on behalf of the military.

During the second week of September nineteen-fourteen, the two elder brothers join twenty-one thousand London men rushing to join up. With their personal animosities temporarily shelved, they stand, side by side, in the long queue outside Woolwich Town Hall. In height, both are inches taller than the puny East Londoners rallying to the call. Older than most, at thirty-six and thirty-four, their experience and expertise with big horses gives them a strong advantage. Among the eager throng of men clamouring to sign up, George and Cal wait, confident in their highly desirable skills and abilities. Cal brags incessantly to those around him in a loud, excitable voice.

"There is no doubt that d' army need men wiv my skills, men 'oo can drive teams of 'orses pullin 'eavy guns over battlefields. Ask me bruver 'ere. 'Ee will tell you there are few better than me at drivin', 'ain't that ri', George?"

Curious eyes turn to George, who appears disinterested in his brother's showy posturing. Despite his calm exterior, George is irritated and embarrassed by Cal's boastful behaviour. He thinks, *I hope d' army brings d' cocky little bastard down a peg or two. It is bound t' 'appen, fer 'ee jus' cannot keep 'is big mouff shut, an' sure as eggs is eggs, d' bloody officers will not like 'im for it, nor will d' uver Tommies.* Cal waits, impatient for George to back up his claims, which, after a short pause, he does, "It is as me bruver says. Ee 'as worked wiv big 'orses since a child, an' 'as driven 'eavy wagons, buses, and cabs all around London. Wha' 'ee says is true alri'."

By the end of the day, Cal has signed up to join the Royal Field Artillery and George, the Army Veterinary Corp. Given just a few days to say their goodbyes to family, they report for training at Woolwich Barracks. Kitted out in khaki uniform, and issued with soldiering paraphernalia, they undertake rigorous drill training, and practise digging trenches on parkland requisitioned by the Government. Giggling girls congregate whenever they are out on exercises and cast admiring glances at the recruits, who, in response, whistle and call out flirtatious invitations.

Morning routines are what Cal enjoys most, for then his platoon work with the horses. For him, this is familiar territory, and he excels at each level of competency; grooming, saddling up, harnessing, riding, leading, and managing horse teams. Immediately, he is singled out by training officers as having advanced skills and fast-tracked onto the level where he learns to identify, handle, and transport shells of all sizes. His excellent horsemanship goes some way, in the drill sergeant's eyes, to compensate for his character flaws. These weaknesses are evident on the parade ground when Cal refuses to follow rules and obey orders. He is truculent, surly, and arrogant, deeming himself superior to fellow squaddies. He considers endless marching practice to be a waste of his time, and shows his contempt by dragging his feet to the barked commands of the drill sergeant,

"Present arms! Fall in! Fall out! Open rank march! Close rank march! Stand to attention! Stand at ease!"

Scowling, and swearing under his breath, it is not long before Cal attracts unwanted attention. Drill Sergeant Billy Sprigg orders the squad to stand at ease. His leathery, weather-beaten, lined face flushes with rage, and his sweeping ginger moustache bristles as he strides towards Cal, roaring, "Private Marchwood, one step forward. Stand to attention!"

As a Drill Sergeant, Billy Sprigg is frustrated by the limitations of the intake of volunteers, and Private

Marchwood's attitude is one such example. Older than most in the squad, Billy Sprigg expects more from this recruit. He knows the type; overconfident, with an inflated opinion of their own worth, paranoid, aggressive, terrified of failure or mockery and prone to violence. Sprigg already knows that Cal is disliked by fellow squaddies because of his volatility. However, he also knows that the army desperately need, men like Private Cal Marchwood. Strong men, who can drive heavy horse teams and load heavy artillery. Men with aggressive natures, useful when fighting the enemy. He is determined to turn Private Marchwood into an effective British soldier. Nose to nose, eyeball to eyeball, he addresses him, yelling, "'Oo d' bloody 'ell do you fink you are, Marchwood? Everyone 'ere, includin' me, finks you are a bit barmy. You are too quick t' fly orff d' 'andle an' d' lads in your troop reckon you are touched in d' 'ead. Did you know that Marchwood? Do you know that they 'ave got a nickname for you?"

"No, Sir!" answers Cal.

"Shall I tell you what it is they call you be'ind your back, you 'igh an' mighty piece of 'orse dung?" yells Sprigg.

"No, Sir! I don' want t' 'ear it," Cal sourly replies, as mocking laughter from his platoon is stifled beneath tightly compressed lips.

Incandescent, Sprigg roars, "What you want is not always what the army finks is best for you. A country man, as yerself, musta seen many a mad buck hare in spring, leapin' an' runnin' abou' d' fields. 'Ave y' seen it, Private Marchwood, standin' on its back legs, boxin' wiv 'is front legs, 'ittin' ou' at imaginary rivels for big-eyed does? Your mates 'ere 'ave nicknamed you '*March Hare*' 'cause y' sure act like a mad ole buck hare."

Struggling to control his impulse to react with fury and walk off parade, Cal barely manages to remain standing to attention in front of the Drill Sergeant. The extreme effort it takes to control himself does not go unnoticed by Billy Sprigg and he surprises Cal when he says, "Well done, Private Marchwood, you controlled your anger. I believe I will make a good soldier of you yet. Nuffin' wrong wiv getting' mad. We all get angry sometimes, nuffin' wrong wiv that. Just do not let rage take command of you, else you will soon be a dead man on d' battlefield."

After his training in the Veterinary Corp, in April nineteen-fifteen, George is posted to the Gallipoli Peninsula. His main duties are to ensure that horses and mules are fit and ready for the battlefield. His working days are spent grooming, massaging, rubbing down and exercising horses. He helps the farrier shoe them, polishes the hooves of officers' mounts, and trains heavy breeds used to transport bulky supplies to and from the frontline. In the field veterinary hospital, he assists the veterinary surgeon and cares for injured animals and those recovering from surgery. When the sun sets, he drives wagons over the scorched battlefields shooting badly hurt horses and burying their mutilated corpses.

The novelty of being in a hot climate soon wears off and George finds the heat unbearable. He loathes the swarms of black flies, and the all-pervading stench of rotting animal, and human flesh. The Corp suffers from the constant lack of clean water to drink and there are outbreaks of sickness among the men. Fellow soldiers, working alongside George, respect him for his stoicism and resilience in the face of unfolding hardship and the savagery of war. Hard-working, and uncomplaining, he is driven by his hatred of the murderous Turks, who kill soldiers and their mounts, before they can even reach the shore. To his comrades, he remains an enigma. At times with them he is sociable but mostly they find him to be secretive and wary. They know little of his personal life, except that he has a wife and children.

Back home, on four days' leave, he briefly visits Rosie and sees the twins, Ben and Henry. Though they are mildly resentful of his other life with Alice, they are proud of him serving in the prestigious Veterinary Corp. He leaves Rosie some cash, mindful that he is soon to be posted to France, where his chance of surviving the war will be much reduced. In the company of his beloved Alice and Arnold, George is emotionally detached. What he has seen of the war so far, the death and destruction, is something he chooses not to talk about. Though pleased to hear about lucrative contracts that Alice and Seth have procured from the military, he shows scant interest in the details; instead, he is restless, anxious to return to his comrades at the Front. There is talk of a huge, allied offensive building up near the River Somme. Word going around is that farmers and male factory workers, until now exempt from call-up, are going to be conscripted. They are needed to replace the tens of thousands of dead and wounded soldiers.

George worries about Albert, for he is not as tough and hardened as he and Cal are. To save his younger brother from becoming too apprehensive, he does not voice his concerns when he meets him in The Wheatsheaf for a drink. There, Albert excitedly tells him news of Cal, received on the back of a saucy postcard that he sent to their mother, Mary.

"D' last word she 'ad were in September, when 'ee wrote a few lines sayin' 'is big gun shells 'ad 'elped break fru enemy lines. 'Ee is keepin' safe, an' says 'ee is not in danger of bein' gassed, 'cause d' Boche are d' ones getting it, not our lads. When 'ee joined up I 'ad me doubts that 'ee would shape up, bu' me an' Edwina, we fink Cal is 'ard an' mean enough t' be a bloomin' good soldier."

A few days later, George returns to barracks, where preparations are underway for the departure of the returning soldiers to France. News reaches him that Ella has left Cal, and her marriage, and sailed away to America leaving no forwarding address. The family are astonished that timid, mousey Ella had the courage to plan, and execute, her escape. Seth and Mary are relieved that, away in France, Cal is in no position to give chase, and inwardly George and Albert hope that he never finds 'poor Ella'.

Four months after this event, Albert is conscripted into the Royal Garrison Artillery to train as a gunner and Mary's worst fears are realised. At twenty-one, he is still a boy in her eyes, too young to go to war. Gripped with intense anxiety, she remains outwardly composed when she meets with him on the morning of his departure to France, but her thoughts are frantic. *Praps I mollycoddled 'im too much, twill be my fault if 'ee don' survive. 'Ow will it be fer me if I lose 'im? 'Ee is all I got, fer George don' care much fer me, Cal ain't capable of caring fer anyone bu' 'imseff, an' Seff spends all his spare time wiv 'is uver woman.*

Seeing the recruitment posters plastered on every billboard – 'Your Country Needs You', 'Come, do your bit. Join Now' – Mary stays resolutely cynical about the patriotic fervour being whipped up, but she keeps those thoughts to herself as she embraces her son for the last time on the station platform. She watches the departing train until it disappears into the distance with a last giant puff of steam. Beside her is Edwina, who weeps loudly, sniffing and blowing into her handkerchief, and Mary's heart aches for her.

Seth rejects the possibility that Albert may be going into danger, believing that he, like his older brothers, will stay out of the line of fire. He prefers to focus his attention on the vast amount of money he is earning from supplying the army. When not away conducting business, he drinks with his brothers, Bill and Bert, or visits Gwen, who is mother to four of his children. With enough money to be generous to Mary, he leaves her plenty to spend when he is away and does not begrudge her any small personal extravagances.

Regarding the war, Mary gets a more truthful account from the new farmhand, Jacob Kerridge. Discharged from the army; after losing a leg during the Battle of Loos, he enlightens her of the true facts behind many troop casualties. He talks of superior German-built trenches, their highly trained, disciplined soldiers, and advanced weaponry. Still handsome, despite many facial scars, Jacob stands six feet two inches tall. Known by the locals not only for his immense size but for the lilting tones of his soft Irish brogue, he is fully accepted into the community, playing his old, battered guitar in the village pub on a Friday night while customers belt out popular, rousing songs.

Needing paid work, he agrees to do daily chores for Mary at Ennis Lodge. He helps her collect eggs from the coop, tend the horses and manage the vast gardens. Doing the rounds each day with him, Mary learns to appreciate nature, to name birds and identify their nests – she is soon able to recognise the blackbird's sturdy concoction of mud, grass and moss and the house sparrow's straw and feathered, grass basket. It is many years since Seth showed interest in spending time in her company, so now Mary is uplifted and her loneliness alleviated when she is with Jacob. When with him, she feels alive, and she sparkles, like she did all those years ago when she sat holding Brian's hand on the Embankment near Westminster.

With Seth so rarely at home, it becomes normal for Mary and her new friend to eat supper together. Afterwards, sitting companionably by the fireside, Jacob strums on his battered guitar while Mary knits socks and mufflers for her soldiering sons. On occasions, when prompted by Mary, Jacob describes the battlefields of Belgium and France and how being there affected him.

"Once I had a fine voice, 'til d' choking yella gas got into me lungs. Now I can barely get a note out me mouth widout it goin' haywire. I can no longer sing for me supper, Mary lass. But life has compensations, an' every mornin' at dawn, I hear d' larks singin' an' me auld heart lifts. Then I remember d' laughs I once had wid comrades, before they turned into twisted corpses, hanging for days on end, entangled in d' wire."

Leaning on Jacob's warm friendship, Mary almost manages to eliminate the spikes of jealously she feels towards Gwen Black. Such negative emotions occasionally bubble up when she finds sand in Seth's clothing, for then she knows that he has taken his other family to the seaside. Picturing the scene, them enjoying a day on the beach, causes her anger and hurt, as Seth has yet to fulfil his promise to take her to the seaside. She vows that when Albert returns from the war, she will persuade him to drive her, and Edwina, to East Cockle Bay where they can walk on the damp sand and paddle in the rock pools. Every day she wonders how Albert is coping. At night she pushes away the ominous feelings she gets as she drifts off to sleep.

On their way to the Somme, Albert, and his fellow conscripts, travel in cramped, draughty trains, carrying horses, mules, and supplies as well as many men. It is Albert's first taste of extreme discomfort, spending days and nights in cattle carriages, sleeping on bundles of loose hay while desperately trying to keep himself warm. By the time the train arrives at its destination, the men, including Albert, are plagued with body lice picked up from the rough bedding. They are unkempt and dirty, having had no clean water to wash in. With infrequent toilet stops, the men urinate in overflowing buckets, kept in the corner of the carriage, and the acrid smell seeps into their clothing, clinging to it for days.

Alighting at Arras, hundreds of soldiers mill about the station platform, smoking and jostling with one another. After a time, they, and Albert, begin the long march to the battlefields of the Somme. Carrying weighty, cumbersome kit–trench–building apparatus, wooden boards, shovels, buckets, and rolls of barbed wire, they march along narrow, twisting, mucky country roads. Hour after hour they traverse the lanes, before dropping, exhausted, to sleep overnight in field tents or ruined village buildings. By the third day, the cocky, defiant, morale-boosting songs are sung less frequently, and any renditions of *Pack up Your Troubles in your Old Kit Bag* are followed by long, heavy silences. Youthful bravado stumbles and falters, as nightmarish landscapes emerge from clouds of dust and acrid smoke.

Fields and meadows, once lushly green and full of grazing cattle, are grotesquely transfigured into a blackish, yellowish, chalk-streaked quagmires. Hedgerows, usually hung, this time of year, with succulent berries, have been replaced by six-feet-high barbed-wire fences. Snared and twisted upon many metal spikes are the purple-black corpses of soldiers, oozing pus; men and boys, machine-gunned as they attempted to climb over the metal barrier. In horror, Albert sees mucky clay fields, ridged, not by a working plough, but disfigured by huge shell holes, filled with dead bodies; torn flesh, blood, entrails and the gore of horses and men. The once rich, fertile soil is poisoned by tonnes of reeking human faeces, expelled by men in the terror-filled moments before bullets hit them and shrapnel shredded their flesh. Lines of mud-sucking trenches straggle the terrain, and emanating from them is a stench like no other, a vile smell that invades the nostrils and makes strong men vomit.

That night, bedding down in a trench a short distance away from the front line, Albert struggles to control his panic. He tries to remember the cheery messages, written on rude postcards, sent by Cal and George, and the way they boasted of pretty, French girls cheering them as they passed through villages on their way to Front. Turning to comrades; Connor Walker, a stable lad from Kent, Albert Short, a docker from Southampton and 'Irish' Pat who loves to recite poetry, Albert tries to be upbeat.

"I fink it might not be as bad as we 'ave been led t' believe, lads. My bruvers wrote 'ome sayin' that our big guns are protectin' d' boys in d' trenches, so we can rest easy, an' not be down'earted. Eh, lads?"

Connor, half crouching, burrows into the side of the trench attempting to get warm.

"I bluddy 'ope y' are righ', Berty. Wha' we seen today 'as given me d' colly wobbles, which ain't like me, I can tell y.' Hey Pat! Tell us again abou' Innisfree, fer 'earing parts of that poem will 'elp us drift off fer a bit."

"Aye, I will take youse all to d' Lake Isle of Innisfree. Close yer eyes and imagine yee are in dat magical place, where *'peace comes dropping slow, dropping from the veils of the morning to where the cricket sings; There, mid-nights all a glimmer, and noon a purple glow, And evening full of linnet's wings.'*

"Listen to me now, boys, although we are 'ere now in dis hellish place, one day soon, we *will arise and go… for always night and day, I hear lake water lapping with low sounds by the shore; While I stand on the roadway, or on the pavements grey, I hear it in my heart's core.*"

For the next three weeks Albert and his troop of Artillery Gunners follow orders to attack German trenches, with little progress made. On the eleventh of October, Albert has four days' leave away from the front line. Laying exhausted on his camp bed, eyes closed, he tries to ignore the light-hearted banter of his comrades playing cards in the next tent. In the distance, he hears chattering metallic noises; Lewis guns firing five hundred and fifty rounds a minute, and the crack of rifle fire. For no reason, an image of Cal pops into his head and, as if by magic, he hears his familiar voice.

"Get up, gee, haw, steady, whoa!"

Sitting bolt upright, he looks towards the lane and sees his brother, Cal, leading a team of twelve big horses pulling a 60-pounder gun through the deep mud of the track. *'Ow strange,'* he thinks, while noting changes in his brother's physical appearance. Cal seems taller, stronger somehow and exudes confidence. Leaping up, he stands and waves, calling out, "Cal! Cal! It is me, Albert."

Dismounting from an enormous black mare, Cal shows his surprise by uttering loud profanities. Telling the men alongside him to water and rest the weary horses, he trudges through the mud towards Albert. Seeing him arrogantly swagger through the thick slime, with a half-smile on his lips, Albert is, for the first time in his life, glad to see him. Stretching out their arms, the men shake hands and Cal speaks.

"Only a munf away from Blighty, an' y' look bloody beaten, Albert. To survive you must ferget yer soft life at 'ome. Finking of it makes you take your eye off d' enemy, an' you are likely to end up a swollen, blackened, 'edless lump of flesh. Be a bit more like me, Albert; tough as old boots, 'fraid of nuvfink, or nobody."

Albert finds himself grinning.

"I am tryin', Cal, bu' I can never be as good a soldier as you. I did not volunteer like you an' George, an' d' 'ole experience is a big shock. Still, I intend t' do me duty an' fight d' Hun 'til they give in. 'Ave you seen George? Do y' know where 'ee is?"

Cal is pleased to give Albert positive news.

"Ee ain't far from 'ere, Albert. Find d' field 'ospital, an' d' animal 'ospital is never far away."

Promising to see each other again soon, Cal returns to his troop and Albert is much cheered by the pleasant encounter with his brother.

A month after this meeting with Cal, Albert is firing shells at an enemy trench from a short-barrelled howitzer. Leaning against sodden sandbags, up to his knees in cold, slimy, rat-infested water, he crouches, reloads, and fires in a continuous rhythm. His movements are robotic; he is detached from everything around him, except the job in hand, oblivious to the putrid stench of the trench he has been in for four days and four nights. In his brief time here, at the Somme, he has witnessed comrades blown to bits and has wiped their blood and splattered brain matter from his uniform and face. He has seen the torsos of men he once joked and sang with cruelly clutched in the upstretched, splintered, blackened branches of dead trees. Suddenly he hears a commotion. From the end of the trench comes a shout from the Lance Corporal.

"Whiz bang coming, Private Marchwood. Look out!"

A thunderous noise, a bright flash, burning heat and flying shrapnel instantaneously plunge Albert into an aura of unearthly silence and complete stillness. Unable to see, unable to hear, he lies face down in the mud, arms akimbo, heat radiating over the small of his back. Then a merciful blackness descends, and he falls unconscious.

Hours later he is found, surrounded by huge, malevolent rodents intent on gorging on fresh flesh. His feet are wet and numb with the cold. In some confusion, he thinks he is back at Laurel Farm, paddling in the pond, laughing, as he watches Nellie slip, fully dressed, into the water. He hears her call out his name, frantically trying to get his attention as she clutches at his arms and legs. Slowly he regains consciousness and is hit by an excruciating pain that twists and slashes through his lower back and belly. Screaming in torment, he calls out for his mother as he is lifted onto a stretcher. He only calms when he hears the soothing voice of his comrade, Pat.

"Berty! It is me, Pat. You 'ave bin 'urt, old chap. Wid luck yee 'ave got yerself a Blighty Wound. Stay awake! Talk t' me 'cause we don' want yee t' fall asleep again."

Days later, as Albert lies in the hospital, the generals stop the pointless slaughtering of young men at the

Somme. Waiting to be shipped home to England, where he will be treated in a London military hospital, Albert gets a visit from George. Bedridden, unable to walk, he watches his favourite brother stride towards him through rows of beds, where fellow soldiers lie wounded, in air reeking of antiseptic. Reaching Albert, George conceals his shock at seeing how thin, pale, and fragile his younger brother looks as he lies on the bed covered by a thin white cotton sheet. Attached to him are rubber tubes and his torso and legs are tightly bandaged.

"Got yerseff a proper war wound, old boy! No more trench fightin' fer you, little bruv. I tried t' get meself one, bu' only managed t' get a cracked rib when an 'orse kicked me. I wish it were me though that was shot. You are not as prepared as me fer 'ardship an' sufferin', Berty. Growin' up in Lime'ouse prepared me an' Cal fer d' cruelties of war but you did not 'ave that advantage."

Albert makes a weak attempt to smile at his brother, but his eyes well up with tears. George notices Albert's hands trembling and shaking. He pulls up a chair, sits down, and, reaching over, clasps one of Albert's hands in his. Endeavouring to bring comfort to Albert, he assures him that he will get the best treatment back in London, in the military hospital, and should recover from his spinal injuries. He tells him family news.

"Ma, Da, and even ole Cal is rootin' fer you t' get back on yer feet agin, an' y' will, Albert, y' will. Money will be no object in gettin' y' top-notch treatment, fer d' old man is rakin' it in, as he said he would."

He stops when he notices Albert trying to speak

and leans his head nearer to his face so as to catch his whispering words.

"Bruver, I fink I mus' be losin' me mind, goin' mad. I see dead bodies in me sleep. I 'ave d' stink of death in me nose. I cannot get away from it. 'Oo will want me if I cannot walk again? D' bastards put gunshots in me back, an' they ripped ri' fru me belly. Will I ever work again? Will Edwina still care fer me? Wha' use will a cripple be to 'er?"

He stops talking and turns his head away from George, who, saddened, feels helpless to comfort him. He thinks it a cruel fate that Albert, after just a fleeting time serving in the army, is the one maimed for life, while he and Cal have escaped injury, despite being involved in the war since its onset in 1914

Touching Albert's hand, George, wanting to lift his spirits, tells him, "This bloody war is ending. When it does, me, Alice, and Arnold plan on goin' to d' United States. My American soldier friends tell me there is land t' buy, an' good money t' be made there. I will go ou' first, buy a farm, or a motor car garage, or bofe, then you an' Edwina can come over an' join us. It will be a fresh start, Albert. We deserve t' 'ave somefing good comin' our way afte' wha' we been fru."

Albert closes his eyes, and George quietly tells him that they will see each other back in England. The parting image of his brother, before he stands up and leaves, is of his chalk-white face and look of despair. Returning to the Veterinary Corp's encampment, he slogs through thick, sucking mud, likening it to a hideous living monster, devouring men, heavy weapons, animals, and all things that fall upon it. He is glad that, at least, Albert escaped that fate. Genuinely distressed at finding his 'little' brother suffering so much emotionally, he feels his eyes burn with a rush of tears at the wretched unfairness of it all. *Why is Albert d' one t' be wounded? He an' d' rest of d' inexperienced conscripts are lambs t' d' slaughter, not prepared enough t' be brought 'ere to face the enemy guns.*

Laying in his bunk that night, he yearns for the comfort of Alice's arms around him.

Whisperings:
Wave after wave of human souls, syphoned up in a torrent of terror, leave their blood and entrails to seed a host of red poppies. In full flower, they stand, a vibrant crimson, reflecting the beauty of men who shed precious blood for freedom.

12

Boom and Bust

It was the best of times, it was the worst of times, it was the age of wisdom, it was the age of foolishness, it was the epoch of belief, it was the epoch of incredulity, it was the season of light, it was the season of darkness, it was the spring of hope, it was the winter of despair.
  A Tale of Two Cities – Charles Dickens

1920–1929

Tears run down Edwina's cheeks as she clutches the small hand of her three-year-old son, Samuel, conceived just before Albert was conscripted in nineteen-hundred-and-sixteen. She runs to catch the bus to Liverpool Street Station, where she hopes to catch the 4pm train to Great Dun. There she will be met by Seth and Mary and driven the two miles home to Ickle Bow. It is the middle of summer nineteen-twenty, and she has just paid her last visit to Camberwell General Hospital to finalise arrangements for Albert coming home. For the past eighteen months, she has faithfully visited the hospital as often as possible, endeavouring to support her husband in his long struggle to rebuild his mental and physical strength. Now that his discharge from the army is imminent, she is worried.

Her nose is red from constant blowing into her handkerchief and her large brown eyes have shrunk into the back of her head from weeping. She tries to stop crying for Samuel's sake, not wishing to scare him, but she cannot. The level of her distress is too high, too overwhelming to be controlled. She is fearful of what the future holds for her and little Sam. The more time she spends with her husband, the more frightened she feels, because his character is changed beyond all recognition. The gentle, shy, sensitive man she married six years ago is gone, obliterated by excessive wartime trauma and the resulting chronic pain he suffers daily. Today, Albert is volatile, angry, paranoid, and bitter, unwilling to accept the changes to his life. He is incapable of expressing how he feels except through rage or self-piteous despair.

Surgeons in the field hospital in France, faced with his catastrophic spinal, pelvic, and intestinal gunshot wounds, performed an emergency colostomy operation. In the years since then, Albert has learned to walk short distances with the aid of a stick and manoeuvre himself around in a wheelchair. For months, he resisted offers from Edwina and his mother to push him outside to the hospital gardens, finding the whole idea humiliating. It is only after George promises to get him the very latest invention from America, a motorised wheelchair, that he agrees to venture out into the fresh air.

Leading up to the date of Albert's release from hospital,

Seth brusquely encourages him to build his arm muscles by using a hand-peddled wicker chair, which he does reluctantly. His half-hearted preparations for returning to civilian life reflect his dread of the future. His night terrors increase in intensity and leave him wide awake, shivering, his body drenched in sweat and his heart racing alarmingly. In the aftermath of his night terrors, Albert wraps his arms around his body, rocks, and cries out his grief and profound misery at losing his dignity as a man.

He feels unable to share his torment with anyone, least of all his wife. His mind continually struggles with his dilemma. *"Ow will I be able to 'ide my predicament from Edwina? I can never make love to 'er again, or to anyone. No-one would want me anyways, not a cripple like me, a man 'oo is no longer a proper man. If Cal were to find out, would 'ee laugh? 'Ee bein' a cruel, 'ard bugger I 'spect he would. Wha' of Da? 'Ee still boasts abou' 'is sexual energy, always wantin' to let us know 'ow great 'ee is wiv women. Will 'ee despise me when 'ee finds out d' trufe; that I am infertile and impotent?* Watching Edwina and Sam leave the hospital on their last visit, he vows to protect himself from mockery with the best tool at his disposal; rage.

Alighting from the train at Great Dun, Edwina is relieved to see her mother– and father-in-law waiting for her as she exits the station. Although her tears have stopped, the anxiety she feels is etched on her pale face. Samuel runs into the embrace of his grandmother, who stands by the car. She pats him on the head affectionately before reaching out to embrace Edwina and pummel her with questions about Albert.

"'Ow was 'ee t'day, Edwina? Is 'ee lookin' forward t' comin' 'ome? Is 'ee 'appier in 'imseff? Did y' manage t' tell 'im abou' 'is father's idea of runnin' a pub, instead of strugglin' wiv d' farm? I 'ope 'ee agrees, 'cause we all know that the backside 'as fallen outta farmin' since d' war finished. Did y' explain that to 'im?"

Seth, still sitting in the car, overhears the conversation and feels irritated on hearing the latest news relayed by Edwina.

"I'm sorry t' tell you bofe that Albert is worse than the last time I saw 'im. 'Ee is not sleepin' and doesn't wan' t' talk to me, or even look at Sam. I fink that 'ee is frettin', not knowin' 'ow 'ee will cope when 'ee comes 'ome. Whatever I said to 'im only seemed t' plunge 'im deeper into a black mood. I was really scared, Ma, at d' way 'ee glared at me, as if 'ee 'ated me. I don' know what I am goin' t' do, I really don't."

Edwina again starts to cry, and Sam buries his head in her skirts, clinging onto her leg needing reassurance. Seth feels a rumbling impatience with his son, disliking the way he is wallowing in his own misery, not trying to adapt to his changed circumstances. *'Ee do not 'ave my backbone, more's d' pity, nor Cal's 'ard 'art,* he thinks. Mary is also disappointed that her favourite son, who she indulged so much, is showing a weakness of character with his incessant, self-pitying complaints. Unable to understand, or truly envisage the horror of trench warfare, she and Seth flounder in knowing how best to deal with their emotionally traumatised, badly maimed, third son.

Seth, as always, is quick to see a way forward for Albert.

He purchases a small pub halfway down the long, tree-lined Brownfield Road on the outskirts of Chivelbank. An established beerhouse, well stocked by Dun Breweries, it serves locals and those working the timber barges on the canal nearby. As a named licence holder, Seth gauges that Albert, with the support of his young wife, can earn a steady income and comfortably accommodate his family in the commodious extension at the back of the pub. Albert agrees, once he accepts that his smallholding and farmhouse are no longer financially viable and must be sold.

Aged forty when demobbed in nineteen-twenty, George makes a promise to Alice that they will soon escape the lingering, shady associations with his father and brother and put the Atlantic Ocean between them and his errant family. He sells Jasper Hall to fund his, Alice's and Arnold's passage to America and give them a financial head start when they get there. Selling the Hall, at an inflated price, to a wealthy racehorse trainer furnishes him with enough money to reinvest in a piece of real estate bordering Epping Forest. This he can rent while he lives abroad. It gives him a safety net to know that he will still have property in England if he ever needs to return.

In September nineteen-twenty-one, having procured the necessary entry documents, he, Alice and Arnold sail for New York before travelling on to San Francisco by train. Before he leaves England, George writes to Rosie telling her that she is welcome to remain in the house owned by him, until such time as he needs to sell it. He tells her to let Henry and Ben know they are welcome to join him in California once he is settled. Cal and Albert learn of George's plans at a meeting held in Albert's pub, just two weeks before he is to set sail for America. As the three brothers sit in a secluded corner of the dark, wood-panelled bar, Cal, true to his nature, begins to brag, trying to impress his siblings.

"Did y' know that I am jus' back from Detroit an' Michigan? I travelled over from Canada, which is d' easiest way int' d' States, 'cause USA visas are now bloody 'ard t' get. Wiv Da's 'elp this end, an' my underworld bootlegger contacts in Detroit, I was able to offload liquor bound for speakeasies an' underground jazz clubs in d' cities."

Sneering his contempt for the unenforceable Prohibition Laws, he excitedly expresses his admiration for gangsters and their crooked lawyers, who make a mockery of the Constitution's Eighteenth Amendment.

"I tell y', bruver, speakeasies, in places like Cincinnati, Detroit an' Chicago are swamped in alcohol, run by men 'oo are big in d' pharmaceutical business 'cause they can bottle it as medicine. They even let women drink in 'em. Though me an' Da are small time in comparison, we are still rakin' in a nice, easy pile of cash"

Laughing loudly, he continues, "Pro'ibition is d' best fing ever 'appened, George. There is money to be made, comin' at a time we need it most, 'avin' sold off d' old farms at a loss. I expect y' 'ave yer own plans to make a fortune in America, George? If ever y' want t' come in wiv me an' Da on a deal, don' worry abou' d' old fellow, fer 'ee is no longer d' boss. You are lookin' at the new boss; me, an' I intend t' expand into 'ouse buildin' an' open offices in Bolster and Chivelbank."

George listens with an impassive countenance, giving nothing away of his thoughts, a fact that irritates Cal who, as usual, is unsettled by it.

"Me an' Alice are makin' plans of our own, Cal. Best I keep meseff away from wha' you an' Da are up to, bu' I wish you well. Fanks for askin' me, I appreciate it."

His words belie his inward thoughts. *If 'ee really finks that I would put myself under d' financial control of 'im, or Da, that I am stupid enough t' fall for 'is bribes, 'ee can fink again. Me an' Alice 'ave the skills to make our own way in America. The only circumstance that would make me join wiv 'em again would be if I were the one in control. Anyways, Alice would never approve of such a partnership, 'avin' suffered the old man poking 'is nose into 'er business during the war.*

Wanting to rattle Cal, just for his own amusement, George asks after Ella and enquires if he has heard from her or met up with her in America since the war ended. Enjoying the dark, angry look that comes over his older brother's face, George continues to goad him by mentioning a rumour going around.

"Some people do suspect, Cal, that you married a woman in Michigan, when you was workin' on the ship. Praps y' married 'er under yer uver name, Stuart Borewood? I am not sayin' I believe it though. Seems a bit far-fetched t' me."

He anticipates an aggressive rebuttal from Cal judging by the furious look in his eyes so to defuse the situation, he alters his tone.

"Don' worry, old chap! My lips are sealed on both

matters, unless you an' Da pull any dirty tricks on me, an' get in me way, fer then I mi' be tempted t' disclose information."

As George, Alice and Arnold settle onboard for the long crossing to New York, Cal and Seth feverishly assess business priorities. The bonanza war years, providing horses and fodder for the military, and growing food on arable fields in Suffolk to boost the food chain for the troops, are over. Rural life is once again negatively affected. Farming is no longer lucrative, and hamlets and villages are erased by roads and increased house building to serve the sprawling London population.

Ennis Estate, Mary's home for so long, is broken up and demolished to make way for a large suburb for the aspiring middle classes; those who commute to their London offices in their own cars or travel by train. Having to leave the place she has made her home, yet again, devastates her. She is neither consoled, nor fooled by Seth when he implies that he is doing her a favour by moving her out of Ennis Lodge.

"I know you always wanted t' be near d' seaside so we are movin' t' East Cockle Bay, beside d' Estuary. Cal 'as found us a grand place t' live; a four-bedroomed terraced 'ouse on d' cliff overlookin' d' Promenade. It 'as a back garden where you can plant vegetables, an' keep a pet dog if you like. There is no space fer a pony and trap bu' there are trams to d' beach an' to d' pier so you can go to town, an' walk down d' Promenade whenever you like. We can afford a housekeeper, Mary, to 'elp around d' place, so you can be a lady of leisure."

Knowing the fruitlessness of arguing with decisions made by Seth and Cal, Mary does as she is accustomed to doing; she adapts. *After all,* she thinks, *I always wanted to live near the sea an' now me wish is granted, I must make the best of it.* She is helped through the transition from Ennis Lodge to East Cockle Bay by Edwina and her grandson, Samuel. Spending much of her free time these days in Albert's pub, The Black Cat, she enjoys supporting her daughter-in-law, who she has much affection for. Her heart breaks when she sees how changed in character her youngest son is since returning from France. His bitterness and irritability spew out in all directions and Mary feels helpless to do anything to alleviate his mental and physical suffering.

Witnessing the cruel, verbal abuse he reigns on his young wife and his son, Mary worries for their safety. Many hours she lies awake at night fretting about how she can make things better for him, Edwina, and Sam. Once she would have vehemently defended him against anyone, now she cannot, for his behaviour is too disturbing and unkind to be excused. Seth refuses to discuss the subject with her. In his opinion, Albert, instead of complaining about his situation, should be grateful that he has a fine pub to run and a roof over his head, thanks to him.

Taking regular brisk walks along the Cockle Bay Promenade, Mary enjoys colourful scenes of activity reminiscent of her childhood years in Tower Hamlets. The stalls, selling winkles, cockles and muscles, and the bustling crowds jostling among the fairground rides, transport her back to London marketplaces. Sometimes she pays tuppence for a deckchair and sits eating an ice cream bought from Mr Frosty's stall. Memories of happier times float in and out of her head. *If only Brian 'ad not been killed, 'ee would be sittin' 'ere beside me laughin' at d' sight of fat-bottomed men and women stretching d' colourful, striped deck-chair canvas until it bulges and sags just inches from the sand.* The sight of pompous gentlemen becoming irate as they struggle to erect their deckchair fills her with stifled merriment.

At other times, she watches the sun set over the bay and is more contemplative. She remembers the babies and children she lost to disease, poverty, and through her own ignorant neglect of them, and then she is filled with sad regret. After the many hurts and disappointments she suffered during her sixty plus years of life, she can now acknowledge her strength of character, and her resilience in the face of sorrow and hardship. She can accept, without bitterness, George's estrangement from the family and his emigration to America. She makes no judgement about Cal's deceptions and verbal cruelties. Regarding Seth's long-standing lack of interest in her as a person, she no longer cares. She is self-reliant and stoic when shouldering her anxieties about Albert's depression and, in comparison to Seth, now depleted by poor health and old age, she is the stronger and more energetic.

Watching Seth one evening, as he slumps in his favourite high-backed Windsor chair in their parlour, head back, snoring, she wonders why Gwen has not tired of him. *Afte' all, 'is 'andsome looks is all gone now,* she thinks, not without feeling a smidgen of sympathy for the man who once made her explode with raw desire. *Look a' 'im now. 'Ee has grown fat around 'is belly an' 'as shrunk by two inches or more in height. 'Is 'air is thin, an' d' look on 'is lined face is bitter an' sulky. I can tell 'ow 'ee 'ates it when Cal shouts an' yells a' 'im, bossin' 'im about. Spendin' time wiv 'is ladylove, Gwen, an' their children seems to be d' only fing gives 'im 'is pride. Wiv 'er, 'ee can show off, impress 'er, an' their children, wiv 'is flashy car.* In a strange way, Mary has sympathy for Gwen, who must, from necessity, pretend a continuing attraction for her old, fat lover, so she can, with his financial support, remain living in the big house in Hackney.

By nineteen-twenty-four, George is settled comfortably with Alice in California; the proud owner of a chain of garages selling petrol and second-hand cars. His twenty-year-old son, Ben, has come to join them and has a labouring job in the thriving, post-war construction trade, north of San Francisco. Arnold and Alice manage a three-hundred-acre ranch, the family home, where they breed thoroughbred horses and keep a modest herd of beef cattle. Culturally, their lives are flourishing. They eat out in restaurants, drink alcohol in illicit jazz clubs, enjoy Charlie Chaplin movies in drive-in cinemas, and, in the company of Arnold and Ben, go to Blues Clubs where they boogie alongside carefree flappers on the dance floor. George's early life in the slums of Limehouse recedes into a distant memory, as does the horror of war, and he is, at last, fulfilled.

In his mid forties, Cal forms a relationship with a girl less than half his age; rosy-lipped Henrietta Monk, the daughter of Seth and Cal's land adviser, Claud Monk. Henrietta bears him three healthy daughters between nineteen-twenty-three and nineteen-twenty-seven. Like his father before him, Cal registers his illegitimate daughters with his surname, seeing no reason not to claim them as his offspring. He and Henrietta occupy various farmhouses in Essex and Suffolk, temporary residences, before Cal sells them for development. The Marchwood Land and Property Development Company is a success during these years and money is plentiful for Cal and Seth.

In appearance, the middle-aged Cal looks distinguished; greying at the temples, with the overall deportment of a ruthless, confident man. Able to make sound business decisions, he enjoys the respect of his father and mother and his self-esteem flourishes. He has grown less volatile, though Henrietta suffers periods of domestic violence at his hands, especially when he drinks whisky. He is often away for months in America, and she is left without financial support for herself and the children and resorts to doing menial, casual farm work, and pawning the gifts of jewellery he gave her.

As he nears seventy, Seth's mood becomes increasingly irascible and bad-tempered, the exception being when he is at the horse races or gorging himself on roast lamb in Gwen's big kitchen in London. No longer able to enjoy drinking, as beer blows him up and fills him with gas, he drinks endless cups of tea, resulting in him taking many trips to the toilet. Worst of all, he is now impotent, like Albert, and he can no longer enjoy his favourite pastime in life; sex. He has become demotivated and has lost interest in seeking out new pieces of land and property, especially now that Cal is the one in charge of the business. Nevertheless, he hopes to beget one last promising idea to impress his son, and remind him that it is he, *Seth Marchwood*, who is the brains behind all their past and current good fortune.

In nineteen-twenty-seven, he pushes Cal to consider selling off most of their stock – even if it entails a loss – and to move all their capital into the booming American stock market. He is pleased and gratified when Cal admits that he has been thinking along the same lines.

"I agree wiv you, old man. My gangland contacts in d' States advise me to do d' same fing. I 'ave not told you, Da, bu' last time I was over there I bought five hundred shares in d' steel industry an' I have seen 'em double in value since then. As I have a permanent address there and am officially a resident as Mr Cal Boreham," he laughs and winks at Seth, "wiv an American wife an' children, I am a bona fide gentleman playing d' stock market. We cannot lose, Da. We cannot lose."

Inwardly sneering, Cal knows that Seth is curious, wanting to ask questions about his other family in America, though reluctant to appear interested. He waits for his father to resume talking.

"Wiv wha' you 'ave jus' tol' me, Cal, an' wha' I 'ave been 'earin' fer weeks now, there is 'ardly any risk investin' all we got in d' American stock market. I trust you to deal wiv d' buyin' an' sellin' of shares, fer you know wha' t' do. I trust you to look after the Marchwood wealth, Cal."

Mary is not told by Seth of his plans, nor is Gwen, and they remain ignorant of the fact that the homes they live in- the house in East Cockle Bay, and the Victorian terrace house in Hackney- are used to procure finances to fund the purchase of shares. *They 'ave no need t' know my business anyways,* thinks Seth, *fer it is my opinion, an' Cal's, that there is nought to worry abou'.*

Cal and Seth persuade Albert that The Black Cat should be sold, and the money used also to buy shares, a sound investment on his behalf. Albert jumps at the suggestion. He has let his pub business run down since Edwina and his son left after a blazing row. The breakdown of his marriage, brought on by his paranoid jealousy and conviction that she was seeing other men, culminated in him locking his wife and child out of the pub on a bitterly chilly night, and refusing them access from then on. For months on end, he broods. *In trufe I 'ave done 'er a favour. It is a relief she' gone. Seein' 'er every day just reminded me of all d' fings I can no longer do. Only 'alf a man now, marriage ain't fer me no more.*

February nineteen-twenty-nine, Albert lives with Seth and Mary in East Cockle Bay. Mary does her best to ease his suffering and discomfort, but it is a thankless task. Albert's overall physical health worsens. He endures sleepless nights, and days full of despair and depression. Every six months, Seth drives him to the London military hospital where his condition is checked and monitored. Apart from controlling his chronic pain, medical teams can do nothing to improve his condition. Knowing Albert's fondness for George, Mary contacts Edwina. She begs her to write to Alice and George and plead with them to write to Albert and cheer him up.

Three months later, two letters arrive in East Cockle Bay from America. One is addressed to Mary and the other to Albert. Sitting down at the kitchen table, Mary picks up the envelope with her name on it, and, with trembling fingers, she tears it open and extracts a single sheet of writing paper. Her emotions are in a state of flux. It has been years since George has communicated with her. The last time she saw him was in The Black Cat when she exchanged just a few cold words with him before he left for America. *What 'as 'ee got t' say to me I wonder? I 'ope 'ee 'as forgiven me fer sidin' wiv Seff all those years ago. I 'ope 'ee understands that I 'ad no choice.* Through teary blurred vision, she reads,

> *Marchwood Ranch, Oak Woods, San Francisco,*
> *17th May 1929*

> *Ma. I hope that you, and the old bugger, Da, are keeping well. I hear you now live near the sea. Me, Alice, Arnold, and Ben live on a ranch with horses. I am doing very well here in America. I own three garages, and I play the stock market like everyone does. I am too busy to make the long trip back to England but when I do, I promise to visit you. Glad you are looking after Albert. No one could look after him better than you.*
> *George.*

Mary is walking on air after reading George's letter. She leaves the kitchen and goes to the garden to give Albert his letter. She finds him sitting, quietly sketching daffodils growing in the flowerbed. Recently, his mood has dramatically improved due to the new friendship he has with a West Country man living next door. Of a sensitive nature, Peter Small, a working artist and musician, moved by Albert's plight, takes it upon himself to try to lift the wounded Alfred's spirits. He teaches him to draw and paint. To the amazement of his parents, and himself, Albert discovers he has an artistic talent. Sitting sketching, or in front of an easel painting, he is pleasantly distracted from his usual morose introspection. On at least two evenings a week he and Peter sit and listen to jazz on the wireless, a modern style of musical entertainment that excites them both.

Approaching Albert, Mary stands by his side and, smiling warmly, hands him the letter. Controlling unexpected tears, she turns away to go back into the house. From the kitchen window, she watches her frail son open the letter, and again her eyes prickle with unshed tears. She sees him pull the letter out of the envelope and bend his head to read.

Marchwood Ranch, Oak Woods, San Francisco
17th May 1929

Dear brother Albert.
It's been a long time since I wrote to you and I am sorry, but time seems to fly and there is so much

to do here that I rarely get the chance to sit down and send letters. I will try and change that and write more often. How are you, old chap? I hear from Cal that you are back living back with Ma and Da. I am sorry you and Edwina are no longer together. I wish I were not so far away and could come and cheer you up a bit. With all the money Da and Cal are making on the stock market, you should be getting the best treatment possible, and I hope you are. I never did get around to sending you the modern, motorised chair I promised you, but today I have shipped one off. You should receive it in about six weeks' time. Better late than never! It will be fun for you to drive about and get yourself down to the local pub whenever you want. If you feel up to it, Al, write me a note and I will make sure to answer it. Your brother George

Between May and the first three weeks of October nineteen-twenty-nine, the lives of Seth, Mary and their three sons seem more financially secure and stable than they have ever been. For Seth's other family– his mistress Gwen, their two adult daughters and three younger children– life, too, is good. Gwen is content to go lengthy periods of time not seeing Seth when he is at home with his wife, Mary. No longer physically attracted to the aged, impotent man he has become, and wary of leaving him alone with their daughters, who dislike his lecherous gaze upon them, Gwen struggles to show any affection for him. Whenever he visits her in London, mindful of her financial dependency on him, she forces herself to make a fuss of him. She cooks him his favourites foods, flatters him, and ingratiates herself to him until he hands her a wad of grubby banknotes, and whatever pieces of gold jewellery he holds in his pocket at that time.

Like Gwen, Cal's mistress Henrietta is beholden to him financially but his support of her and their children is erratic. When not in America on business, and flush with money, he is generous, buying her and the girls expensive clothes and treating them to days out at the seaside. Moving from property to property, neither she nor the children can settle into a stable home life. By the time of the birth of their third daughter, Henrietta has become used to Cal's cruel verbal and physical abuse. She dreads the periods of time when he is in England, fearing for the safety of herself and the children. Consequently, she is relieved when, suddenly, at the end of October nineteen-twenty-nine, he disappears from her life forever. Within days of the collapse of the America, stock market, he is gone, back to the United States.

Seth is alarmed by the frightening rumours circulating. Receiving an urgent telegram from Cal, sent from Southampton, which read, DO NOT PANIC STOP GOING TO NEW YORK STOP WILL SELL SHARES IMMEDIATELY STOP CAL, he experiences fear. By the following Tuesday, fourteen billion dollars is wiped off the value of stocks, and, to Seth and Cal's horror, their world of material wealth collapses. Millions, duped into investing everything they had into shares, face economic ruin. A lifetime of opportunistic success in the Marchwood family catastrophically implodes.

When the bank calls for repayment of loans taken out on his properties, Seth is forced to take radical decisions. He moves Gwen, and their remaining dependent children, into a humble, two-room thatched cottage in a small hamlet in Suffolk, a property Cal knows nothing about. He, Mary and Albert are forced to move into a similarly dingy, cramped, three-bedroom end of terrace Victorian house in a run-down street in East Cockle Bay. The last message Seth receives from Cal, using his pseudonym 'Stuart Calum Boreham', is from Detroit; a telegram with the words, WILL NOT BE COMING BACK TO ENGLAND STOP STAYING HERE WITH FAMILY STOP CAL. Seth and Mary reel from the callous abandonment by their son at a time when they need him like never before.

George's businesses in California folds under the impact of the financial crash, though he and Alice manage to hold onto their ranch and both properties back in Essex, England. Seth braces himself to somehow survive the catastrophe alone, without the moral and practical support of his two older sons, whose treachery he will never forgive. With a war-wounded younger son to support, Mary, and an obligation to try to help Gwen when he can, he faces the biggest challenge of his life as poverty raps on his door.

Whisperings:
For him, and him alone, there is only one opportunity worth grasping: Repentance.

13

Retribution and Reconciliation

Does wisdom appear on the earth as a raven which is inspired by the smell of carrion?
– Friedrich Nietzsche

1930–1939

Reeling from the loss of all his wealth, so painstakingly acquired through the twists and turns of the last fifty years, Seth is devastated. Having to part with his grey Ford T hurts him more than anything else. Attending his brother's funeral during the third week in December in nineteen-twenty-nine is to be the last time he drives it. In many ways, he is glad that Bert is dead, for now he need never know of his humiliating financial situation.

For the service, held in St James's Church, Selden, he insists that both Mary and Albert accompany him, ordering them to dress in their best black funeral finery. Their manner and appearance must, he tells them, belie the fact that they are affected by the financial crash. They are to pretend to nieces, nephews, and cousins, who make up the bulk of the mourners, that their circumstances have not changed, and money is still plentiful. Ruminating, as he sits listening to his brother's eulogy, Seth's thoughts are on Bert; *'ee never did get over losin' 'is two boys on d' battlefields of France, poor bugger. Not 'avin' Agnes, dead this longtime, t' 'elp 'im fru 'is grief musta been 'ard. Wish I 'ad visited 'im more often, an' been kinder to 'im after 'is loss. Anyways, too late now, so no point bein' sorry fer it 'cause there's nought t' be done.*

Mary, sitting next to him, is also suffering pangs of remorse about her past feelings of jealousy and resentment towards her brother- and sister-in-law, who were kind and caring to her older boys and, most especially, to Sally Anne. They looked after her children when she was locked up in Millbank Prison and never did they once give the impression that they judged her harshly for it. Taken by surprise at the strength of her regret, she has a sudden urge to fall forward in the pew and loudly sob out her painful remorse for the way she had once behaved towards them.

Triggered by the sombre atmosphere inside the hallowed space, the same church where she and Seth were married, her mind is flooded with stark, fleeting images, not of her wedding day, but of her long dead children; Cedric, Charlotte, Elizabeth Rose, and Sally Anne. She imagines Agnes standing alongside her deceased children in the afterlife. Inexplicably, she has a sense of their presence all around her, enveloping her in love and forgiveness. At first, she dismisses these feelings as wishful thinking, but on closing her eyes, she is consoled by her train of thought. *Why would they want t' send me love? I don' deserve it. Fer d' mos' part I neglected me poor children. I was not a good mufver. Am I jus' a silly old fool fer finking they love me from beyond d' grave? Maybe it is 'cause they 'ave 'eard me say 'sorry, in me 'ead, an' aloud, many times these las' twenty years. I'll say it again now fer I 'ave a strangest feelin' they are here, listnin'.* Bowing her head, she whispers with deep sincerity.

"Sorry, Cedric."

"Sorry, Charlotte."

"Sorry, Elizabeth.

"Sorry, Sally Anne."

To hide any outward sign of her intense inner emotion, she covers her thin, trembling lips beneath the fingertips of her gloved hand, before casting a surreptitious, sideways glance at Albert, who sits slumped in his wheelchair in the aisle. *Poor sod, it is an ordeal fer 'im bein' 'ere, alone, wivou' 'is bruvers, or 'is wife t' support 'im,* she thinks.

Sitting through the service, Albert feels nauseous and is afflicted by spasms of searing pain across his lower back. When the organ plays *Chopin's Funeral March*, and his uncle's coffin is carried from the church, he wishes that George were there beside him. He has heard nothing from him since those catastrophic days in October last, when all their family wealth vanished. Nor has Cal been in touch since his rapid exodus from England to New York just days after the notorious 'Black Tuesday'. He went, promising that he would salvage enough collateral to pay back Seth's bank debts and save some of their fortune.

Since the day of his speedy departure, not a single word has been heard from him, no message to give them hope of a financial resolution. Albert is ambivalent about Cal's absence, but his father detests his eldest son for his callous desertion at a time of crisis and he refuses ever to mention his name. After Bert's funeral, as winter moves into the spring of nineteen-thirty, Seth's fury at Cal for deserting them, knowing their financial ruination, is taken out on Mary, and, to a lesser extent, on Albert.

Day after day, they endure his outbursts of violent rage when he makes threats to kill Cal if he ever claps eyes on him again. Unable to travel far without a car, in desperation, he resorts to using a donkey and cart to go to the pub each evening, where he drinks cheap cider and rants about the unfairness of his misfortune. Too gloomy to think his way out of their dramatic return to poverty, he relies on his old age pension of thirty shillings a week, and on pawning odd bits of gold jewellery he accumulated over the years, pieces intended for Gwen in lieu of child maintenance.

Each time he selects an item to sell, he thinks about her; *No need t' fund Gwen no more. She 'as t' look after 'erself. Apart from young Charlie, d' older ones are grown up an' workin', so she don' need me t' support 'er. She got plenty from me over d' years. At least I 'ave given 'er a country cottage to live in. I am mighty glad I kept that property a secret from Cal, as 'ee would 'ave 'ad it sold, or probably burned it down out of spite to Gwen an' me. Best not fink of that. I reckon d' cunning sod will never come back, fer 'ee be 'fraid t' show 'is guilty face. Bofe 'im an'*

George run out on me an' d' family, an' they are a bloody disgrace.

Albert, encouraged by his friend Peter Small, starts a modest business down by the pier, near to a bohemian, good-natured stall holder, Susannah Levi. Her stall, laden with conch shells, seaside souvenirs, straw hats, buckets, and spades is one of the more popular with visitors to the pier. Albert's trade is sketching miniature portraits for customers inside his tiny booth. It earns him enough to pay his mother towards his keep and buy art materials for his new-found hobby. Drawing and painting gives him back a feeling of self-worth and pride. Mary notices a marked improvement in his mental state and a lessening of his night terrors and outbursts of rage. Her happiness at his improved mood is enhanced further when he speaks to her about Edwina and fourteen-year-old Samuel. During their conversation, Albert expresses remorse for the way he callously treated his wife and son, driving them out of his life the way he did.

"'Ow could poor Edwina understand, 'ow could anyone 'oo weren't a soldier in the trenches like me? Back then, I was trapped in a nightmare, Ma, an' could not wake up from it. I was thrashing abou', rememberin' 'orrible fings, fings that went round and round in me 'ead, never stoppin'."

"I'm glad to 'ear you speak 'er name, Albert. Yer wife is a good woman an' I fink she loved you. She knew it were d' War that made y' behave bad, an' I know she forgives y' fer it."

In the summer of nineteen-thirty-two, with his health

rapidly deteriorating, Albert surmises he may not have long to live. He writes to Edwina and sends her a gift of two small miniature drawings, a small token of regret for his past cruelty towards her. Sitting alone in his bedroom, he picks up his pen and writes.

> *56 Hampshire Road, East Cockle Bay*
> *Sunday 28th August 1932*
>
> *Dear Edwina,*
> *I hope you do not rip up this letter before you read it, though I would understand if you did for I hurt you and Sammy after the war ended. It was not your fault that you could not cheer me up when I came home. The war changed me forever. I was angry at the world, and I took it out on you. I am sorry for the horrible things I said and done to you. I cannot change anything that happened then. I wish I could. All I can do is say I am sorry. I will not ask you to visit me because it would upset us both. I often wonder what Sammy looks like and if he still looks like me. Since learning how to draw, I do portraits. I am sending you two miniatures, one of you on our wedding day, and one I copied from an old photograph of Samuel when he was about three years old. Say sorry to him for me, Edwina. Thank you. Albert x*

Parcelling up his gift ready to post, suddenly he is overwhelmed with tiredness. A wave of sickness causes him to break out in a clammy sweat. Temporarily abandoning his task, he closes his eyes and leans back in his chair. After a while, he is unsure how long, he opens his eyes and clearly sees his grandmother, Lottie, standing in front of him, her arms outstretched, and hears her voice.

"Do not worry, Albert. I am here waiting for you. Everything is going to be all right."

He is dismayed, thinking it a figment of his imagination, though much comforted by it. As Christmas approaches, he finds it difficult to swallow food and drink. Thin and exhausted, suffering chronic pain and discomfort, he is taken into the London Military Hospital at St Pancras. There doctors tell him he has terminal cancer of the liver and cannot expect to live much longer. Stoically, Mary travels by train, twice a week, to sit with him, hold his hand, and give him what solace she can. She writes to George, telling him how ill his younger brother is, and pleads for him to write to him before it is too late. When she does not get a reply, deeply disappointed for Albert, she weeps bitter tears into her pillow each night.

The thirty-first of January nineteen-thirty-three is bitterly cold. Mary arrives at the hospital and sees a man, accompanied by a youth, sitting either side of Albert's bed. *'Oo can it be?* she thinks, as she pushes through the swing doors into the ward to walk down the central aisle towards her son's bed. From the back, the man sitting by the bed looks like a Seth when he was younger. Her heart misses a beat. *George, 'tis George! I can't believe it! 'Ee 'as come over from America t' see 'is bruver an' got 'ere in time. Fank Gawd! Bu' 'oo is d' young lad? Is it Arnold?*

No, 'ee is too young to be Arnold, 'oo must be a grown man by now. Drawing closer she notes how yellow and gaunt Albert looks but is cheered to see his eyes are shining with pleasure. Turning his gaze to her, he says weakly, 'Ello, Ma! See 'oo 'as turned up to see me. It is George, wiv me son, Sam. Come t'gever, they 'ave, to giff me a double surprise."

Rendered speechless at first, Mary bombards George with questions.

"'Ow long are y' stayin', George? 'Ow are fings in California? 'Ow are Ben, Arnold, and Alice? Did you lose money in d' crash?"

Turning to Sam, she exclaims, "Look at you now. You 'ave grown up since I las' saw you, lad. Nearly a man, I'd say."

Leaving Albert at the close of visiting time, George offers to drive Mary to the railway station where she is to catch the train back to East Cockle Bay. Knowing that he plans to stay in England for a month, she is not distressed at leaving him, as she expects she will meet him again before his return to America. Smiling, she addresses Sam.

"Give yer mufver me bes' wishes, Sammy, an' tell 'er I am glad she agreed fer y' t' see yer da. It 'as made 'im 'appy, an' me too."

One week later, a telegram arrives from the hospital informing Mary and Seth of the death of Albert. Both, in their own inimitable way, grieve over his death at such an early age. Seth is embarrassed that he cannot afford to give Albert a lavish funeral but, under pressure from Mary, he agrees to allow George to pay the burial expenses and purchase a headstone.

Standing around the open grave in Ickle Bow cemetery, watching Albert's coffin lowered into the ground, the emotionally disparate family group avoid looking at each other. The air around them palpates with heavy, mixed sentiment. Mary feels sad, though relieved that Albert no longer suffers. Edwina remembers happy times she had with Albert before the Great War. Samuel is pleased he saw his father before he died. George, holding a floral wreath from him and Alice, looks pale and drawn, as he remembers seeing his young, wounded brother in the military field hospital thirteen years ago. *It should 'ave been me or Cal who got wounded, not poor Al. It ain't fair that it 'appened to 'im. Now, all these years later, the German gunshots 'ave finally killed 'im. Here's 'oping that they don' start another bloody war,* he thinks, half listening to the vicar reciting a prayer at the graveside.

"O Father of all, we pray to thee to grant Albert thy peace; let perpetual light shine upon him, through Jesus Christ our Lord, Amen."

Seth, muffled up against the cold, leans heavily on his walking stick and broods about having two elder sons who have gone their own way, in selfish disregard of him and Mary. Losing Albert, the only son who was loyal to them both, is a bitter pill to swallow. *Wish I 'ad been nicer t' young Albert. It weren't 'is fault d' way 'ee behaved jus' after d' war. Shell shocked, 'ee was, an' I should 'ave been more patient wiv 'im. D' other boys sailed fru d' bloody war wiv 'ardly a scratch.* Grimacing at his thoughts, he hobbles back to the chauffeur-driven funeral car, his gouty foot giving him a lot of pain. He throws George a cold look, making no attempt to speak to him, as he and Mary settle into the back seat of the car, ready to be driven back home.

Mary misses Albert. She liked accompanying him down to the pier when he was sketching. There she would watch over him and chat to stallholders, mostly London cockneys; her people, as she considers them to be. Her friend, Susannah Levi, was always the first to help Albert whenever he took a bad turn, and Mary loves her for the generous support she gave him.

When the summer season begins, and the promenade comes to life with summer traders and seaside entertainers, Mary takes the bus to the pier to see Susannah. She suspects she already knows of Albert's death, as sad news travels fast. She hears her friend's loud voice before she sees the familiar, plump, bosomy figure, with the untidy mop of black hair piled on top of her head in a loose bun. Spotting Mary coming towards her, Susannah calls out, "Well! If it ain't wee Mary Marchwood, come t' see me an' 'ave a natter. Come 'ere darlin' and join me in a cup of Rosie Lee. I've plenty in me flask, an' sandwiches enough t' feed a bleedin' army."

She laughs. Then her expression turns solemn. "Sad I was t' 'ear of poor Albert, Mary. Poor lad, 'ee suffered too much, an' fer too long, 'ee did, an' that is a fact. Yer 'art mus' be broke in two, Mary. 'Ow are you keepin in yerseff anyhow? I 'ope yer old man is treatin' you kindly fer tis a terrible fing fer a mufver to lose a chil' whatever age they are at."

Sitting on a three-legged stool behind the stall, Mary talks about how relieved she is that her *dear* Albert is at peace, after years of pain and torment. Eventually, she gets around to asking Susannah about the rumours she keeps hearing about fascist marches in Tower Hamlets lately.

"Me an' Seff 'eard rumours about men in black shirts marching fru d' Jewish area in Tower 'Amlets, makin' trouble an' scaring 'ard-workin' Jews livin' an' workin' there. 'Ow is yer dear bruver Issac an' 'is missus, Abigail? 'Ope their boy Daniel is avoidin' any trouble. Is it true they are bein' attacked, an' 'avin' their windows broke?"

Her arms folded defensively, Susannah answers,

"What y' are 'earing is true Mary. Isaac 'as 'ad 'is windows smashed, twice in free mumfs, an' d' police don' seem to know wha' t' do. It is because an 'orrible toff, Oswold Mosley, stirs up hatred agin the Jews. 'It is said that 'ee is pals wiv Adolf 'itler, another one 'oo hates all us Jews. These are worryin' times fer us, Mary, I am sad to say. Worrying times to be Jewish, 'specially in East End."

Confused and enraged by what she hears from her friend, Mary repeats it to Seth that evening and is gladdened when he seems as annoyed as she is about the way the Jews are being bullied and threatened.

"Jews I done business wiv were okay wiv me, an' glad I was of their knowledge, 'specially in d' jewel business," announces Seth. "Never did they do me a bad turn so I will 'ave no truck wiv 'em bein' attacked by mobs. I 'ave no complaints abou' 'em neither."

Sighing, he goes quiet.

"Mary, we is too old, an' I am too poorly wiv me gout an' belly pain to be gettin' worked up over it. I 'ave enough to worry meseff over."

Mary nods in tacit agreement.

"Every time I ask y' t' see a Doctor, Seff, y' swear an' shout at me, but we need t' know why y' 'ave los' yer appetite an' are findin' it 'ard to pee. You used to love yer food an' drink. It must be somefink bad to stop you eatin.' You need to see Doctor Bugden. 'Ee will giff y' medicine t' pick you up."

Seth initially resists following Mary's advice because he does not want to hear unwelcome news. Then, the decision is unexpectedly taken out of his hands. In December nineteen-thirty-three, eleven months after the death of Albert, Seth collapses in acute pain on the red-tiled kitchen floor. Unable to lift him up, as fast as she can, Mary runs next door to use their telephone. She calls a local taxi company which runs 'hospital' cars with specialised equipment, able to transport sick and injured people to hospital. Within a few hours, Seth is admitted as a patient to Rickford General Hospital where he undergoes tests.

Told he has incurable prostate cancer, Seth is shocked, angry, and frustrated. He fumes, *I cannot be dyin' jus' when fings is startin' t' pick up an' I can see new ways t' make a bit of money. I want t' liff a bi' longer, a' least so I can get me revenge on that braggard, Cal, an' show smarty George I am still a force t' be reckoned wiv.*

His aspirations are doomed when, still a patient in hospital, the following March, he finally accepts his fate and faces up to his imminent death. Every second day, Mary makes the three-mile bus journey to be by his side. Stricken with dismay to see her once muscular, strong, arrogant husband so emaciated, weak, and listless, she struggles to hide her dismay. Hour after hour, she wipes his forehead with a cool cloth and strokes the back of his bony, blue-veined hand. Many times, she catches him looking intently at her and wonders what he wants to say, though he is too reduced to speak.

The last twenty-four hours of his life, repetitious thoughts go around and around in Seth's head, *Mary, little Mary, 'oo 'as put up wiv me all these years. I wish I 'ad been nicer t' 'er, especially after she lost 'er babbies. Why 'as she put up wiv me? I don' deserve 'er loyalty. No matter wha', she always stuck by me, an' 'er just an orphan girl born in d' gutter. Still, I did give 'er nice 'ouses t' live in, three sons, an' ponies to love. Shame abou' what's 'appened to George an' Cal. Is it my fault they turned ou' d' way they 'ave? Am I to blame? An' Albert, poor Albert! I won' fink of 'im now fer I mi' cry an' that would be a first fer me. I don' wan' t' look weak in front of Mary or others in d' ward.* From his parched mouth, Seth musters up just enough energy to speak what are his last words to her.

"You 'ave been a good wife t' me, Mary, when I 'ave not always been a good 'usband. Fank you! Be 'appy afte' I am gone, fer you deserve t' be 'appy, girl."

In the early hours of Friday 30th of March nineteen-thirty-four, Seth slips in and out of consciousness. During his last moments of lucid thought, he remembers good-natured Gwen, and the five children they have had together. He feels sorry at the way it had to end, but losing touch with his illegitimate sons and daughters was for the best, he believes. *They done better wivou' me, fer I mi' 'ave led them down d' wrong path in life. Best t' 'ave deserted 'em. Gwen is a good mufver. No regrets. We 'ad fun t'gever.*

Mary, who sits by his bed in the silent, dark ward, surrounded by sleeping patients, sees a faint smile flit across his face before he falls into deep unconsciousness. At the first flicker of dawn peeping through the high windows of the ward, she is startled when he, suddenly and unexpectedly, sits up and, looking straight ahead, excitedly shouts out, *'Rosie! Whoa, Rosie!'* before laying back and exhaling a last, long, rasping breath.

Leaving his bedside that morning, Mary wonders how she will acclimatise to being a widow. She is astonished that she, despite all the trials and tribulations in her life, has outlived Seth. *'Oo would 'ave believed it? Me, born an' raised a pauper on d' streets an' in d' slums, an' still alive at d' grand age of seventy-free. There must be a reason, somefink God wans me t' do afore I go t' meet me maker.* With that in mind, she stands up, and, straight-backed and determined, she leaves the hospital with a sense of renewed purpose.

On arriving home, she sits at the kitchen table and writes to George, knowing that by the time he receives it, Seth will be buried in a communal paupers' grave, for she has not the wherewithal to fund a proper tomb or even an inscribed headstone. On an old sheet of Albert's writing paper, she starts,

56 Hampshire Road East Cockle Bay Essex.
30th March 1934

George, I am writin to tell you that yer farver is dead. He passed away today in Rickford Hospital. I

wos wiv him. Before he died I swear he saw the first horse he ever owned fer he sat up and shouted er name, ROSIE, before he fell back and wos gone. He is to be buried in the graveyard near ere next week. I ave no money to get him a posh hedstone so he will be laid wiv uver paupers. I am glad he is not ere to see it George, fer his pride wood take a nocking to be brought so low. I hope you are well. Ave you seen Cal? There as not been a word from him. Tell im if you see him that his da died today. Sinserely Ma. PS. I ad a visit from Rosie and yer son Henry after the funeral. They are well.

Three years go by before Mary hears back from George, three years in which her life moves on in quite remarkable ways. Despite her advanced years, she has a renewed burst of energy, regularly visiting London with her friend Susannah. When there, they stay with Susannah's brother Isaac and Abigail. During one visit, Mary experiences, first-hand, the horrific level of abuse and physical assaults on Jews, carried out by the Black Shirts.

On returning home to East Cockle Bay after a week in London, Mary listens to news bulletins on the wireless. She is shocked, when on the 4th of October nineteen-thirty-six, there is a violent clash between Oswald Mosley's Black Shirts and anti-fascist groups in Cable Street, Whitechapel, a street she knows well. Next day, walking home from her local greengrocer, where the topic of conversation among customers was only about the London riot, she ponders the events, *'Ow can such a fing be allowed t' 'appen t' Gawd fearin', 'ard-workin' Jews? If I were younger, I would join d' anti-fascist movement. Poor Isaac, an' Abigail mus' be scared t' deff.*

Suddenly, she has an idea. She will tell Susannah that she has two bedrooms to offer to Jewish lodgers, those who want to flee the violence in London and find a safe place to live until they are back on their feet.

Within weeks of the Cable Street riot, she has her first lodgers; Reuben and Elizabeth Golding and their twenty-year-old son, Daniel. She is more than happy to allow them space of their own in her humble kitchen so they can adhere to their Jewish dietary requirements. Within six months, they find a new home of their own in Cockle Bay and their rooms are then occupied by Mary's new lodgers; two young, male jazz musicians who, to her delight, fill the small house with music every night and remind her of Albert. Strangely, as she thinks of him one morning, waiting for the kettle to boil, a letter drops through the letterbox. Picking it up, she sees it has an American stamp. Her heart misses a beat.

Marchwood Ranch, Oak Woods, San Franciso,
California USA
15th September 1937

Ma. It is a long time since I wrote. I hope you are keeping well and managing to get by without Da. It is odd to think of him being dead. I thought the old fellow would live forever. Alice and me are well. We managed to hold onto the ranch and keep breeding horses after the Crash, but it was hard at times. Arnold and Ben are in the American army. They are both American citizens now. Ben married an Irish girl, and they have a boy, Michael. I am a grandfather. I seen Cal a year ago. He is living in Detroit. He would not tell me what he is doing or how he makes his money, but he was driving a nice car and bragged that he is back on his feet again. He goes under the name he used years ago, when he was working on the big liner. We met up in New York when I was there doing business. I have not heard from him since. I told him Da was dead and gave him your address. You might hear from him. He told me he plans to go back to England one day so he could turn up looking for a place to live. Thought I should warn you because you might not want to see him after so long. Sincerely George

Mary is relieved to know that Cal is alive, but her bitter feelings towards him are regurgitated as she remembers that he did not bother to get in touch, even when Albert and Seth died. She believes he would have known about Albert, so to ignore his younger brother's death was unforgivable. She recalls his young mistress, Henrietta, and their three small daughters. '*Ow could 'ee abandon 'er wivou' any money and see 'em 'omeless when 'ee sold 'is 'ouses? Seff did giff 'er some gold trinkets to sell once, bu' we were 'ard pushed t' survive ourseffs. Cal is more selfish than 'is da ever was, an' that's a fact. Finks only of 'imseff. 'Ee always was a bloody problem, an' I spect when 'ee comes back, 'ee will still cause me trouble. Well, I aint afraid of 'im, never was, never will be.*

By nineteen-thirty-nine, Susannah and her family, along with hundreds of Jewish East Enders, leave London and resettle in East Cockle Bay. When Mary's Jewish lodgers leave, she feels lonely, bereft of company; each day she goes to the church hall to drink tea and chat with her elderly peers, sometimes taking over the job of making tea for them all. Still blessed with youthful agility, she does not look seventy-eight years of age. Her slim frame, straight-backed posture, piercing blue eyes and head of wiry, grey curls are admired and envied by others, many of whom are crippled and bent into old age.

When at the Hall, Mary sits beside Fritz Hansel, a tall, well-built German man in his fifties, who was once a prisoner of war on a holding ship down by the pier. After the war, he chose not to return to his home country. Instead, he worked on local farms and married an English girl. Having no children to comfort him, he is entirely alone since his wife passed away a few years ago. Mary likes him. He reminds her of the many kindly German bakers who gave her and Molly free bagels from their market stalls in Whitechapel all those years ago.

Animosity towards German immigrants is on the rise among the local, and wider, population. People are fearful of another military engagement with Germany. As tensions increase, Mary tries to protect Fritz. She knows people are reluctant to employ him, so it becomes her mission to persuade neighbours to pay him to do odd jobs; gardening, cleaning windows, mending walls and fences, and, as he is good with wood, even carving wooden toys for children. Fritz appreciates Mary's kindness, but when he tries to express his gratitude to her, she brusquely dismisses his overtures with an embarrassed look and an impatient wave of her hand.

On the third of September nineteen-thirty-nine, Mary's worst fears, and those of all British people, come true. Listening to the mid-morning public announcement on the wireless, she, and millions of others, hear the words of the Prime Minister, Neville Chamberlain.

> *"This morning the British Ambassador in Berlin handed the German Government a final note stating that, unless we heard from them by 11 o'clock that they were prepared at once to withdraw their troops from Poland, a state of war would exist between us. I have to tell you now that no such undertaking has been received, and that consequently this country is at war with Germany. I am speaking to you today from the Cabinet Room at 10 Downing Street..."*

"No! No! No! Not again! Not again! Dear Gawd, not again!"

Mary, rocked by the news, howls out. Trying to recover her composure, she presses a frayed piece of the kitchen towel over her mouth to stifle her shocked gasps and sobs,

> *"-------We have a clear conscience. We have done all that any country could do to establish peace.*

The situation in which no word given by Germany's ruler could be trusted and no people or country could feel themselves safe has become intolerable. And now that we have resolved to finish it, I know that you will all play your part with calmness and courage."

Those words, *calmness* and *courage*, resonate with Mary and snap her out of her fear and trembling. She knows, with certainty, that Fritz, along with other Germans she has known during her long life, will suffer badly from discrimination and abuse. The authorities will round them up, confine them to camps, and treat them all with suspicion. Even those who have served in the army on the side of the British will suffer.

Pulling herself together, her thoughts tumble about as she wonders how she can cope with another world conflict. W*ha' is d' worst that can 'appen t' me? Nuffin! Because d' worst 'as already 'appened. I lost me first love, Brian, I lost gentle George, I lost Albert, Seff, four children. I 'ad no mufver, was brung up on the streets. I seen fings I should never 'ave seen as a child, an' done bad fings too. I 'ave been 'ungry, poor, cold, lonely an' afraid. Did I not see me darlin' Molly dragged off t' d' mad'ouse, wiv no-one there t' 'elp me? An' 'ere I am, an old lady, 'avin' survived it all. No, I aint 'fraid of nought, not even anuver war.*

Resigning herself to whatever lies ahead, Mary resolves to bravely confront whatever life has planned for her. She will befriend German neighbours, when others turn against them, and contribute to the war effort. She will try to forgive Cal for his selfish behaviour and welcome him when he returns to Britain. *It is wha' d' Good Book do say, an 'oo am I to argue wiv God?* Such are her thoughts, as she says her morning prayers. On sunny days, throughout the year, she takes the pony and trap and visits Seth in the graveyard where he lies, and talks to him more openly and honestly than she ever did when he was alive.

Whisperings:
Repentance and forgiveness lift the latch on the gateway to eternal peace.

EPILOGUE

Footprints

You never know whose life you may touch with the footprints you leave behind.

– Anon

1945

The old-fashioned clock on the hallstand at the bottom of the stairs chimes five times. The first faint infusion of the rosy blush of dawn rises over the horizon. Quiet as a mouse, the old, enfeebled woman turns the shiny brass doorknob then pulls open the front door. She steps outside, quietly, and furtively closes it behind her. Her actions are instinctive for she is confused. She is not sure why she is standing on the step inside her porch, or where she intends to go, except she knows with certainty that she does not want Cal to wake up and make her go back inside. Carefully, she steps down off the tiled doorstep and hesitates. *What am I doin'? I cannot remember where I 'ave to go.* She thinks hard, trying to puzzle it out.

Dressed in a long, grey, old-fashioned overcoat,

stained and frayed in parts, she is unaware that beneath this outer garment, she wears nothing but a voluminous, pink, long-sleeved flannel nightdress. Her skinny legs and ankles, porcelain-white and blue-veined, appear too fragile to hold her upright. The soles of her small bony feet are thickened with layers of hard, dry skin, thus protecting them from feeling any sharp pebbles on the ground.

On hearing a soft snorting sound coming from the yard at the side of the house, she is galvanised. *That is Nobby. Nobby knows I am 'ere an' 'ee will know where I need t' get to. 'Ee will take me there.* She shuffles down the short, tessellated path, through the open wooden half-gate and onto the pavement. Turning left she goes around the corner of the house and enters the yard where her neighbour, Paddy Conroy, keeps his donkey.

Paddy stables the donkey in Mary's shed and has done so for many years. In return, she is free to visit or use Nobby, whenever she wishes. It is an arrangement that suits them both. Every year, from late spring through to mid autumn, children take tuppenny rides on the donkey up and down the beach. Stationed near the pier, Paddy and Nobby are popular additions to the varied entertainments in and around the busy promenade. During the war, when entertainments were curtailed, Paddy, for a small fee, rented out his donkey and cart and so managed to avoid penury.

This morning, Mary greets Nobby with soft words and a gentle scratch around the base of his long grey ears. Her mind clears. Momentarily, she recalls the purpose of her early departure from the house.

"We is goin' fer a ride Nobby. I 'ave an' 'ankerin' to go an' walk on d' sand. Am I mad do you fink? Anyways, I did 'ear d' sea'orses calling me las' night, jus' b'fore I fell asleep. I 'spect you 'eard them too, Nobby. So, you an' me, we is goin' on a dawn adventure down on the sands."

With decades of experience in handling horses, ponies and donkeys, Mary, though now painfully slow at the task, manages to harness and hitch up Nobby to the single-seat cart. The animal stands quietly, as she, with the aid of a stepping block, climbs up onto the seat and gently lifts the reins. Preoccupied with settling herself, once more she forgets the reason for taking this early morning ride. She is not troubled by her sudden blank confusion because Nobby sets off at a confident pace. She is immediately reassured that he, at least, knows where she needs to get to.

In the half-light of the evolving dawn, they pass silhouettes of bomb sites on their journey down to the estuary basin; the school, a heap of rubble, and the old church, now a broken ruin. She shivers, and a frisson of fear floods her veins as she recalls the early days of the war when one hundred German bombers flew in over the bay, destroying ships anchored there. Passing, dark memories fade from her fluttering mind as golden fingers of light spread their magic out across the morning sky. Her old heart beats fast as she excitedly anticipates her first, clear glimpse of the sea. Rounding a corner, she is awestruck on seeing the water's night-time blackness being chased away by waves of emerging daylight shimmering over its surface.

A solitary bus picks up factory workers doing early shifts, while groups of children, with bulging satchels on their backs, begin their long trek to school. Seeing their tiny figures, and hearing shrill, childish chatter wafting her way on the morning breeze, she is full of gladness. *They are back again, d' little 'uns. Back wiv their mams and dads, livin' once more in Cockle Bay. D' war took 'em away bu' they 'ave returned. I did miss seein' 'em playin' in d' streets, like I did when I was a wee one.* Meandering thoughts of Cal, living with her since his return from America, intrude on her enjoyment of the ride. Simultaneously, an expression of faint disquiet flits across her lined face and her eyes are bleak, an expression that stays on her face until they arrive at their destination, the pier.

Slowly she levers her stiff legs down, over the cart step, and, with a sharp intake of breath at the excruciating pain in her joints, she drops to the ground. Once composed, she leads Nobby to his usual tethering post, the front left stanchion under the pier. Fondling his pointy ears, she feeds him the small carrot she had in her pocket and checks there is enough fresh water in the drinking trough beneath the pier. Once satisfied that all is as it should be, she turns towards the outgoing tide that has receded to a point far out from the promenade. Straining to hear the tumbling waves in the distance, she stops, suddenly apprehensive, until she hears a familiar voice calling her.

"Mary, Mary, me darlin', do not be afraid. Everyting will be all right. I am waitin' fer yee to join me, to come back home where yee belong."

"Molly, Molly, is that you? Is that you callin' me?"

Her voice carries, high-pitched and shrill, quickly absorbed into the cool dank air. She feels the cold, silky, wet sand beneath her feet. With an overwhelming sense of joy and relief, she walks across an expanse of beach, sprinkled with shards of broken shells and pieces of drying seaweed, out towards the ebbing waterline. Despite the intrusion of huge concrete blocks, placed there during the war, as if under a spell, she glides between them on her journey. A strange thought comes to her, *I am goin' backwards, just like d' tide is rollin' backwards. I am goin' back to my beginning, back home t' find Molly.*

The sand darkens, oozy with the increased volume of seawater the closer she gets to the line. Her feet sink deep into its cloying brown essence, leaving behind prints of her gnarled toes and feet. The hemlines of her coat and nightdress are saturated, encrusted with globules of wet sand, and weigh heavy on her thin, diminutive frame. She is tiring and wonders if she can make it to the edge and catch Molly.

She feels the scalding tears cascade from her eyes and down her cheeks and neck, drenching the yoke of her nightgown, and she wonders why she is crying, surprised by it. Then, in a flash, she realises that they are cleansing her of all sorrow, all fear, all pain and all past childhood traumas. Uplifted, lighter in body and soul, her feet leave the sand, and she is floating. She calls to Molly, though no words leave her thin lips. *I 'ope you can 'ear me, Molly. I am almos' there. Look! I can see 'em, d' white 'orses you tol' me about. I wish you were 'ere wiv me. Why did y' leave me, Molly? I want you to come back fer me this very minute.*

In response to her plea come words, softly whispered, into her ear.

I am here, me darlin' chil'. I am beside yee now. Take me hand an' we will go together to ride dose galloping horses. You and me, Mary, as I promised.

Grasping hold of Molly's hand, Mary floats above the breaking waves. All around her, she sees other souls dancing and tumbling in rapturous release from earthly bondage; Brian, Albert, Seth and her long dead babies and children.

I am free, Molly. I am free and I am coming home with you.

A woman, heavy with child, together with her husband, takes an early morning stroll along the beach. At first glance, the couple assume the crumpled mound lying near the edge of the incoming tide, is a dead animal. Then, as they draw closer to it, they are shocked to see the body of an old, emaciated woman lying, curled in a foetal position. Mesmerised, they watch how her grey, straggling curly hair gently undulates with the movement of the foamy brine and how her piquant face holds an expression of profound peace and contentment.

Whisperings:
A life begins with a single step and leaves a trail of footprints on its journey.

This book is printed on paper from sustainable sources managed under the Forest Stewardship Council (FSC) scheme.

It has been printed in the UK to reduce transportation miles and their impact upon the environment.

For every new title that Troubador publishes, we plant a tree to offset CO_2, partnering with the More Trees scheme.

For more about how Troubador offsets its environmental impact, see www.troubador.co.uk/sustainability-and-community